RED
HOOD

ELANA K. ARNOLD

BALZER + BRAY
An Imprint of HarperCollinsPublishers

Balzer + Bray is an imprint of HarperCollins Publishers.

Red Hood
Copyright © 2020 by Elana K. Arnold
All rights reserved.

www.epicreads.com

ISBN 978-0-06-274236-0

Typography by Chris Kwon
21 22 23 24 25 PC/LSCH 10 9 8 7 6 5 4 3 2 1
❖ First paperback edition, 2021

For my sister Mischa, with love

"Why do men feel threatened by women?" I asked
a male friend of mine.
"They're afraid women will laugh at them," he said.
"Undercut their world view."
Then I asked some women students in a quickie
poetry seminar I was giving, "Why do women
feel threatened by men?"
"They're afraid of being killed," they said.

—MARGARET ATWOOD, "Writing the Male
Character" (1982)

CONTENTS

I: FIRST BLOOD

II: WHAT SYBIL SAYS

III: OVER AND THROUGH

I

FIRST BLOOD

THE BETTER TO EAT YOU

O nce upon a time, just hours ago, the doorbell rang.
You were ready—lipstick on, hairpins in. His dear face
smiled as you opened the door for him, his bright dark eyes, his
wide sweet mouth, and small diamonds twinkling from both
pierced ears. His bow tie—red, to match your dress—was tied
just so. Your grandmother, who you call Mémé, took your
picture by the door, James's arm around your waist, the fresh-
cut-grass scent of his deodorant familiar now—six months,
tonight, since last spring, when he asked you to be his girl.

As you posed for the picture, the smell of him was familiar,

3

and the feel of his arm around your waist, and the warmth of his breath on the top of your head. And the way he laced his fingers through yours after you said goodbye to Mémé, his right hand with your left as he led you to his wagon. His old blue wagon, that was familiar, too. The way the door squeaked when he opened it for you, the way he had to slam it hard to get it to latch, the way the driver's seat was pushed way back to make room for James's long legs, the way he folded those legs as he climbed in, the way he turned to smile at you as his hand turned the key, the light brown of his skin, the black of his eyes, the curl of his lashes. As familiar as the sound of the engine revving.

It is a cloudy night, this night, homecoming night, and clouds obscure the moon. When you arrived at the school, the parking lot was already full; music poured from the gym like the desperate thrumming of a heart. You would rather have stayed in this car, with just James; it's not in your nature to join a crowd, and you knew the crowd in there, the thickness of it, the pack of it. But it means something to James that you go to these things—the dances, the soccer games, the house parties, the gyrations of the high school machine. And James means something to you and so, for him, you climbed out of the car, you took his hand, you went toward the music.

A table was set up outside the gym, staffed by three of the PTSA moms, the group that lobbied to hold homecoming on a Sunday. They displayed large, laminated photographs of car crashes—one, a car wrapped around a streetlight, another, a car crumpled beneath the grille of an enormous red transport truck. DON'T DRINK AND DRIVE was printed in bold letters beneath each photo, and the women pressed flyers into the hands of everyone who passed.

One of the mothers waved a flyer in your direction; you ignored her, but James took it and said, "Thank you, ma'am," before folding it neatly, slipping it into his jacket pocket, and sliding his hand into yours once again.

Inside, it was as you expected—there they all were, half shrouded in shadow: James's teammates and their dates, the group he pulled you toward, one you are part of now, one that opened to receive you, for better and worse. Tucker and Maggie, perpetually off and on, his hand on her arm, either pulling her in or pushing her away, or maybe both at the same time. Big Mac, with that smile and swagger. Flame-red Darcy on the fringe, wanting so desperately to be in the center. And others, so many others, anxious faces and happy faces and excited faces, too. On the dance floor, couples swayed—mostly boy-girl pairs, but some girls with girls, and one pair of freshman boys in matching tuxes, pressed close together. Dresses in all colors, suit jackets and ties and the smells of perfumes and pomades and pizza, commingling and pungent.

You let James lead you to the basketball team's circle, next to Big Mac, you let their laughter and conversation wash over you without soaking it in. Big Mac is funny. He's expansive, gregarious—a leader. You have always liked him, in spite of his swagger. He plays center, and that's what he is off the court, too, among his friends. Close by stood Landon and Caleb—good guys, both, and both forwards. It was no surprise to see them together, here at the dance—as far back as you can remember, where one of them went, the other followed. Landon and Caleb are a duo—best friends and, lately, maybe more. The three of them—Big Mac, Landon, and Caleb—are as close as brothers to James; standing there, you felt him relax into the familiar rhythm of their shared banter.

You watched James's brilliant smile and you felt the warmth of his fingers twined through yours.

You went through all the motions—the chatter, the dancing, the giving and receiving of compliments. It made James happy, being there. But you were already somewhere else—remembering James's car, and the soft quilt folded in the back. That was where you wanted to be—with James, unfolding. But you could wait for James, who loves everyone. It is one of the things you love about him.

It was loud and sharp and almost painful, the entire exhibition of it: the display of bodies, dance moves, coupling and uncoupling.

You accepted it for James's sake, and each moment there brought you closer to where you longed to be. And not all of it was terrible; feeling James's hungry eyes on you in your dress, that was not terrible. The way his fingers pressed between yours, spreading them apart, such a tiny and intimate act—not terrible. Listening to his laugher with his friends. Pulling each other close on the dance floor, your cheek against his chest, each breath rich with the scent of him, that was not terrible. You allowed yourself to be led, you allowed yourself to follow. Your bodies moved together rhythmically, as if in an act of premonition.

But then—"Looking fine, friend o' mine!"

It was Tucker, who'd stumbled onto the dance floor. If he had been sober when he had arrived, that state had left him. He laughed loudly at his own stupid rhyme and slapped James hard on the ass.

James clenched his jaw and shook his head, and together, you turned away from Tucker, who was well known for getting only worse as an evening progressed. The best thing to do, if at all possible, was to ignore him.

But Tucker did not want to be ignored. He tried again. "Hey," he said, shoving James's shoulder, "Lemme cut in. I want to dance with Bisou."

Your hands were laced behind James's neck; his were around your hips, and the music was loud enough to pretend not to hear Tucker's demand. But as the song ended, Tucker was still there.

"Where's Maggie, man?" James asked, trying to deter him

in the friendly manner that was his way.

But Tucker would not be deterred. He reached out again, a third time—"Whatever, fuck Maggie. I wanna dance with Bisou." He was belligerent, as if his desire to dance with you was all that mattered. And you were done ignoring him, and into the moment of silence between songs, you said loudly, "Jesus, Tucker, you can't even dance when you're sober."

Everyone within earshot laughed. Tucker's face reddened and he spat, "Fuck you, Bisou," and James put his hand on Tucker's chest, saying, "Hey, now," and you said, "Wait," and then there was a moment that could have gone either way. The crowd seemed to smell it on James and Tucker, the possibility, and a low, laughing rumble of "fight, fight, fight" began and grew, but you pulled James away and someone else pulled Tucker away and then, a moment later, he was nowhere to be seen. It might have ruined the night, if it hadn't been something you and James had seen from Tucker a thousand times before, if either you or James was willing to let the night be ruined. But you wouldn't let Tucker have your night, and you could see in James's eyes and his smile, gentle and true, that he wouldn't, either.

At last, the dance is over and done, and the others scatter— to their homes, to after-parties, to back seats . . . you don't care, you don't care, you don't care. You don't even care that Mémé might be waiting up for you, though you told her not to.

All you care is that you are, at last, away from that gym, alone with James. Already, the dance is almost forgotten, so unremarkable it was, even that unpleasantness on the dance floor.

Now—now, in James's wagon, parked on the edge of the woods, where the air is cold and fresh, where the scent of damp pine is sharper and better than any perfume, you watch James spread the quilt. *This* is remarkable—lying on the blanket with James, feeling his hands in your hair as he finds and pulls free each hairpin, undoing you. These are remarkable—his kisses, tracing a path down your neck, his hands pulling low the sweetheart neckline of your dress, his nose brushing your right nipple, and then, a moment later, his lips capturing it, his tongue circling, circling, his teeth skimming and biting, not hard, just enough to make your hands tighten into fists and clutch the blanket, enough to make your legs begin to quiver.

And then he pushes up the tulle and satin of your skirt, rustling like wrapping paper coming undone, and his hands reach and find the lace panties you bought just especially for this occasion, and slowly, so slowly, he pulls them down your thighs, and you lift your hips to help him slide them free. Your feet are already bare, high heels abandoned in the front seat, so there is nothing to stop your panties from coming all the way off.

Oh, how much you want this. Whereas before, at the dance, you had been there for James, at his side as he enjoyed himself, now—here—you are your body. How much you want him to put his mouth on you, there, right there, at the crux of you.

Your combined breaths have fogged the windows of the wagon, the air is damp. Your head rolls with desire, frustration, as he moves his kisses from your right thigh to your left, as his fingers run up and down your legs, all the way down to your toes but never up all the way to your aching center.

Outside, on the other side of the cold, steamed-over glass, is the forest. Inside, there is just you and him, your James, the boy you love, the boy who loves you.

Do you shiver from desire? Do you shiver because it is cold? Do you shiver from anticipation, for the moment when—at last, at last—his mouth finds his way to the center of you?

At last, at last, he's found his way there, a hand on each of your thighs, his head buried between them, and he's not teasing you, not now, not anymore, he's earnest in his desire to bring you desire, and yes, you think, as his tongue and lips press into you, as his fingers pull you apart, as you come undone beneath his hands, it is important to be earnest if this is what earnestness brings.

Yes, the smell of him, the sight of him, the feel of him, all of it familiar, but not this—the hot firm pressure of his tongue against your center, the insistence of his hands on your thighs, the building wonder of your pleasure rising, oh, that is not familiar, that is new, brand-new.

You gush—that is the word, the only word—you gush as

the pleasure becomes too much to survive, and it bursts like a shaken-up can of soda, it tickles and it burns and it ripples from your center outward, in pulses of sensation so intense you are pinned by them, and your left hand curls into a fist and your right hand flails, hitting the damp cold glass and streaking away the steam, and your eyes open as the pleasure ebbs, and just then the clouds outside part, revealing the full white moon, unblinking, staring down at you from a black velvet sky.

James laughs, his gentle, happy laugh, and he looks up from where he's crouched between your thighs, and he smiles, and you see his face in the moonbeam that pours through the strip of window you've wiped clean, and at first you don't know what you're seeing, you don't know what to make of the redness on his chin.

It's blood.

It is *your* blood.

But why would you bleed? It's pleasure you felt, not pain, but now the pleasure is gone and in its place is dread, and disgust, and shame, and though James does not yet know that your blood is on his face, he sees your expression change, he sees your brow wrinkle and your mouth purse. His own brow furrows in response.

"Bisou," he says, "you okay?"

You don't answer. At sixteen, you have waited long enough to start your period that you had all but given up on it ever

coming—"Mine was late, too, don't worry," your grandmother has said—but here it is, this blood. You fumble with
the door handle, ripping back a nail as you struggle, and then
the door flies open with that familiar squeak, and you tumble
out of the wagon and onto the pins and needles of the forest
floor.

"Bisou!" James calls, and you hear him behind you, climb-
ing out of the car, you feel his hand on your arm, but you yank
free, you find your feet, you pull up the bodice of your dress,
and you run, you run, ashamed and afraid, away from the boy,
away from the car, away from the blood, and into the copse of
trees that will hide you.

THE PATH OF PINS AND NEEDLES

You have a long relationship with blood, but not your
own.

Your first memory is red rich: Your mother scooping you
from bed in the deepest velvet of night and cocooning you,
still wrapped in blankets, in the back seat of the car. Rolling
down the hill, the car in neutral almost to the corner before
she turned the key and the engine growled to life.

Only when the car was nearly to the freeway, stopped at a
red light just before the on-ramp, did she turn to look back at
you, and there, in the red glow of the traffic signal, you saw

that she was somehow both mother and not-mother, her face bathed in red from the light outside and from the cut above her right eyebrow, weeping blood, that whole side of her face distorted by the blood and the swelling of her jaw, and in the place of her nose, someone else's nose. You pulled the blanket up over your head and squeezed tight your eyes, and then the car began to move again, speeding onto the freeway and away, away.

Now, among the trees, you are away again. You run, here in shadow and there in moonlight, through the woods behind the high school and toward your home, as fast as you can go. Your dress slips down as you run, and you hold it up with one hand to cover your breasts even though there is no one here to see, and you feel the slick-soft wet of your blood dripping from the core of you, down the insides of your thighs.

You picture James as he looked in the car—his sweet face, his eager smile, the blood—and you shake your head violently, as if you could shake the image and the shame away, away.

The forest floor is thick and sharp with pins and needles, and they pierce the pads of your bare feet, the tender skin between your toes. It's all shadows and angles, the forest, with the moon-full sky above making everything eerily not-dark. Moonlight illuminates your path, and you can make out the long-limbed bodies of trees all around you, the way their arms reach as you pass, the way their fingers brush against you, the way they caress and claw you.

Your heart hurts, it beats so fast, it is beating you from the inside, each drum a punishing blow—how dare you bleed, how dare you be so gross. James's face flashes behind your eyes and you hear the little cry you make, like an injured animal, so ashamed that it seems anything would be better than this, anything, anything, even death.

Death.

You smell it, though you cannot see it. Over there, up ahead and to the left—something has died. Not today, but not that long ago. It is beginning to rot, that is what you smell, flesh breaking apart beneath fur, maggots that plump up the carcass, doing their work.

Bigger than a squirrel, bigger than a rat. A possum, maybe, or a raccoon.

You don't know how you know this, only that it is true.

There—on the right, forty feet up—a nest. You hear a pair of owlets stirring. Their mother is away.

And there, behind you, is the fall of running feet. James, coming after you.

But . . . wait. Not two feet.

Four. Ba-ba-ba-*bum*.

Not James.

You don't know how you know these things—the smell of the dead animal, the presence of the nest, that something is pursuing you and that it is not James. Right now, it doesn't matter how you know them, only that you *do* know them. Just as you know that the animal that pursues you is faster than you are, that soon it will be at your back, and that you cannot flee, you will have to turn and fight.

There. A femur-thick felled branch. You scoop it up, you turn and heft it over your shoulder. Your dress was not made for this; the bodice is slipping down again, your breasts half out, and you have more important things to do than maintain modesty.

Your eyes scan, your ears listen. You wait.

Ba-ba-ba-*bum*, ba-ba-ba-*bum*.

It is coming.

Your feet are hip-wide, right slightly in front of left, branch swung up over your left shoulder, like a baseball bat. Though you have been running, though your heart has been punishing you for bleeding, now it is obedient, its beats steady and controlled.

Ba-ba-ba-*bum*.

Your heartbeat? Footfalls? Both, twined together.

And then—there—in a glint of moonlight, *there*, a wide grinning mouth full of teeth, a thick red tongue, a huge pewter-pelted wolf.

You have three seconds before he is upon you. He will go for your throat.

Three seconds is less than a breath.

You have only seen one other wolf in your entire life. At the Zoo de Granby. You were four years old. Mama held your left hand in her right, both ensconced in mittens. First snowflakes floated around you, promises of winter. You wore the rabbit-fur coat and matching cap that Mama had bought for you at the friperie, though she herself still wore a too-thin raincoat belted over her thickest sweater.

That wolf was honey brown and sleeping, curled like a dog in its enclosure.

"Un chien!" you called, pleased that you knew the word, in this new tongue you were learning.

"Non," Mama answered. "Un loup." And then, kneeling beside you so she could whisper in your ear, "A wolf."

Two seconds. Your toes grip the earth, the path of pins and needles, the best they can. You dig in your heels.

One second. Your fingers tighten on the branch, your muscles assess the heft of it. Your dress has slipped now beneath your breasts, your nipples tightened against the cold.

And then he leaps, the pewter wolf, he pushes off his powerful haunches and flies through the air toward your throat.

There is, in that moment, an instant of silence. The beast's feet are off the ground and beat no more; in your chest, your heart holds its breath. The owlets in their aerie freeze into stillness; the raccoon corpse says not a word.

There is nothing but the wolf's enormous mouth full of teeth—the better to eat you with—and your own self, and the awareness of another hot pulse of blood emerging from your center, dripping down your thigh, and landing, like a premonition of more blood to come, on the pins and needles of the forest floor.

And then that moment is over, as all moments are, and the next begins, as all moments do.

The wolf's eye shines cruelly, his hot breath steams and stinks.

You swing the branch, the muscles in your arms and shoulders exploding into action as if they have been waiting all their sixteen years for just this moment. It's a good swing—solid, strong, timed just right—and the branch connects with the wolf's jaw, twisting his head hard to his left, a spray of spit and blood erupting from his mouth.

His whole body is knocked off course, away from you, and he falls to the ground and rolls slowly to his feet.

It was a clean hit, but you can tell by the weight of the branch in your hands, without your eyes ever leaving the wolf, that the blow has compromised your only weapon. It is ruined, the top third disappeared into a shattering of splinters, the shaft sharp-tipped and jagged now, so you change your grip, holding what remains like a spear rather than a bat, and you change your stance, too, from the defensive posture of a batter to the offensive position of a fighter.

The wolf shakes his shaggy gray head as if to right his brain. He's gotten all four feet under him now, and he looks up at you from beneath his pewter brow. His near-black eyes assess you.

Despite the blow you've struck, the wolf's hackles rise and

a growl gurgles up from his throat, menacing but unafraid. He does not fear you. He does not respect you. Do not mistake the stance he now takes, the pause in his attack, as proof of either. You are prey to him. You are a consumable object.

You do not wait for him to attack again. Maybe he is still rattled from the blow to the head. Maybe his feet are still unstable beneath him. Perhaps this advantage will last no more than a moment, and so you take it.

Breasts bared, teeth bared, you scream. It's high, your scream, unmistakably female, and it propels you forward, the sharp-spiked stick jabbing as you lunge, and you aim for the eyes—the better to see you with—and the wolf is still slow from the first blow, still off-balance, for though he sees you coming, he doesn't dodge quickly enough, and you feel the meaty wet *squish* of his right eyeball skewered on the point of your stick.

The wolf yips in surprised pain, and he bats away your weapon with a sharp-clawed paw, and though you're gripping it as best you can, it's torn from your fingers and gone.

The wolf's right eye is swelling closed around the mean sharp splinter that pierces it. It's not nothing, the blow to the head and the splinter to the eye, but it's not enough, not by far.

You are alone in the woods, seen only by the unblinking yellow moon. Your hands are empty. You are nearly naked. And the wolf is angry.

Hackles up, the wolf advances. If he underestimated you,

if that was an advantage, it is gone now. Each step brings him closer, brings the potential of your death closer.

But that is true, wolf or no, of each moment.

There is a tree at your back. It rises behind you like all of history—your history, the history of girls in forests, the history of wolves and fangs and blood.

Another gush of blood flows from you, and you see the wolf's nose twitch as he smells the iron in the air. You are made of blood and your blood is made of iron.

You bleed, but are not injured. Not yet.

"Not today," you promise—yourself? the moon?—as the wolf attacks again. But it is as though you know what his moves will be before he makes them, and you can adjust according to this knowledge—he will go for your throat, because that is what wolves do, and you will step toward him, not away, because you are not his prey.

Your hands shoot out, empty but not powerless, and as his jaw snaps at you, so close you feel the skim of his teeth on your flesh, the slice of his claw at your breast, you find his neck, your fingers plunge deep into his lush fur and you lunge past him, using his power to propel him, head first, into the enormous trunk of the tree behind you.

There's the sound of his head on the tree, and the sound of the snap of his neck, and the thud of his body as it falls upon the pins and needles.

And then there is just the ragged sound of your own breath.

He is beautiful, the pewter wolf, dead at your feet, except for the splinter protruding from his once-shiny eye, and the way his head angles too far to one side, connected to its body by flesh but no longer by bone.

You find the bodice of your dress way down by your waist, and you pull it up, back into place, as you turn away from the wolf and toward home.

i

you don't know why mothers leave
you don't even know that they *do* leave

but they do

N'OUBLIE PAS D'OUBLIER

You were always cold in Quebec. When you and Mama first arrived, it was on the edge of winter. Dead grasses and gray skies and a mean, biting wind. It was a different color, the landscape, lavender-gray in a cold, cruel way, too cold to be green like back home in Washington State. It was another country of coldness. It was another world.

But you weren't to talk about home. You learned that quickly. "N'oublie pas d'oublier," Mama said over and over again, as if it were a line from a storybook, from a song. She said it as the two of you walked through the trees that rimmed the property; she said it as you bent to collect smooth, round stones; she said it as you skipped the stones across the small pond behind the barn; she said it as she kissed you good night, loosing a cupped stone from your palm. *Don't forget to forget.*

Then the snow came, the hush and rush of winter. It fell with the dense weight of sleep, covering all your tracks. Tree branches curtsied with the white weight upon them. *Shhh,* said the winter, the quiet, shining winter. When the sun broke through the overcast sky, its brilliance on the snow was blindingly bright, but it couldn't ever stay out for long, the snow-heavy clouds gathering thick and gray in the sky. With each snowfall, Mama's bruises lightened. The air grew colder and colder, and the pond grew a crust of ice, so that stones thrown slipped across it and skidded atop its surface. As the ice hardened, Mama's face softened. She looked more like before, but not quite the same. Her nose was different, raised in the center with a hard, ugly bump that you didn't like, that she stroked with her left index finger when she was thinking about something, staring out the window into the blank snow.

The windows—they did not help. They were thin, made of old glass, Mama said, and frigid air crept in around the old wooden frames, rattling them like chattering teeth.

Ah, but they were beautiful. Each morning, though the bed you shared with Mama in the sleeping room was a cocoon of shared warmth, you'd wrap your special blanket around your shoulders like a cape and you'd run to the window to see what the night had done.

Each morning was different, but always beautiful—frost ferns, Mama called them, the pictures sketched in ice on the glass. Feathery leaves and trees and flowers bloomed across the window, magical gifts from nature, Mama said.

Or fairies, you imagined.

You would travel down the stairs and into each room, to see each miracle—the twin tall rectangles of glass in the dining room; the squat, square window above the kitchen sink; the wide, paned windows of the sitting room, each squared-off panel its own little work of art.

Landscapes in white unfolded all around, sparkling and impossibly detailed.

You loved them, and the cold seemed a small price for such beauty. But Mama frowned in the mornings, shivering as she worked to build the fire.

You remembered the house Mama had taken you from, the house with Papa in it. That house had been warm—sometimes suffocatingly so. Hot and stuffy and full of Papa in a way you did not miss.

You could bear this cold.

Still, Mama shuttered the windows, going down to the basement to retrieve sets of green-painted wooden panels and trudging with them around the perimeter of the house, affixing a set to each window. You watched from inside as one by one the windows went dark, as the house grew dimmer and dimmer.

But she left bare the sitting room window, the one that faced the driveway, and though she didn't say why, you knew the reason. So she could watch.

For though she urged you to remember to forget, she did not forget, not for a moment, as she sat by that window, looking out, one finger tracing the uneven ridge of her nose.

You wake but do not open your eyes. The sheets are tangled. Your hair, tangled too. Eyes squeezed shut, you make a wish that it was a dream, last night, all of it—that today is yesterday and that tonight is the dance, that James has not yet come for you, that you have not yet come for James, that there is no blood on his chin, that there has been no run through pins and needles, that you have not seen the wolf.

But you know that today is today and not yesterday. You know time flows only in one direction—onward—and that you flow, too, that the stickiness between your thighs is proof that all of it happened.

When you got home last night, you put on your biggest underwear and you lined the crotch of them with one of the pads that have been waiting for you in the back of your bathroom cabinet for four years now. But you know even before looking that the pad was an insufficient barrier between your blood and your bed. You'll have to deal with the blood. You'll have to open your eyes.

And so you do, though they are dry and painful to peel open. You blink, you rub your palms against them, you sit up.

There it is, the press of the pad in your underwear. You throw back your cover and swing your legs over the edge of the bed. You stand.

The bottom sheet is marked with an uneven red-brown stain. It's dry, and you throw the duvet back up to conceal it. Later, you'll deal with that. First, you must deal with your body.

In the bathroom, on the toilet, you watch with fascination as the stream of your urine mixes with the thick rivulet of blood that emerges from you. Viscous, it moves slowly; your urine shoots and sprays, but the blood languishes, takes its time. Unhurried. On its own schedule, as you suppose it always has been.

Every girl you know has had her period for years. You must be the unluckiest girl in the history of girls to begin menstruating at the absolute worst moment, the most mortifying, terrible instant.

But thinking of that instant brings with it the memory of the press of James's tongue, the brush of his dense, dark hair against your thigh, the blinding, confusing pleasure that washed over you, that made you tremble. The memory is a mix of pleasure and shame, and you wonder: For the rest of your life, every time you experience that pleasure, will shame be its shadow?

The loud pulse of water from the shower separates you from this thought and you step beneath the cascade of warmth, closing your eyes and resting your forehead against the cold, hard tile wall. You give yourself a long moment to just stand there, your hair straightening under the weight of water, falling into curtains around your face.

Then you do all the things one does—washing and rinsing and conditioning and shaving. You would give anything for it to not be a school day, but alas, it is, and as you prepare your body for the day, you try to heed your mother's imperative from so long ago: don't forget to forget. If you could forget the last twelve hours, oh, you would.

For though you have done your best not to think about it, there is, alongside your blood and shame, the question of the wolf.

You killed it. That, you know. It must have been rabid. That is the only reason it would have attacked you. Or maybe it was starving.

It didn't *look* rabid or starving. It looked . . . smart.

But you were smarter. Or luckier. You don't know.

You crank off the shower. You grab your towel and rub it over your hair, across your shoulders, between your legs, just as you always do, but this time there is a streak of bright red blood. You close your eyes against it. It's okay. You'll just wash the towel along with your sheets, and you'll have to remember, next time, that this is your body now. It bleeds.

You will have to relearn your morning routine. You wrap the towel, bloody side out, around your waist, and you go to the cabinet under your sink, where you found the pad last night. You kneel in front of the cabinet and poke around, the sink drain in the middle of everything, push aside the extra bottle of shampoo and the mouthwash and the pink plastic bag of pads you tore open last night, and then you find it—a small box of tampons, pushed way in the back by time and disuse, and you take it out, sit back on your heels, open it.

They are lined up like white plastic-wrapped bullets. No applicators. Why your grandmother chose this brand for you, you have no idea, but this is what you have.

You find the edge of the plastic wrapping and twist it off. The box contains a little page of directions, which you glance at but don't read; after all, how hard could it be? There is really only one thing to do with a tampon.

You hold it, one hand on the cotton shaft and the other on the long blue string, and you pull the string in a circle to widen the cotton fibers at the base. Then you balance it on your left pointer finger, sit back on your bath mat, and open your legs, the towel falling wide.

There is the pelt of your pubic hair. You keep it trimmed

close and neat around the edges, but you like the way it looks and have bucked the fashion magazines that advise you to shear it completely. There is the nub of your clitoris, and again you push away the memory of what James did last night with his tongue. With your right hand, you pull apart the lips of your vagina, and with your left, you angle the tampon toward its opening. You are slick with blood, and so the tampon slips in easily. You push until you're knuckle-deep in your own body, the first time you've touched yourself like this—though you have rubbed your clitoris and touched the outside, you've never put your fingers inside, somehow feeling like it was not right, like it would be trespassing.

It's warm in there, almost hot. It feels like what it is—a muscular tube, made of flesh.

The tampon's tip pushes against the wall of your vagina, and you straighten it out, and then it feels like nothing is there at all. You stand, rinse the blood from your index finger, and survey yourself in the mirror. The towel has fallen, and you are naked. The slope of your shoulders, the wet brown curls that drip onto your chest. The thrust of your small breasts. Nipples that seem darker than you imagine they should be, the right one smaller than the left. Round hips, thick thighs. The light blue string emerging from your center. You tuck it up, and it disappears.

There. Now no one could guess, by looking at you, how

different you are this morning from yesterday's morning. Now you look just the same. Identical to that girl, the girl you were.

N'oublie pas d'oublier.

Mémé is at the kitchen table with her cup of tea. Always tea, never coffee. She is reading poetry, you can tell from the way the words scatter across the page. You stand in the kitchen doorway, watching her read.

She is the only grandmother you know who keeps her hair long—longer than yours, even, nearly to her waist, steel gray and white with a few last sweeps of brown, and clear white around her temples, braided.

Right now, she is wearing the bathrobe you gave her for her last birthday, her sixty-first. It is thin, silk, not quite pink but not quite gray, and is knotted firmly at her waist by a scarlet sash rather than the matching belt it came with.

This is Mémé—that scarlet sash.

"You got home late," she says, eyes still on the poem. "How was the dance?"

She looks up then, and you love that face so much. You love the thickness of her eyebrows, still dark. You love that her eyes are hazel-flecked, like yours, like your mother's between you. You love the soft skin of her cheeks, the deep lines in her brow and around her mouth, the lips that have kissed and comforted you nearly all your life.

Those lips tighten. "Bisou," she says, "what's the matter?"

And there's a moment where you nearly tell her everything—*everything*—the blood, the shame, the race through the forest, the attack by the wolf, your escape. She is the sort of grandmother you *could* tell such things. She has been, for these past twelve years, since you returned to Washington and moved into her home, a vessel for almost all your feelings, your fears, your concerns. She has become the voice you hear inside your head, better than a conscience—Mémé is cautious and smart, always fair, tough sometimes, yes, but true. It is a good voice to carry with you, and you yearn to hear it now, telling you everything will be okay.

But every relationship has its limits, you realize suddenly, as you swallow back the words that wish to spill out. You are not going to tell your grandmother about the feel of James's mouth between your legs. You are not going to tell her about your orgasm in his old blue wagon, or about the moonbeam that illuminated his face just as he looked up to see your pleasure on your face and showing you your blood on his.

And you are not going to tell her about what happened after.

"It was fine." And you go to the kettle for water for your morning tea.

"I didn't hear James drop you off," Mémé says. "That clunker of his usually is loud enough to wake up the whole street."

You scoop some English breakfast into the infuser, lower it into your favorite mug—the fat-bottomed one with a lid—and pour a stream of boiling water over it. Aromatic steam billows up and you breathe it in.

"You must have really been asleep," you say, and there, you have lied two times to Mémé in the span of ten seconds.

The water in your mug turns to tea as you slice a piece of bread from the loaf near the sink. Mémé bakes twice a week, and today, Monday, is a baking day. Already dough is rising in a bowl on the countertop, draped with a blue checked dishcloth. There will be fresh bread when you get home from school.

"I'll be going out to market today," Mémé says, sipping her tea. "Do you need anything special?"

You shake your head and slip the slice of bread in the toaster.

"If you think of anything, call me before noon," Mémé says. "I'll be heading out then."

Mémé's bone-deep distaste for cell phones means that she almost always forgets hers at home and barely ever checks her messages; if you need to get ahold of her, you have to catch her on the landline or leave her a note. It's then that you realize you don't have your phone; you must have left it, along with your shoes, in James's car.

When the toast pops up, you slather it with butter and drizzle honey both on the bread and into your tea, now near-black, dump the loose tea leaves into the compost bin, and snap the mug's lid into place.

Mémé has been watching you move about the kitchen—you feel her watching you—but this is not unusual. Mémé watches people. It's just the way she is.

You zip a jacket over your sweatshirt, shoulder your backpack, wrap your toast in a cloth napkin, and take up your tea. "I've gotta go," you say. "I'm late for the bus."

But you would never leave without kissing her goodbye, and so you turn, lower your face as she turns hers up, and you kiss, left cheek, right cheek.

"Des bisous de ma Bisou," she says, as she always does. "Kisses from my kiss," a play on your name.

It's the familiarity of the routine, probably, a force of habit, that prompts you to say, just before you leave the house through the kitchen door, "Oh, I got my period, finally."

Your hand is on the doorknob, and you turn back to smile goodbye, and Mémé's face is open in a way you have never seen. Her eyes are wide, her forehead deeply wrinkled, her mouth round.

You open the door, and a brace of wet, cold wind knocks you back a bit, so you struggle out to the porch to close the door quickly, not wanting to let too much of the outside in.

Hood up, eyes down, you descend the steps and head toward the sidewalk, hurrying now to make your bus.

Your steps slow as you contemplate Mémé's expression.

The wide eyes. The open mouth. She looked . . . surprised? Yes, that. But also, something else.

You get to the bus stop just in time to see the plume of exhaust as your bus pulls away. You could run after it and yell for it to stop. Maybe it would. But what is the hurry? You don't want to hang out in the hallways before class, and James shares your homeroom . . . are you really so eager to see him again?

You will walk. You'll arrive late, but so what? It's drizzling, but that's nothing here in the Pacific Northwest, where rain is constant throughout the fall, winter, and even spring. You've got the hood of your sweatshirt to protect your hair and your mug of tea to warm you.

So you cut right, across the misty park, and you bite into your still-warm bread, sticky with honey.

School, when you arrive, is quiet, classes already in session. The wide swath of steps that leads up to the door of the old stone and brick building is dark with wetness, and you take it slowly. You are already late—why rush now?

Raphael, the security guy, sits on his stool just inside the purple, glass-paned front doors, paper folded open. He's got a cup of coffee squeezed between his legs. He must be reading something interesting because he barely registers your entrance, raises his chin slightly without raising his eyes, and waves you to the admissions office.

You're not the only person arriving late today; there are a few bleary-eyed stragglers in the hall, and Big Mac pushes out of the attendance office just as you reach for the door to go in, a gray cast across his usually pink skin telling the story of how much he must have had to drink at whatever after-party he went to last night, and how he must have woken up feeling this morning. He raises his chin at you in a halfhearted greeting, something he wouldn't have bothered doing last year, before you were James's girlfriend.

Inside, the office feels off. Everyone is there who is usually there—Ms. Nguyen at the front desk, a couple of student aides pretending to file things but really checking their phones, the half-closed door to the principal's office no different than any other morning. But you sense something, something you don't have the words for. A disturbance.

Ms. Nguyen shakes her head when she sees you standing in front of her desk. "Really, Bisou, you too? I would have expected better." She dashes her signature on a tardy slip and tears it from the pad, handing it to you. "Off to class," she says, and so you go.

"I don't know if it's any better this way, having the dance on a Sunday and all of them showing up late and hungover," she complains behind you as you push through the door.

"Sharing, Valuing, and Caring About Each Other's Feelings," reads the banner above the entranceway into the main hallway. It's a new sign, bright yellow background, letters all in blue except for *Caring*, which is an enormous looming red word in the middle of the banner, its *i* dotted with a red heart.

The floor is speckled gray-white linoleum, scuffed here and there, and slashed across with bands of brick red, for contrast. All down the right side of the hall spans an enormous mural—a visual history of Washington State. Here, a gathering of Native Americans incongruously holding aloft a sign that reads "The Garfield High School History Project"; there, a group of unsmiling Chinese immigrants; farther down, a half-finished building on the edge of the water, a ship in the distance.

The hallway is silent but for your steps, the occasional squeak of your sneaker on the linoleum, and the tinny, faraway slam of a locker. You pause outside your chemistry classroom.

You're grateful that the door opens in the rear of the class. You slide into your seat. Ms. Walker is turned away from the students, doing a problem on the board, some molecular equation, and you take out your notebook and copy it down. Toward the front, near the window, you see James. His head is down, he's writing in his notebook, and the back of his neck is exposed. Seeing it fills your eyes with unexpected burning tears—the vulnerability of it. The bareness of his skin.

He's wearing a red-and-black checked flannel with a black puffer vest. His long legs, stretched out, reach underneath the seat in front of him—Keisha Montgomery's seat—and are in a pair of deep black jeans. He's wearing his basketball shoes, the high-tops.

He wore those same shoes last night, with his jacket and tie. The same jeans, too.

Maybe he feels your eyes on his neck, because he brings his hand up and rubs it.

You look down. You don't want him to turn around and see you staring at him. What will you say? He's going to be disgusted by you, by last night. He probably won't break up with you, though, because he's not that kind of guy. You'll have to do it. There's no way he could be with you again, after last night. How *could* he? After you . . . bled like that?

You imagine the blanket he spread in the back of his wagon, bloodied by you.

Disgust. He must be disgusted. *You* are disgusted. Disgusting.

Then—shit. It occurs to you that you should have packed some tampons into your bag. That was stupid, not to do that.

You scan the class. There's Maggie, playing with a long strand of her flaxen hair, dreaming out the window. You could ask her, but you don't want to maybe have to deal with whatever feelings she might be having about what you said to Tucker at the dance last night. Your eyes return to Keisha, in front of James. Her hand moves quickly across paper on her desk, taking notes. Her twists are wrapped into their characteristic low bun, out of the way. You can ask her. She's the prepared type, always with an extra pencil, happy to hand out a sheet of paper to anyone who needs it.

You don't really like the idea of asking anyone for a favor. It's just not the way Mémé has raised you, to need anything from anyone. It's not that she had actively discouraged you from asking for help; she didn't have to. Just looking at the way she lived her life—practically a hermit, making for herself things that she could easily buy, never bringing home friends or going out to eat—told you all you needed to know about how best to live.

Your mother told you the rest.

Someone's phone beeps—an incoming text. Ms. Walker looks around, annoyed, but it's impossible to tell whose phone it was. Her gaze lands on you.

"Bisou," she says. "Do you have a tardy slip?"

You hold it up. She folds her arms and raises one eyebrow. You sigh, stand, and deliver it to her at the front of the class.

"Not like you to be late," she says, accepting the pink slip of paper.

Behind you, suddenly, phones begin to vibrate, all across the class, like a breaking wave. People pull their phones out of backpacks, out of jacket pockets. A gasp. And then another. Students begin to murmur.

They are talking about you. The certainty of it is a crash of nausea in your gut. James must have told someone, just one someone, about what happened last night, in his car, after the dance. And that someone—one of his basketball friends, probably—told somebody else. Who told someone else. And now *everyone* knows, and right behind you, they're all laughing. They're all covering their mouths and laughing at you.

You lift your chin and prepare to face him. You will level him with your gaze. You know how. You got it from Mémé, the ability to wither with a glance. She doesn't need anyone, and it was a mistake, you feel with sudden clarity, to want James as much as you did. It leads to pain, love. Always. You should have known.

But when you turn, it is different than you expect. Yes, they all are holding their phones, James included . . . but their faces are wrong. Not laughing, not disgust—shock. Horror, even.

Ms. Walker feels it, too. She doesn't reprimand the class for having their phones out. "What is it?" she asks. "What's going on?"

"It's Tucker Jackson," Keisha says.

"What about him?" Ms. Walker folds your tardy note, absentmindedly, into the pocket of her blazer. "What happened?"

"He's—it says he's dead."

FLOCKING

The class erupts. A noise comes out of Maggie, an animal wail that raises the hair on your neck. Three girls jump up to cluster around her. She says, "I can't believe it. I can't believe it," over and over again, and tears streak her face. She has her phone in both of her hands, like a prayer book, and text after text lights up its screen. She shakes her head and cries and thumbs through them, one after the other.

"What happened?" Phillip demands. "Was he in an accident?"

"I don't know. Wait." Keisha is scrolling through something—an article? a text? She looks up, her glasses flashing.

"What happened?"

"How did he die?"

"What do you *mean*, he's dead?"

Everyone is asking questions, talking over each other, forming little groups clustered around phones, looking for answers.

An uncomfortable tingling begins in your brain, as if it is trying to recall a forgotten dream.

You are still standing at the front of the room. You start back toward your seat, but when you walk past James's desk, he puts a hand out, touches your hand, squeezes it. You stop.

"Everyone, stay here," Ms. Walker says. "I'm going to the front office. Just stay here."

She leaves, closing the classroom door behind her. Maggie is wailing, and the girls tighten their circle around her, making shushing noises and patting her back, holding her hand. Lorraine takes Maggie's phone, gently, and sets it facedown on her desk. This is as nice as you've seen the others act toward Maggie in a while, since the rumors started up a month or so ago. You'd overheard Lorraine gossiping with Darcy about Maggie—how the things she was into were too weird even for Tucker, that she was a nympho, that she begged Tucker to have a three-way with her and some guy from her job, which was why Tucker finally broke up with her. But you suppose none of that matters now.

You stand in the aisle, the warm familiarity of James's hand in yours. He leans his forehead into your hip.

"I can't believe it," he murmurs. Then, "You scared me last night."

"I'm sorry." You squat down on your heels so you can look into his eyes. "I didn't mean to—I mean, I didn't know that I—I've never done that before. Any of that. I mean"—and here you whisper—"I've never had my period before. I am so, so sorry. It's so gross. I don't know what to say."

"That's not what I meant," James says, his voice lowering to match yours. "I tried to find you after you ran off, but you were gone. And I texted you like five times before I realized that your phone was still in my car." He reaches into his vest pocket and fishes it out, hands it to you. "It's dead now," he says.

"Oh," you say. "Thank you."

"That other thing," he says, his voice dropping even further, like he knows you wouldn't want anyone to hear. "It's no big deal. Actually, I was kind of relieved when I figured out that that must have been the reason. I mean, I didn't know why you'd run off like that. I thought—I was afraid I'd done something wrong."

His face is so dear, so open. You bring your hand up against his cheek. "No," you say. "You didn't do anything wrong."

He smiles, and then you can see that he remembers the news about Tucker as the smile collapses.

"I can't believe it," he says again. "Tucker. I wonder what happened."

You shake your head. There is a feeling in the pit of your stomach—dread.

Ms. Walker comes back into the class and you squeeze James's hand once more before returning to your seat.

"Everybody quiet down," she says, and it's comforting, the way she takes charge, that authoritative ring to her voice. "I don't have much more to tell you. It's true—Tucker is dead. His body was found, early this morning, in the woods nearby."

She keeps talking, but you can't get past those words—*his body was found, early this morning, in the woods.*

In the woods.

You can still hear the pounding pace of the wolf at your back.

You can still see the wolf's flashing eyes. His flashing teeth.

Your legs are weak, and you are grateful to be sitting. Your hands are gripping the edges of your desk. You tell them to release, you fold them in your lap.

Ms. Walker is still talking. "Principal Evans has called a school-wide assembly. Everyone, pack up your things." She goes over to Maggie, puts her hand on her shoulder. "Maggie, honey, do you want to skip the assembly and go to the office? See the nurse?"

Maggie shakes her head, swipes her hand across her eyes. "I want to hear what happened."

Ms. Walker nods. "Okay. Take a friend and go to the bath-room. Splash some water on your face. Then come join us."

Maggie sniffs loudly. She shoves her notebook into her satchel and gets up. Keisha gets up, too, even though you didn't think she and Maggie were particularly close, and they make their way to the doorway. Before they disappear around it, Maggie turns back for a moment and looks right at you.

"All right," Ms. Walker says, "decorum and patience, everyone. Let's do this right."

Everyone gets their stuff together and heads out the door, up the hall toward the gym. James waits for you just outside the classroom, laces his fingers through yours, and you walk together with the crowd, the whole herd of you moving as one, and the other classes emptying out into the hallway, too, merg-ing with your class, all of you going together to the gym to hear what there is to hear.

It's a big school. There are more than a thousand of you, pouring out of doorways all up and down this hallway, and every hallway. You don't know everyone, but you do know lots of people, and they know you. Though you don't play any team sports, though you're not a *joiner*, really—not of clubs or societies or teams—people have always seemed to listen when you talk, and kids in younger grades have always known your name. "Hey, Bisou," boys always say, some with shy grins, some with sly grins. Today, though, no one is saying your name. Only one name is on their tongues: Tucker Jackson.

The gym teachers are already there, pulling out the bleachers. Coach Arthur, the assistant basketball coach, wipes his face against his sleeve after he pulls out the last set on the left. James lets go of your hand and heads over to where the basketball players are clustering.

"Don't just stand around, gentlemen, help us with the bleachers," Coach Arthur barks, his voice rough with emotion.

So it is that those closest to Tucker—his teammates—arrange the seating for the rest of the students, who file, quieter than usual and with a sobriety that leaves the gym echoey and hollow, into the stands, one by one, as they accordion out from the walls.

You consider saving a spot for James, but it looks like he's going to stay with his team, so you angle into the bleachers along with the herd, sitting on the hard silver bench and tucking your backpack between your feet. It's cold in the gym.

The basketball team sits in the front two rows of the last set of bleachers. Other than the football players, they're the school's biggest guys, some of the most grown-up looking, most of them taller than the teachers; but sitting together in the wake of the news about Tucker's death, they look like very large children, faces stricken with uncertainty, sadness, fear. More than one of them is crying, and they put their arms around each other's shoulders, teammates even in grief . . . though, if you're being totally honest, you don't recall that many of them actually *liked* Tucker. James could hardly stand him.

Keisha and Maggie come in through the far door and end up next to you on the bleachers, Keisha on your left, with Maggie on her left. On your right is Graham Keller, who you haven't spoken a word to in at least a year. Keisha is holding Maggie's hand, and she offers you her other, and you take it. Because it seems like the right thing to do, you offer your other hand to Graham, but instead of cupping it, he laces his fingers through yours.

Freshman year, you said yes to Graham when he asked you to be his date to a dance, even though you didn't want to. Mémé, who was driving you to the school to meet him, kept looking at you out of the corner of her eye, until at last she said, "Dear one, why did you agree to go out with this boy when you are so clearly unhappy about it?"

"Because," you said, "I felt sorry for him, and he wouldn't take no for an answer."

Mémé had pulled the car into the next parking lot and turned off the engine. She turned in her seat to face you. "Darling," she said, and her hazel eyes were electric, her mouth a straight flat line, "it is not your job to make boys happy."

You were already mad at yourself for saying yes, and the last thing you wanted was a lecture from Mémé, who always had some feminist axiom at the ready but didn't seem to understand how the world really worked.

"It's no big deal," you told her. "It's just a school dance."

Mémé had wanted to turn the car around and take you home. "Making one mistake does not oblige you to make another in the same direction," she had said, which made no sense to you at all. You had said yes, and you would go, you insisted, and so, reluctantly, Mémé had driven you the rest of the way to the school.

"I will be waiting for you right here at ten o'clock," she had said, and three hours later, when ten o'clock arrived, you had never been so grateful for a night to end.

When Graham had asked you to go see a movie with him a week later, you said that your grandmother had decided you were too young to date, that she was just old-fashioned that way, and you'd shrugged and feigned annoyance. He'd followed you like a puppy until the end of the semester, when he suddenly decided you were a bitch and moved on to adoring some other girl. But in this moment, your fingers meshed with his, you feel like that freshman girl again, with Graham nudging, pushing, nosing his way in.

"Listen up, people." Principal Evans steps forward, looking, as ever, too important for his position. He's handsome like a movie star, tall and dark skinned, dressed in a navy suit with a pink pocket square and neatly knotted tie. His shoes, black and pointed, gleam. "Quiet down," he says, but everyone is already nearly perfectly still, no one has their phone out, everyone leans forward, listening.

"This is what we know," Principal Evans continues. He's speaking into a microphone, and so his voice comes from all around you. "Tucker Jackson was found dead this morning in the woods off Claiborne Avenue at 6:05 a.m. by a runner and his dog. You've probably heard rumors, so I'm just going to give it to you straight. Tucker was found naked. Based on various injuries to his body, it appears as though he'd been running, and the working theory is that he couldn't see the path clearly, because it appears he suffered a blow to the head, most likely from hitting a tree, and broke his neck."

Maggie sucks air in, high and sharp, and buries her face in Keisha's shoulder. Keisha lets go of your hand so that she can wrap her arms around Maggie, and that leaves you sitting there in the bleachers, fingers entwined with Graham's.

Naked. A broken neck. Alone in the woods.

The tingling feeling you felt earlier, in the classroom, is back, stronger. It's accompanied now by a high-pitched ringing in your head. You swallow hard, as if you can swallow it away.

"His parents have been alerted, of course, and there will be an investigation," Principal Evans continues. "Tucker, like all of our students, was an important and beloved member of our community."

You hear the words, you hear the murmurs that begin to swell up around you, but the electric buzz and sharp ring inside your own head seem stronger, louder.

It was a wolf, you tell yourself, a *wolf*, not a boy, that attacked you in the forest. It was a wolf you threw into that tree.

"Quiet down," Principal Evans says, and everyone does. "Counselors will be available this afternoon and for the rest of the week if you'd like to speak with someone; the library will be open to accommodate you." He glances at his watch. "We'll resume classes in . . . fifteen minutes, when second period begins. Are there any questions?"

"Will there be an autopsy?" Maggie says, not raising her hand. "Are they going to have to cut him open?"

The students' voices break into discussion, their words indecipherable. You pull your hand away from Graham, who doesn't want to let go right away, but finally does.

"Quiet!" Principal Evans booms, and this time he sounds angry.

When the gym is silent again, he says, "I don't have that information, Maggie. I'm sorry. We will do our best to give you updates as they come in." Then he says, "Last night, you all know, was the homecoming dance, and Tucker was there, as were many of you. Somebody in this room likely knows something that will help the investigation, something that could help Tucker's family understand what happened. Any information you might have about what may have occurred— at the dance, and after—we need to hear it, guys. Things you might not think are important could be of interest to the police. We're not saying anyone is in trouble. But if there was a dare, or a prank, or anything like that—any reason Tucker would have been alone, without clothes, in the middle of the night—well, we need to know about it. Understood?"

All around, people begin to murmur, to whisper to one another.

"He came to the dance alone," you hear from a voice behind you. "But I saw him leave with Maggie."

"He was drunk off his ass," says someone else.

You remember seeing Tucker, the way he grasped Maggie's arm. And later—when he'd stumbled onto the crowded dance floor. You remember the last words you ever exchanged with Tucker, and now he is dead.

Naked, with a broken neck, in the woods.

"Quiet down," says the principal again, and his deep voice booms through the gym. He keeps the microphone just under his chin and waits a beat until the room is still again. Then he nods. "Okay. Gather your things. Make your way to the library if you'd like to talk to a counselor. Investigators are on campus, and they may have questions for some of you throughout the day." People start to rustle around, gathering their things, but then Principal Evans says, "Tucker's friends from the basketball team, hang back. The investigators would like to interview you first. Please head to my office."

And then he switches off the microphone, and the assembly is over, and you are free to leave. James looks up and finds you in the stands, gives you that sweet, kind smile you love, and then follows Principal Evans and his teammates.

Ahead of you, Keisha leads Maggie out of the gym. It seems that everyone wants to stop Maggie—ask her a question, give her a hug, say something about Tucker. Maggie cries and nods and wipes her face.

In a flash, you remember a day last spring, not long after you and James had gotten together. You had walked halfway home before realizing you'd left your history textbook behind and turning back toward school.

The hallway that late afternoon seemed particularly empty; it was an unusually fine day and everyone—the students and the adults too, it seemed—had left as soon as the final bell tolled, in search of sun. You turned a corner toward your locker and there they were—Maggie and Tucker, her pushed up against the row of lockers, him pinning her there, his mouth on her throat and one hand disappeared up under her skirt. Maggie squirmed like maybe she wanted him to stop, or maybe she was just embarrassed to be found there by you like that, so undone.

But Tucker didn't pull away; he kept his hand where it was, up under Maggie's skirt, buried between her thighs, as you walked past them, as you turned the dial of your padlock, as you extracted your book, as you relocked your locker, as you passed them again on your way back up the hallway.

He kept his hand where it was, but his eyes followed you.

You had felt them on your face, your neck, your back. And no one—not Tucker, not Maggie, not you—said a single word. And a few days later, when you saw Maggie at a party, she didn't say anything about it, and you didn't either.

"Tucker was such a good guy," Graham says to Maggie, his hand touching her shoulder, just for a moment, as he passes.

Maggie nods again.

In the hallway, groups break off from the herd and head in separate directions. Three girls from French are making plans to go to a coffee shop at lunch, and another cluster of kids is talking about heading over to Tran's house after school. Both groups invite you to join, but both times you shake your head. You suspect it's the fact that you're James's girlfriend—just one degree of separation from Tucker—that's eliciting the invitations. You have no stomach for the gossip. Finally, the hallway clears when the bell rings, signaling the beginning of second period. You hesitate, alone, for a moment. You should be going to British lit, but you can't head that way, not today. Instead, you push out through the purple doors and head down the steps.

You're not the kind to ditch class; you've never skipped before, actually. School is fine, and you wouldn't want to worry Mémé like that. But you can't be in that building, not a moment longer. Not today. Not now.

It's strange to be out on the street in front of the school on a Monday, midmorning. The sun seems like it's in the wrong place in the sky. The air is cold and wet, and a sharp wind blows your hair, opens your undone jacket. You zip and button against the wind the best you can. You hoist your backpack onto both shoulders. You pocket your hands.

You walk.

Not home.

You know where you must go. Of course you do.

It was a wolf you killed in the woods last night—a wolf, not a boy. Not Tucker.

All you need to do is go back to the woods, back to the path of pins and needles, and find the wolf's body. You will see the wolf there, beneath the tree, his neck bent at that life-ending angle, and then you will unclench. You will soften, your pulse will slow, and you will laugh at yourself for being so ridiculous. You will shake your head and maybe even you will kneel beside the broken wolf and lay your hand upon his pelt, wet now from the morning's rain. And then you'll go back to school. If you're lucky, no one will even notice that you've been gone.

Except that when you make your way to the forest, to the place you faced the wolf, you are not alone. And there is no wolf.

Yellow caution tape winds around tree trunks to form a rough rectangle. Three officers—two of them uniformed, a man and a woman, and another man, this one in a jacket and tie, a badge strung around his neck—stand inside the taped-off perimeter.

You see them before they see you, and you take the moment to rearrange your face and then your story. Were you quick enough? What do they see, when they sense you there, when their heads pivot and their eyes pin you? The Latina officer—midthirties, low ponytail, sharp and tight in her uniform—sees you first. She's standing with another uniformed officer—Asian, maybe forty, a camera in his hands—looking down at writing in a notebook, when she seems to feel your presence. She looks up, then around, before her gaze finds you.

You step out from behind the tree that half hides you. You make yourself conspicuous.

Now the third cop—this one plain-clothed, soft bellied, thinning red hair, in his early fifties—sees you, too. He has been walking the perimeter, slowly, slowly, eyes on the ground, scanning.

"Oh no," you say. It wouldn't do any good to feign ignorance about Tucker's death. Too easy for them to check, later, if you were in school today, if you had been in the assembly. "Is this where you found him?"

"What are you doing here, young lady?" the plain-clothed cop asks. His voice is slow, but not stupid. It's careful, that's what it is. "Why aren't you in school?"

"I'm not feeling well," you say. "I'm going home sick." You pause, and then you say, "They told us—they said that Tucker was found in the woods. But not *here*?" It sounds convincing to your ears—your tone. It sounds surprised, a little scared.

"It isn't safe for a girl to be alone in the woods," the female officer says gently, with concern. "You should stay on the street."

At this, you bristle, despite your precarious situation. Why should you be denied the pleasure of a solitary walk in the woods, just because you are a girl? What about Thoreau? Did anyone warn *him* away from the forest?

But you know enough to keep your tongue. There is no good way to answer this rebuff. And the cops' lack of surprise at your question gave you your answer. You clench your fists inside your pockets, tuck your chin, and turn in the direction of Mémé's house.

"Not so fast," calls the plain-clothed officer. "We'll need your name. In case we have questions later."

You stop. You feel your nails form moons in the flesh of your palms. Do they have the right to ask for your name? Must you give it?

It would, of course, be terribly suspicious if you were to refuse. "Bisou Martel." Then you turn your back to them.

"Martel?" It's the same officer. "You related to Sybil?"

You turn back. Another question you are not necessarily *required* to answer, but again, you know better than to refuse. "She's my grandmother."

"No shit," he says, and now he's looking at you, *really* looking—assessing your hair, your face, the push of your breasts against your jacket, the way you stand.

This is not a question, and so you say nothing. You bear the weight of his gaze. Then he says, "You're sick, huh? What's wrong with you?"

"I have cramps," you say. "My period." This causes him to shift his eyes, and so you turn away again, and this time, no one stops you.

There was no wolf at the base of the tree. There was no boy, either, and you wonder where they have taken it. Tucker's body. To the hospital? To the morgue? Your city must have a morgue—maybe it has several, Seattle is a big place—but you have never thought of it before.

You're walking away from the officers, away from the caution tape, away from the tree, as if nothing has changed for you, holding yourself carefully, so no one can see that everything has changed.

Boys do not become wolves. Wolves do not become boys. These things do not—cannot—happen. And that leads you to one ineffable conclusion: you have killed a person. Somehow, you murdered Tucker.

Maybe you had been hallucinating because you were so upset about what had happened in James's car. Maybe you thought you saw a wolf when really it was Tucker, and maybe he had been in the woods for some entirely innocent reason. Maybe he hadn't been following you, no one had been. Maybe it was all in your head, and you are a stupid girl, and you misread the entire situation and now Tucker is dead.

It must have been a dare, you tell yourself, walking faster, suddenly needing to get home, to *be* home. Someone must have dared Tucker to run through the woods naked. And maybe he was drunk, or maybe he'd taken something—what was it that made people act so crazy and aggressive? Bath salts. That was it. Maybe Tucker had taken bath salts, and he'd gone a little crazy last night, too.

You reach the tree line and then you are back in civilization. There is the pizza place and there is the bus stop and not far beyond is your own curvy little street. You take a deep, cold breath, taste the coming rain.

Maybe you are not a murderer. Maybe it was manslaughter. Or, if Tucker was high, maybe it was self-defense, or just a terrible accident.

But now you've lied to those officers back there. You should have told them what happened—not the wolf part, that would just make you seem crazy (*are* you crazy?), but the rest of it— about Tucker running at you, naked, about him lunging for you, about how you stabbed him in the eye, but how even that didn't stop him, how he turned and attacked you again. How he hit the tree. How his neck snapped.

You dig your house key out of your backpack and turn it in the lock. Home embraces you—warmth, the smell of rising bread, the particular light that comes into the hall through the stained-glass panels that flank the front door. Your eyes burn with tears. You drop your backpack to the bench and sit to loosen your boots.

"Bisou?" Mémé calls from the far back room, her little library, where she writes. You hear the scrape of her chair pushing back, the gentle steps of her stockinged feet. She comes into the front hall. Her hair is loose, damp from the shower. "What are you doing home?"

At the sound of her voice, and then the sight of her face in the doorway, your tears spill. Your boots are unlaced but still on your feet, and you put your face in your hands and let the tears come, and the ugly sounds you make when you cry.

Mémé is beside you, moving your backpack off the bench, wrapping her arms around you. "Shh, shh," she croons. Mémé does not push you for information. She just holds you, your wet cheek pressed against the warm soft indentation of her throat, the weight of her chin on the top of your head, and you are cocooned by her embrace, by her arms and her voice and the panels of her silver hair.

"Did something happen?" she asks, finally. "With James? Last night?"

"No," you say, answering the second question, and not the

first. "James is wonderful. He didn't do anything."

You feel Mémé's chin press into your head as she nods. You love her for not insisting, for holding you quietly.

You could sit right there on the entry hall bench for the rest of your days. You and Mémé could fossilize, you in her arms. That would be fine. That would be good.

But you are made of flesh and blood, and you are reminded of this by the urgent hot pulse that pushes from you now. The body must be tended to. You take Mémé's warm hands into yours and bring them to your face, kiss them, place them back into her lap.

"I'll be okay," you say. "I have to go to the bathroom."

And you stand, and you stumble over the undone laces of your boots, and you feel as if your body is completely out of your control, as if it's not your body at all, but someone else's, as you trip and bleed your way to the bathroom.

On the toilet, you find the blood-clotted string and pull. The tampon emerges, a triumph of gore, bloated now to more than twice the size it was when you put it in, a clump of some gelatinous red thing adhered to its side. It dangles like a hooked fish, swinging slightly, and you stare at it. Finally, you wrap it in toilet paper and push it to the bottom of the trash can.

Mémé will want to know why you were crying. You will have to tell her something. You wish that you could tell her everything—how it all started with James in the car, how you might be losing your mind, how you thought you killed a wolf but maybe instead you killed a boy from school. But there are good reasons not to worry Mémé with such terrible possibilities. One very good reason, actually.

Your father.

ii

i was alone
in my booth
selling tickets to dreams
alone
needing to be found

he came
bought two tickets
to the five o'clock show
and slid one back to me

when our fingers touched
he smiled, white and strong
strong enough to keep me safe
if he wanted to

CRYING, WOLF

Your house in Quebec was not built of straw nor sticks, yet still the wind rattled it like the rageful breath of a hungry wolf.

It was a big house—endlessly big, it seemed to you—but Mama kept most of the doors closed.

One afternoon, after the shutters were up, when the bruises on Mama's face had turned a mottled green, you snuck out from beneath the weight of her sleeping arm and slipped from the bedroom you shared. It was the only upstairs room with an open door.

Mama needed lots of sleep. "The body heals when it's at rest," she said. But you did not need lots of sleep. Your legs felt itchy and twitchy from so much rest. You needed to climb, and run, and jump, and play. You longed to return to the pond, to practice skipping stones, though the ice by now was far too thick for such things.

"We won't stay indoors forever," Mama promised.

But the howling wind and the piling snow and the stubborn bruises seemed to conspire against you, keeping you locked inside the strange old house.

Down the long, narrow hallway you walked, away from Mama. The doors were tall and thin, paneled and painted, though the paint was faded. Each door had a tarnished silver knob.

Mama had never told you *not* to open the doors. You walked all the way down the hall, as far away from the sleeping room as you could, and then you reached up for the knob of the farthest door. It turned, and you pushed open the door.

Behind the door, the room was full of ghosts. A tall, thin ghost, a short, fat ghost, a wide, low ghost. As the door yawned open, the ghosts began to dance, weaving eerily back and forth.

With ice-cold clarity, you knew that they would come for you now that you had opened the door. They would circle you, and swoop down on you, and they would consume you, pulling your skin away from your bones and your eyes from their sockets and your nails from their beds. It would be slow and silent and so simple for them. You were frozen by this knowledge, paralyzed, and they danced closer, and closer, and closer.

And then, you screamed. You screamed so high and loud that the sound set your own ears to ringing. Mama came running down the hall, you heard her steps behind you. She was a thousand miles away. She would not get to you in time. No one could save you. It was just you and the ghosts.

But then she was there, and she grabbed you up, and you were in her arms. You wrapped your arms around her neck and your legs around her waist and you held on so, so tight, as tightly as she held you.

Your scream turned to tears and jagged breaths. Mama held you safe and high, and she carried you away from the ghost room, back to the safe sleeping room, and she sat on the edge of the bed, and still you held tight, arms and legs clenched around her, and she didn't complain, she didn't tell you to let go. She held you until the tears were done and your muscles fell limp, and then she laid you in the bed and lay beside you, pulling the blankets up over both of your heads, making a safe little cave where no one could find you, no Papa, no ghosts, no one and nothing but you and Mama, and then you were tired, at last, and your eyes, swollen from crying, fell shut, and you slept.

Later, when you woke, Mama took you back to the ghost room. You did not want to go—you begged her not to make you—but she said you needed to see that everything was okay, that there were no ghosts. She pushed open the door as you held tightly to her hand. "See?" she said. "Look."

You looked, and you saw furniture covered in sheets—a tall mirror, a fat armchair, an old bureau.

"No ghosts," Mama said. "Just as I told you."

But the room did not fool you, even as it fooled your mother. Yes, of course, now there was a mirror, and an armchair, and a bureau. Now there were regular things covered in regular sheets. But before, when you had been alone, the room had been full of ghosts.

And you would not open the door again.

The next morning, you return to school. Mémé has written a note to excuse your absence—"I had cramps, and I left," you told her, the same lie you told the cops. Inside the school's front doors, someone has set up a memorial for Tucker. It's a folding table, maybe the same table the moms were sitting at the other night at the dance, and in the center is his basketball jersey, in the school colors, black and gold, with his last name—Jackson—and his number—45—emblazoned across it. There's a framed picture of Tucker, his official team portrait, with him wearing that jersey; he's half smiling, like someone just said something funny, some inside joke that he gets but you probably wouldn't. Surrounding the jersey and the picture is a motley collection of things Tucker liked—a round green can of Copenhagen chew, last month's issue of *Thrasher*, a few bags of Cool Ranch Doritos, a black box of Trojan condoms.

Of course, there are flowers, even though you have no memory of Tucker ever mentioning an interest in botany. Arrangements in vases, bought from stores; cellophane-wrapped bunches, laid on the table; single blossoms, picked from home gardens.

There are cards, too—the store-bought kind, with pictures of sunsets and flowers, these filled with the loopy cursive of girls, but also notes written on regular lined paper, and one, a single word scrawled on the back of a receipt—*Dude*.

You stand near the table, out of the way of the flow of incoming students, and watch as people walk by, some stopping to read the notes, others pulling something out of their bags to add to the mix.

Maggie comes in. She stops in front of the table, hands on the straps of her backpack, and stares, unblinking, at the table. You shift your focus from the display of inanimate objects to the real person now regarding them. Though she's usually a makeup girl, today Maggie's face is bare, save for some light pink lip stuff. Her hair is raked up into a bun on the top of her head. Her expression is inscrutable, totally blank.

You watch as she loosens her hands from the straps of

her backpack and reaches behind her neck, unclasps a chain, reclasps it, and lays it across the can of Copenhagen. Then she walks away.

After she's gone, you step forward and pick up the necklace. It's a heart-shaped locket, one you don't remember ever seeing her wear. You slide your thumbnail into the crack and the locket pops open. There is nothing inside.

The chain pools on the table as you set the locket down. You stand beside the table, staring at the locket, trying to name the feeling in your chest.

Not guilt.

Not horror.

Should you be feeling those feelings? Most likely, yes. But they do not come. There is a caginess inside your heart; an awareness of danger, and a desire to avoid being found out.

Does this make you monstrous? A monster?

That day, you avoid the lunch crowd; you don't have an appetite. But the next day, Wednesday, you take your place in the cafeteria next to James; he squeezes your knee under the table to let you know he's glad to have you back.

"It'll be a few more days before they get the results of the autopsy," Caleb says from his usual seat next to Landon. A few other basketball players share the table, too. And there, next to Big Mac, is Keisha Montgomery.

This is not usual. Keisha isn't one to hang out with the athletes. Most of her friends are of the student council/yearbook committee/school newspaper variety, and she rarely makes an appearance in the cafeteria.

You aren't close with Keisha, but you find her interesting. In some ways, she reminds you of your grandmother, and maybe that's why you notice things about her. Though the school doesn't require one, Keisha wears her own uniform every day: jeans or cords, in black, gray, or dark brown; a button-down shirt, white, floral, or denim; underneath, either a T-shirt or tank, depending on the season. Doc Martens, eight-hole, or Mary Janes, black. You have never seen Keisha in shorts or a dress. She wears her twists in either a bun or a simple braid. She has three pairs of glasses: one pair round and tortoiseshell; one pair ovular and white; and the pair she's wearing today, slightly cat-eye, black, with inlaid mother-of-pearl floral patterns on the bridge of the nose and along the outer rims.

Last year, over the summer, Keisha went to Latvia on a student program, and when she came back, she spoke marginally decent Latvian. She gave a presentation in history class about Latvian foods, cultures, and traditions, including a slide show. "This is the Pokaini Forest," she'd said. "No one is sure why there are all these piles of stones, but one theory is that ancient pilgrims brought them there as penance for their sins." Keisha is a collector of facts.

Next year, when you graduate, Keisha will be valedictorian. You don't doubt that four years after that, she'll be at the top of her class wherever she goes to college.

She is a nail biter, a fact she tries to hide by balling her hands into fists, but when she disappears into thought, her fingers loosen and find their way to her mouth.

Unlike Keisha, who is an unusual addition to this lunch table, you have sat, on and off, with the basketball team for a while now, even before you and James began dating last spring. Not because you were some fawning girl, but because you'd long been friends with James—not close, but comfortable.

Finding a place to sit at lunchtime, or a lab partner, or someone to dance with, has never been a problem for you, but neither has it been a priority. Still, you're aware of the social order, the groupings, the usual movements of your classmates—and Keisha at this table is not usual.

Something else that strikes you as unusual: though you have, almost certainly, killed a human with your bare hands, you still have an appetite. You register this and wonder at it. What kind of a monster does this make you?

"What did the cops ask you about the other day?" Keisha says to the boys. Her lunch bag, unopened, sits on the table. She perches on the edge of the bench, all of her energy forward. Her hands, in fists, rest in her lap.

Caleb rips a bite from his sandwich, speaks around a wad in his cheek. "They wanted to know about Tucker. You know . . . who saw him at the dance. What he was acting like—if he was weird or anything."

"*Was* he acting weird?" Keisha asks.

"Maybe you'd know if you'd been there," Landon says.

Keisha shrugs this off. "I had better things to do. What else did they ask?"

"You could totally tell they were trying to find out if he'd been on something," Landon says between handfuls of potato chips. "They were all, 'Did Tucker seem out of sorts or unusual? What were you all doing before going to the dance?'"

"And they wanted to know where we went after the dance, too," Caleb says.

You set your water bottle down. You force yourself not to look over at James. But you don't have to ask the question—he answers, unasked.

"Bisou and I headed back to her place after the dance. We barely even saw Tucker that night, other than when he tried to get her to dance with him."

James doesn't look at you, but you feel the message he's sending: he didn't tell the cops that the two of you had been parked near the woods. He didn't tell them that you got out of the car and ran away.

He is protecting you, but it hurts your heart. Because he

71

doesn't know what he's protecting you from. And now he has lied. He's lied, and maybe that makes him guilty by association. Maybe that makes him complicit.

You don't contradict him, though. You don't say, "No, babe, remember? We parked for a while by the woods, and I walked home from there." You don't say anything at all. You pick up your sandwich, unwrap the waxed paper, and you force yourself to chew, to swallow.

When you look up, you find that Keisha is watching you.

James drives you home after school.

He puts the car in park and turns off the engine. He turns to you and smiles his dear smile, reaches over and brushes a curl back from your temple. "It's Wednesday," he says, which it is. But you know what he means: Wednesday is the day Mémé volunteers at the library. Wednesday is the only day that your house is reliably empty; on days other than Wednesdays, Mémé spends her afternoons in her writing room, or crisscrossing the living room, working out the plot for whichever novel she is drafting.

On other Wednesdays, you have invited James inside. You have played house, fixing him a snack, pouring him a glass of iced tea from the jar kept in the refrigerator. You have curled in his lap on the couch, kissing until your chin is raw from his stubble. You have lain together in your bed, first him on top, then you, then him again.

But today, though you hold his hand against your cheek, you say, "I'm tired. I think I'll go inside and take a nap. Okay?"

"Okay," he says, though you know he is disappointed. Still, what does he expect? You have your period, and now that you've done the things you did in the car the other night—this same car—you think that it's not like he'll want to go back to kissing and cuddling.

"I could nap with you," he offers, but you force a laugh and shake your head.

"I'll see you tomorrow," you say, and you kiss him, and then you go inside.

It wasn't your intention, but after you close the door and take off your boots and coat, you go to Mémé's room. The door is open, as it often is, and her bed is neatly made, the white chenille bedspread tucked up and over her pillows. There is her highboy, the one you used to sit beneath when first you came to this house, a dozen years ago. The first time you climbed under there, when Mémé found you, you thought she would make you get out. But instead, she opened one of the drawers and pulled out four long silk scarves, bright panels of flowers and birds, and she taped them just beneath the bottom drawer to form a little hideaway. Then you were safe and hidden, and she passed you a pillow from her bed and the blanket from her sitting chair, and that became your spot for months and months, whenever you needed it, until, one day, you did not need it anymore.

You need it now, but when you try to curl beneath the high-boy, it no longer feels like a safe little hideaway. Your legs are too long; your body too big. You try to fold yourself small enough, but you feel your ribs pressing together, you can't take a full breath, and rather than feeling safe, you feel claustro-phobic.

You roll out from beneath the highboy. You suck in a full deep breath, feeling your lungs and ribs expand. You splay your arms and legs. You take up room, as much as you need.

Better.

Eventually, you climb to your feet. You should leave Mémé's room—not that she would mind your being here, but just because it feels wrong to be in her space without her per-mission (though you have, over the years, pulled open every drawer, dug through every pocket). But rather than leaving, you go to her closet and slide open its door.

The space smells like Mémé. You close your eyes and breathe, and as you focus on the scent, it is as if you can pick out each element: the rose water Mémé sprinkles on her skin after her bath; the lemongrass and patchouli she dabs on her pulse points; the cocoa butter she rubs into her face each night. And something else, something unnameable but distinct, some particular Mémé-ness.

You open your eyes. You run your hand across the row of blouses and sweaters and skirts. Most of the clothes hanging in the closet, Mémé only breaks out when she volunteers at the library. The rest of the time, Mémé doesn't dress all that differently from you: jeans, though she wears hers looser, T-shirts and flannels, good socks, sturdy boots.

"You don't need to dress up to be a writer," Mémé is fond of saying.

When you were younger, sometimes Mémé would humor you and let you dress her up. You'd paw through her clothes and find the prettiest dresses, drape her in all her chains and beads, curl her hair, paint her nails and powder her face. "There," you'd say, when you were finished, and you would step back to admire your work—she looked beautiful, her gray-and-brown-streaked hair loosed from its everyday braid, her eyelashes darkened and thickened with mascara, her shape defined and emphasized by tight-nipped waists and flowing skirts.

And she would even go out with you dressed like that—to the store, to the sandwich shop, to the park. You would hold her hand proudly, noticing everyone who noticed her as you passed.

But as soon as you returned home, off came the fancy clothes, back went the hair, away went the makeup. And though you were a bit sorry to see your work undone, mostly it was a relief to see your own Mémé back again—no nonsense, sleeves rolled up to her elbows, bare-mouthed and booted.

You slide closed the closet door.

You told James you needed a nap, but you're not tired, not really. So you decide you might as well start dinner. Maybe you can surprise Mémé with something delicious.

You've barely poked your head in the refrigerator when you hear Mémé's key turning in the lock. It's not even four o'clock; on Wednesdays, she is usually gone until at least half past six.

You hear the door push open, then shut, and then Mémé's footsteps crossing the sitting room. She has not stopped to take off her shoes by the door.

"Bisou?" she calls. "Are you home?"

"In here." You shut the fridge.

Her expression when she crosses the threshold into the kitchen—for a moment, you are taken back to your child-hood, so clearly does Mémé's face, in that instant, resemble your mother's.

"Are you okay?" you ask her.

When she sees you standing there, Mémé's face rear-ranges, and whatever it was—whatever ghost, or shadow, that made her look so much like the woman who is always, always both between you and missing—disappears. "Of course I'm okay," Mémé says. "Actually, that is what I was about to ask *you*."

Now her face is all Mémé: sharp; appraising; thoughtful; curtained.

"I heard about the boy," she says. "You knew him, yes? Why don't we have a cup of tea and you can tell me all about it."

SICKLE MOON

What is the right tea for this sort of conversation? Not English breakfast; it is midafternoon. Not Earl Grey; you don't want to set that serious a tone. Chamomile is for sleeping, peppermint is a digestive . . . white tea, you decide, is the best choice. Clarity, energy, some caffeine, but not nearly as much as black.

Mémé fills the kettle and sets it to boil. You spoon white tea into the ceramic pot. While you wait for the water to heat, you get down teacups, and Mémé arranges a few cookies on a plate. Just before the kettle screams, you twist off the gas and pour the water into the pot, breathing in the aromatic steam that rises up, then settling the lid into place.

You sit at the table with Mémé. She passes you the plate of cookies; they are ginger snaps. You take one.

In three minutes, the tea is ready. Mémé pours and passes a cup to you.

All this time—while the water heated, while the tea steeped—neither of you has said a word. Now, each with a cup, each with a cookie, Mémé says again, "Tell me about the boy."

You lift your cup and sip your tea. Too hot—you feel the flame of it brush the roof of your mouth. You set the cup back down.

You are not a practiced liar, so you begin with truth. "His name was Tucker Jackson. He was on the basketball team with James. They found him—dead—in the woods." You look up at Mémé through the rising steam from your cup. "They say his neck was broken."

Mémé holds her cup in both hands. With both hands, she raises it to her lips.

You wait. You wait for her to say something. You don't know what you wait for her to say, but you feel yourself clenched in anticipation. And suddenly, you have a name for the expression that was on Mémé's face when she rushed into the kitchen, the expression that made her look so much like your mother, her daughter: *fear.*

"This boy," Mémé says at last, "Tucker—he was naked when he was found?"

Your tea burns the tips of your fingers through the ceramic, but you do not set it down. You hold it perfectly still.

Then, at last, you speak. "Yes," you say. "It's true. That's what they told us, anyway. At the assembly yesterday. Where did you hear about that? Were people talking at the library?"

Mémé does not answer. She is gazing somewhere over your shoulder, at the cabinets behind you, but you can tell that she is not really seeing what she is looking at—she is somewhere else, somewhere far away. It feels to you as if she is wrestling with something. Trying to decide something.

Then she snaps back into this moment, and it seems her decision is made, for she looks right at you and says, "I have a gift for you. Something I'd like you to have." She takes another sip of her tea, then sets her cup in its saucer, pushes back her chair, stands.

When she leaves the kitchen, you set your cup in its saucer. It rattles. You curl your hands into balls and pull them into your lap. You flatten your fingers against your thighs and spread them apart. You tell them to still, and, after a moment or two, they do.

When Mémé returns, she is holding something in her closed

fist. She sits again, places it on the table, and pushes it across to you.

It is one of her necklaces—while she has many, she has no others like this. It is the only piece of jewelry that Mémé has worn with some regularity. The chain is thick, each link a quarter-inch long, and there is no clasp. Its only ornament is a large, rather heavy sickle-shaped moon in lapis blue, each tip affixed to one end of the chain. You remember the weight of that lapis moon from your childhood, from the occasions when Mémé would let you dress her up. Once, when you were eight or so, she found you playing among her things, and you had draped this piece around your neck.

"Not that one," she had said, and gently she had lifted it up and away. "Any but that. You don't want such a weight on your neck. Perhaps another? Some pretty beads?"

But now she has given it to you. Before you lift it from the table, you look up at Mémé. She is watching you. Her eyes flash green and gray.

You pick up the necklace. It is, as you remember, heavy. You turn the sharp-tipped moon over and over, enjoying the weight of it. Then, for no particular reason other than to see if you can, you pull on it, one hand grasping the lapis-blue moon, the other on one end of the thick chain.

And it pulls apart, the lapis-blue moon revealing itself to be sheathing something—a needle-sharp claw of burnished metal, a half-inch thick at its center, tapering to a deadly point. It is about four inches long from its base, still attached to the chain, to the tip.

You look up again at Mémé—did she know the secret of this necklace? But her face—its lack of surprise, the way her green-gray eyes still watch you—tells you she has opened it herself.

"No need to tell anyone about that," she says. "It can be just a pretty ornament. I think it belonged to my grand-mère before me. But I'm not sure. It was given to me long after she was gone."

"It looks like . . . a weapon," you say, touching the tip of your finger to the claw's sharp tip.

"I used to wear it during my menses," Mémé says. "I liked to imagine that the blade could cut the pain. It worked for me, for many years. Now, perhaps, it can do the same for you."

"Thank you." You fit the sharp-tipped claw back into its sheath, you push them together until the claw has disappeared inside the lapis-blue moon. Now it is just a pretty ornament again. You string it around your neck. You tuck the moon beneath your T-shirt. It is cold, first, between your breasts, but it warms quickly to the temperature of your skin, and soon you cannot feel where you end and it begins.

"All right," Mémé says. "Let's finish our tea."

* * *

Later that night, after dinner, after Mémé has gone to her writing room to work on her latest novel, this one set entirely at sea, you unstring the chain from your neck and examine the moon beneath your desk lamp. Could it be that all these years this piece of jewelry contained this secret heart, that all this time it looked like just another pretty thing, tucked in among Mémé's strings of beads? You run your finger along the tiny raised shapes that edge the moon. What do they represent? You've never clearly looked.

You squint your eyes and adjust the lamp to shine more fully on the piece, and then you see that all along the edge of the sickle moon runs a series of tiny images—the phases of the moon, waxing and waning, again and again.

This piece of jewelry has hidden its secret heart from you all these dozen years, since first you arrived at Mémé's house. And now, you wonder—what secret heart might Mémé be hiding from you, as well?

In the morning, the pad you've worn all night is dry. It's just been three days—short for a period, you suppose, but it is your first, and you remember from health class back in middle school that it's not unusual for a girl's first few cycles to be short.

Perhaps you'll bleed more today, once you're up and about. It's possible. But you know it isn't true. You don't know *how* you know, but you are certain that, for this month, your period is behind you.

It's a relief, but it's something else, too. Some quality of . . . awareness seems missing. Dulled. You have heard about pregnant women developing a hypersensitive sense of smell, and you wonder if perhaps the same thing happens during menstruation. Do all bleeding women experience the same thing—the heightened perception you have had the last few days, that you find yourself rather missing now? If so, it's odd that no one has ever mentioned it to you.

Tucker's memorial table is still set up in the school's front hallway, but now Raphael, the security officer, is keeping a close watch over it, his legs in a wide stance off to the side where he can watch both the front door and the traffic at the table.

The condoms are missing, as is the Copenhagen. You wonder what other things must have been taken from the table, what gifts to Tucker's ghost have been removed that the administration has deemed "inappropriate."

It's not hard to come up with a list—you didn't know Tucker closely, a deliberate decision on your part, but he was at every party you had been to with James since the spring, and probably many others. He liked to drink—beer, of course, usually Bud Light. Jack Daniel's as well. Those were his favorites. He wouldn't pass up an edible, either, or dip. But he didn't smoke—not pot, not cigarettes, nothing. Lung capacity was too important to him, as an athlete.

You slow as you walk by the table, but you don't stop.

James is waiting for you by his locker. He's leaning against the bank of them, scrolling through something on his phone.

"More kitten pictures?" you joke, peering down at the screen. James does have a sweet affinity for adorable animal memes. But it's not pictures; it's a stream of texts, and the group chat is named "B-Ball."

James has no guile; he doesn't put the phone away or try to keep you from reading it. "Hey, Bisou," he says, and he leans in to kiss your cheek. "They finished Tucker's toxicology report. A preliminary one, anyway."

"Oh," you say. "Wow."

"Yeah," James says. "Caleb's uncle is a cop. He told Caleb all about it."

"Well, what does it say?"

James scrolls up to one text, the longest one. "Tucker wasn't sober," he says, showing you the text. "But that shouldn't be a surprise to anyone."

His blood alcohol concentration, you read, was .12. "Is that a lot?"

James shrugs. "Yeah, it's pretty drunk. Probably not black-out drunk. Definitely hangover drunk."

You don't say what perhaps you both are thinking—that

Tucker did not wake to a hangover. Down below, you see words you don't know—methylone and cathinone, followed by the word "Detected."

"What are those?"

James shrugs, powers down his phone, tucks it away. "Don't know. Caleb's uncle says it's going to take longer to do a full toxicology report. But Tucker was definitely on some shit." James's face, already serious, looks even more concerned. "Bisou," he says, leaning in close, his voice quiet and deep, "I just keep thinking what could have happened if you'd run into him out there. That night, in the woods. After you . . . ran off like that. Tucker could be kind of out of control when he was drinking, and that other shit they found in him . . . who knows what that might have turned him into."

You remember the pewter wolf—the hate in its eyes, the thick, sharp, yellowed fangs. The aggression. No, you tell yourself. Not a wolf. Tucker. But this perhaps explains how he could have attacked you the way he did.

"It's a good thing I didn't, then," you say, and you lace your fingers with James's. His hand is warm and feels so good in yours.

He leans in to kiss you, this time on the top of your head.

News spreads fast, and by lunch, everyone knows about Tucker's toxicology report. Mr. Davidson, the math teacher, talks disapprovingly about "the culture of teenage drinking" and how "everybody loses."

During last period—US History—a messenger comes to the door with a note. It's Darcy, the redheaded sophomore try-hard. She hands the note to Mr. Willis, and even though she doesn't need to, she says, "There's a couple of cops in the front office. They want to talk to Maggie."

The class bursts into whispered discussion. Maggie is sitting two rows back, so you don't see her reaction, but you see Mr. Willis sigh and pinch the bridge of his nose. "Thank you, Darcy," he says dryly. Then, "Maggie, you may as well take your things. This could take until after the bell."

At the front of the class, Darcy looks like a ginger cat who's caught a fat blue songbird in her mouth. Maggie passes down your aisle on her way to the front of the room, and though you don't crane your head up to look at her face, you do watch the set of her back as she heads out the door. Her backpack, thrown over her left shoulder, almost slips down her arm; her neck is curved forward; she looks afraid.

After the door closes behind her and Darcy, the volume in the class ratchets up. A guy's voice says loudly, "That girl."

Just two words. But the way he says them—the way he draws out the second word, "girl"—it's clear what he's saying about Maggie.

"Did you see what she wore to the dance?" This from

Lorraine. She is speaking to you.

You narrow your eyes, say nothing.

"Whore." It's a boy's fake cough, but the word is clear, it's loud, and three answering voices laugh in response.

"All right, settle down," Mr. Willis says in his "I mean business" tone that no one takes seriously. But that is all he says.

The class returns to work, which means trying to outline an essay due next week about the three-world convergence—how European conquest of North America linked Native Americans, European whites, and enslaved Africans into an unsteady triangle. You rest the tip of your pencil on the page in your notebook where you've started writing, but your eyes drift toward the window.

It is raining outside, that soft misty rain that is part of Seattle's DNA this time of year. Usually the first few weeks of school have the kind of fine weather that sharpens the sting of being stuck inside, but by early October the days have grown noticeably shorter and the sky cloudier. Last year's homecoming was the first really rainy night of the year, such a storm that, though the football game went on as planned, the parade—usually scheduled at halftime—had to be canceled.

Staring out into the misty rain, you consider how today might be different if this year's game and dance had been held on a different night. Had the dance been a day or two earlier, if the PTSA moms hadn't petitioned for the date change, you and James might have gone to some after-party, might not have driven to the woods instead. The blanket in the back seat might have stayed folded. James might not have dipped his head down between your thighs, and if he had, he would not have looked back up with blood on his chin. You would not have run from the car, into the woods, barefoot. There would have been no need, no shame. You wouldn't have been alone; there would have been no encounter with the wolf—with Tucker, there was no wolf, you imagined that, you must have.

You wish you could rewind time and recast last weekend. Such a little thing, the date of a dance, and such long-unspooling consequences.

The bell rings. Around you, everyone has already packed up their stuff, and the moment school is officially over, there is the flurry and shove of them leaving. You close your notebook and cap your pen, tuck your things into your backpack.

It's amazing how quickly a school hallway can clear out after the final bell. You walk slowly by the front office, trying not to look like you're peeking inside.

The vice principal's door is closed. Is Maggie behind it, still being questioned by police? What could they want from her? You bend down and retie your shoelaces, though they don't need retying, hoping that when you stand, that door will be open and you will be able to see inside.

No luck. You walk past Tucker's table again, and you see

that Maggie's locket is still there.

Whore.

Someone had said that about Maggie, and no one said anything in her defense. *You* hadn't said anything in her defense.
What kind of person does that—lets such a shitty thing stand,
without saying anything? A monster? Is that what you are?

A heaviness settles over you, a dark cold hand. The feeling—
the hand—is guilt.

You try to tell yourself that it's none of your business, any
of it—what people say about Maggie, whether or not she'll be
sorry later that she left her necklace on Tucker's table. It's not
like Maggie is your *friend*; you've known her a long time, but
until you started dating James, you and Maggie had barely
ever seen each other outside of school. She's never been to
your house and you've only been to hers once, right after you
and James started dating, for a party when her parents were
out of town. Honestly, you knew almost nothing about Maggie, except what you'd heard other people say about her. And
the person who had the most to say about her in the past few
months was Tucker.

"It's better to let people's business be *their* business," Mémé
has said to you, many times. And she's lived her life by those
words. You can't remember Mémé ever having friends, or
talking about her past—your grandfather, or your mother, or
her childhood, or anything like that. Her work, too, Mémé

keeps apart from the world. "Poetry doesn't pay the bills," she says when you ask why she's never published a poem, why instead she churns out a romance novel a year, and all with the name Selene Couteau instead of her own on the cover.

You've taken your lead from Mémé, staying close to home, not taking much interest in the other people at school, not having any close friends at all—and, for the most part, you've liked it that way. Until you and James started talking last fall, and flirting last spring, and your body woke up, slowly at first, and then with insistent desire. Then, it became your business to be close to him, and that meant opening doors—not all the way wide, but a crack, at first, that had widened with time.

You could crack the door to Maggie, you think, watching as your hand reaches out to take the locket. It is almost weightless, gold-colored but probably plated rather than solid. Maybe you don't need Maggie . . . and probably it's not smart, right now, to make someone else's business your business. But maybe Maggie needs someone. And maybe that someone could be you.

You push the necklace into your jacket pocket.

When you head to her house after dinner, however, you find that Maggie is not alone after all.

"That's weird," Maggie says when she answers the door. She's changed into track pants and a sweatshirt, and her hair, still in a bun, lists slightly to one side. Her face is puffy, like she's tired or maybe she's been crying. "Keisha just stopped by, too."

"I can come back another time," you offer. You would prefer to have as little contact with Keisha as possible, especially after lunch yesterday.

"No, that's silly," says Maggie, and she turns away from the front door, heading into the house, leaving you no real choice but to follow.

Maggie's home is much bigger than yours and Mémé's. The downstairs, where last spring's party was held, is decorated in sleek, muted modern colors and shapes—a dark mahogany coffee table, curved edges and legs; a cream leather couch and matching side chair; a long black-framed mirror above the fireplace. You follow Maggie up the staircase. Her room is at the top of the stairs, its door open, and you're glad you didn't pull out Maggie's locket yet. You definitely don't want to return it to her now, in front of Keisha, who is sitting cross-legged in stockinged feet in the middle of Maggie's bed, her opened notebook in her lap.

Maggie's bedroom is different from the polished, minimalistic decor downstairs. The walls are painted light pink, and all her furniture, including her four-poster bed, is white. It's overfilled with stuffed animals on the bed and piled in each corner; a collection of music boxes is displayed on a high shelf above the window; there's a corkboard crisscrossed with concert and movie tickets. Her dresser spills clothes from each half-open drawer. There are six throw pillows, maybe more. Above, a ceiling fan slowly whirs.

If Keisha is surprised to see you, she hides it well. Her face is hard to read, anyway; maybe it's her glasses, the thick-rimmed white ones today. Maybe it's the stillness of her mouth, how her lips barely ever move into a smile or a frown. She's a watcher, Keisha, which isn't surprising, since she's the editor-in-chief of the school paper.

"Hey, Keisha," you say.

"Keisha's doing an article about Tucker for this week's paper," Maggie says. "Like an obituary."

"Something like that," Keisha says. "What are *you* doing here, Bisou?"

"I just thought I'd stop by and check on Maggie," you say to Keisha, and then, to Maggie, "How are you doing?"

Maggie shrugs, and smiles, but then her face twists and she begins to cry. She sits down on the edge of her bed, almost on Keisha's foot, and drops her head into her hands. You don't know what you are supposed to do in this situation. You and Maggie may not be close, but you are here, and here she is in need of comfort. And Keisha is watching.

"Oh, Maggie," you say, and you slide yourself next to her on the bed and put your arm around her shoulders. Maggie collapses into you, and her cries go up an octave, a breathy, gasping sound. You tighten your grasp around her shoulder, and you bring your other hand up to enclose her in a hug.

She stays like that, crying, for three or four minutes, but it's so awkward that it feels longer. Eventually, she takes a few jagged breaths, sits up, and smiles at you. Her eyes are red and swollen.

Behind you, from the center of the bed, Keisha reaches out and waves a tissue. Maggie takes it, wipes her eyes, blows her nose.

"It's really nice of the two of you to come over like this," she says, mostly calm now. "It's been so weird since Tucker and I broke up. All the girls I used to hang with are still dating Tucker's friends; I'm not sure what he told them, but whatever it was, everyone has been really 'busy' the last few months." She smiles, but not happily. "Of course, they're all calling *now*, but they can go fuck themselves."

You wonder if she's saying *you* should go fuck yourself, because you've never made an effort to get to know Maggie before this, and you're one of the girls who's dating one of Tucker's teammates, even if you two were never exactly friends. It's true you've mostly ignored the gossip, but it's also true that you didn't do anything to shut it down. You're not interested in drama, you've always held yourself to the periphery, and that's had its benefits—you've never been backstabbed, you've never found yourself the center of a controversy. You catch Keisha looking at you over Maggie's head.

"I mean," Maggie says, sniffing, "Mercury's in retrograde, so if shit was going to hit the fan, I guess now's the time."

"Anyway," Keisha says, ignoring Maggie's astrology reference and seeming to pick up where she left off, before you came in, before all the crying. "What sorts of drugs would Tucker get into on a typical weekend? And about how often would you say that he drank?"

These don't sound like questions for a puff-piece obituary. You don't say anything, but you scoot out of the way so that instead of Keisha sitting behind you and Maggie, the three of you form a semicircle.

Maggie sniffs again. "Tucker didn't really do drugs," she says. "He wanted to play college ball. He liked edibles and beer and stuff like that, but nothing really heavy. Well, I guess I don't know what he was into lately. I mean, we broke up over the summer."

"Mm-hmm," Keisha says. "So you hadn't been hanging out with him lately?"

"It didn't end great between us."

"Yeah," says Keisha. A pause. Then, "But, that's kind of weird, because people saw you talking together at the dance. And Lorraine said she saw you getting out of Tucker's truck in the parking lot. After the dance." She kind of shrugs, like she's embarrassed to contradict Maggie but had to say it anyway.

You turn to look at Maggie. Her features, which had been softened by emotion, harden. She doesn't say anything for a long minute. Then, "I think maybe you should go. Both of you."

"Can I just ask—" Keisha says, but Maggie's lips are pressed into a line, and she shakes her head. Keisha shoots you a look, as if it's your fault that Maggie won't talk to her after she was super rude and nosy. She flips her notebook closed, tucks her pencil behind her ear, and scoots off the bed. "Call me anytime," she says, slipping her feet into her shoes, "if you want to talk."

You follow Keisha out of the room. Before you go down the stairs, you look back at Maggie, who is still sitting on her bed. She has her head in her hands again, but this time she isn't crying.

"Hang on," you say to Keisha as she hurries up the street to her car. "I want to talk to you."

She stops, but she's fishing through her pockets for her keys. "What do you want, Bisou?"

"What was that about? Why are you hassling Maggie?"

"I wasn't hassling her. I was just asking her some questions."

"What does it matter if she was in Tucker's truck?"

"Maybe it doesn't. Maybe it does. I was just giving her the chance to explain herself. For the article."

"So, not an obituary."

Keisha blinks, says nothing.

"So, what is it then?"

"Investigative journalism," Keisha says. "Tucker's death is the weirdest thing that's happened in our town in years. Tucker Jackson, star of the basketball team, naked in the woods, running into a tree? Sounds pretty interesting to me. And what about his eye? Do you know about *that*?"

"His . . . eye?" You hope Keisha cannot hear the frantic beating of your heart.

"His eye," she repeats. "They're saying he'd been stabbed in the eye, before his neck was broken."

You do your best to keep your face even. "Wow," you say at last, but you sound unconvincing to your own ears.

"And do you know what's *really* weird?" Keisha doesn't wait for you to answer. "This isn't the first time that a dead guy was found in the woods around here. It was a long time ago, back in the seventies. Not far away. A student at the university named Dennis Cartwright."

"What do you mean?"

"He was found naked and dead, just like Tucker. With a broken neck."

Your mouth opens and closes. You have no words.

Keisha looks at you more closely. "Why are *you* here, anyway?"

"I wanted to check on Maggie," you say.

"Uh-huh. Because the two of you are such good friends." She finds the keys at the bottom of her bag and pulls them out, goes around to the driver's side door. Before she gets in, she says, "You know, Bisou, there's a special place in hell for women who don't help other women."

Before you can think of a response, she slams herself into her car and drives away.

At home, you tuck Maggie's necklace into the top drawer of your dresser. You don't really want it in your house, but after the run-in with Keisha, maybe it's not the smartest idea to give it back to Maggie. You could take it back to school and slip it onto the Tucker table, but that seems like an unnecessary risk with no reward—there's no reason to draw attention to yourself, no upside to putting yourself closer to the whole situation.

Just stay away from Maggie and let the whole thing play out. No one knows—except for James—that you were out in the woods that night, and even James doesn't know the rest of the story. It's better to let people's business be *their* business, as Mémé liked to say.

You'll avoid Maggie. And you'll avoid Keisha. You shut the drawer with a bang.

＊　＊　＊

When you get to school on Friday, almost everyone in the halls is reading the school paper on their phones. Keisha's article, it seems, was posted overnight. Like she said, nothing this interesting has happened at your high school in years.

You pull up the site on your phone.

Varsity Basketball Star Tucker Jackson Found Dead in Woods

Beneath the title, another line reads:

Authorities Tight-Lipped as Investigation Continues

ELLE A VU LE LOUP

It's not the article that upsets you—not exactly. Mostly it contains a summary of the events, with a few quotes from students. "Tucker was acting sort of strange at the dance," says Mackenzie Carter, a senior who was crowned homecoming king. "He seemed really angry, but no one could get him to say what about." Then there's the description of how his body was found, and a quote from the jogger who found it: "It was just so awful. The way his head was twisted on his neck, bent off to the side in a way necks don't bend. My dog found him first, actually." Farther down, there's a line about how investigators found scraps of Tucker's clothing near the entrance to the woods. And then there's a summary of the toxicology report, along with something you didn't already know from reading the rumor chain on James's phone: though substances similar to methylone and cathinone were detected—two common ingredients in bath salts—they weren't formulations previously seen by toxicologists.

Keisha hasn't mentioned what Lorraine told her about Maggie getting out of Tucker's truck that night, but maybe that's not so much an act of generosity as it is a chess move. She also hasn't written anything about the other death, that guy she told you about, who was found in the woods back in the seventies. You guess that's not because she's decided it's unrelated, but because she's got more investigating to do.

But the final line of the article, just three words long—these three words are what unsettle you:

To be continued.

You thumb through the rest of the paper to see if there's anything else about Tucker, but there isn't, just a roundup of scores from recent games, a puff piece about the homecoming decorations, and letters to the editor. The first letter can't help but catch your eye—it's titled "Whatever Happened to Manners?"

It's basically a whine-fest about how hard it is to get a girl to say yes to dancing anymore. "It's called a *dance*," the letter reads. "People are supposed to *dance* with each other, but even the fours and fives say no these days. I think there should be a rule that if a girl is attending a school dance and a guy asks to dance with her, she has to say yes. Otherwise, what's the point?" It's signed "It's Not Cool to Evade Love."

You turn back to Keisha's article and read it again.

Everyone talks about the article all day, but then the weekend comes, and with it comes Tucker's funeral. Half the school, it seems, turns out for it, and you go with James, holding his hand through the service.

Tucker's family is Catholic, and large. He was the youngest of four boys, and all three of his brothers are home for the funeral. They form a circle around Tucker's mom, a tiny round woman who cries silently and endlessly throughout the service. When it's time to carry the casket, Tucker's three brothers take one side, and three of his closest friends take up the other.

You'd entered the church service under a gray-blue sky, but it doesn't take long for things to change. It's raining at the cemetery, and everyone gathers tightly together under the plastic shelters that have been erected near the grave. James stands behind you, his hands on your shoulders, and you watch together as the casket descends into the ground.

When it reaches the bottom, with a dull *thud*, you feel

James's hands tighten on your shoulders. Silent until that moment, Tucker's mother wails, high-pitched and terrifying, a sound without words. Louder and louder, higher and higher, and her remaining sons, those not in the ground, envelop her.

Everyone stiffens, the air seems to freeze as you together bear witness to her pain, and though the rain pours down, you cannot hear it. All you hear is Tucker's mother's cry for a son who will never come home.

The sound she makes—it vibrates your bones. It shakes something awake. It's the sound you made once, years ago, for your mother.

By Monday, the memorial table is gone, and pretty much everyone seems ready to move on from talking about Tucker to getting excited about Halloween, which is just three weeks away. It surprises you how quickly everyone seems to jump to the next thing, how life resumes even after something like this, but as it's in your best interest for the whole thing to fade away, you do not make a point of it.

This Wednesday, when James drives you home after school, you don't wait for him to ask if he can come in. When the car pulls to a stop at the curb in front of your house, you put your hand on the gearshift and push it into park.

James smiles. It's raining hard today, but it is not just the rain that spurs you both to run up the driveway and into the house. You hang your coats, one on top of the other, on a hook beneath the mirror. Your hair drips onto the wooden floor of the front hallway as you unlace your boots; James's high, tight curls glisten from the rain. You line up his boots next to yours on the rubber mat beneath the bench, and then you take his hand and lead him through the house, into your bedroom, and, from there, into the adjoining bathroom.

James leans in to kiss you, his warm, soft mouth on yours, and then you take a towel from the rack and lift it to his hair to dry it. He tips his head so you can reach, and, gently, you squeeze the water from his hair.

When you've finished, James takes the towel from your hands and drapes it over your head, massaging the wetness away. You close your eyes and feel his fingers working through the towel. It has been a long time since anyone dried your hair for you.

He sets aside the towel. Now there is nothing between you but clothes. You work on loosing the buttons of his blue-and-green plaid flannel, and though he could do it more efficiently himself, he waits and watches. Then the last button is free, and you push the shirt off his shoulders. There's a white T-shirt underneath, tucked in, and, with a sudden rush of urgency, you pull it roughly from the waistband of his pants, up and over his head. He lifts his arms willingly, and you see the dark curls of his armpit hair, which seems like maybe the most intimate thing you have ever seen.

He is hard, you see the shape of him through the thick denim of his jeans. You reach out, you put your hand there. You squeeze and look up into James's eyes. They shine down at you, and you read them well—desire, pleasure, love.

Hand still wrapped around his erection, you lean up to kiss him. This time, when James's lips touch yours, there is urgency there, yours and his, together. His hands are on your shoulders, then your back, then lower, on your butt, and all of this feels so good, so exciting and wonderfully good.

You don't stop kissing as you walk together back into the bedroom, you pushing forward, him stepping back, and then you are at the edge of your bed, and James sits. His face is at your stomach, and, slowly, gently, he pushes up your sweater and the T-shirt underneath to reveal the skin of your mid-section. He kisses you there, and you feel warmth spreading downward.

You pull off your sweater and shirt, toss them to the side. Outside, the rain pounds down, clouds darken the sky, and a rumble of thunder sounds as urgent as your own hot desire.

The rest of your clothes come off, and James's. You are together in your bed, and he is naked before you in a way you have never seen this clearly—his dark, flat chest, the tight black curls of his pubic hair surrounding his erection. It's wet-tipped and urgent, and you stroke it with your fingers. James makes a sound, a moan, and he falls back against your pillows, giving his body up to you to explore.

You take your time. If James wishes you'd do something more, or faster, he doesn't say. Instead he strokes your arms, gently, as you run your hands across and over him.

He doesn't ask you to, but you want to, and you reach into James's discarded pants and find his wallet, find the condom he's tucked inside. He grins then, and he watches as you tear it open.

You've never used one of these before, but you've been told how, and anyway, it's not hard to figure out; you roll it down James's penis, all the way to the base of hair. James adjusts it, making sure it's rolled completely down and pinching the tip a little, stretching it. He's still lying on his back on the bed, and you kneel over him, letting your hair hide your face as you reach between your bodies, find his penis, and guide it toward the entrance of your vagina.

It feels thick there, sort of scary, and there is a moment when you wonder how on earth it will fit inside, but James doesn't rush you, and you lower yourself onto him, his hands gentle on your hips, not trying to tell you what to do. His eyes are closed, his head is back, and you look at him through the soft curtain of your hair as you sink all the way down, as you feel a tear deep inside you, painful but not terrible, as you feel yourself full of him, of James.

And then you move, careful and slow, your hands on his chest, his on your hips, your thighs, and it's not long before his face tightens up, he makes a low groan, and he shivers beneath you.

You stay there, above him, for a moment longer, and inside you, you feel his penis beginning to soften. James opens his eyes. He smiles. You smile, too.

Then he grasps the base of the condom while you move off him, and then you sort of look away, a little embarrassed, while he pulls off the condom, knots it.

He gets up and goes to your bathroom. You hear him pulling off a piece of toilet paper, and you see him tuck the wrapped-up condom into your trash can. You hear him running the water in the sink. You get under the covers, and when he comes back into the room, still naked, that's where he finds you. He's got a warm damp washcloth, which he hands to you, and it feels so good when you press it between your legs.

He climbs in next to you, pulls the covers up over your shoulder, pulls you close. You lie there together, listening to the rain, watching the occasional flash of lightning through the window. The sky has gone nearly completely dark since you and James came into the bedroom; days are getting shorter and shorter, and between the cloudy sky and the waning moon, the day is nearly done.

But James is not; he kisses you again, on the mouth, and

then he readjusts the blankets and begins to move his mouth down your body, across your breasts, down your stomach. You clench your legs together, remembering last time, but James looks up at you and says, "Relax, Bisou, I'm not worried," and so you let your legs fall apart, you let James kiss you there, and it is wonderful.

It is dark when you say goodbye with another long, slow kiss at the front door. He's dressed again, flannel buttoned as if it had never come undone, but you are wrapped in a blanket from your bed, your hair tangled in the back, your lips swollen from kissing.

After he is gone, you run yourself a bath, feeling slow, feeling luxurious, and you lower yourself into its steaming embrace, all the way up to your chin. You close your eyes. Your arms float.

You don't need to tell Mémé about James, about the sex. But, sitting together at the table that night for dinner, you find that you want to.

"Mémé," you say, "I want to tell you something. About me and James."

She puts down her soup spoon. She gives you all her attention.

You clear your throat. "You know that we've been dating for a while now . . ."

"Yes," Mémé says, "I like your James. He is a kind young man."

"He *is* kind," you say. "That's one of my favorite things about him. Also, he is such a good listener, and he's smart, and he's . . . I don't know, *loyal*, I guess."

"Good qualities, all," Mémé says.

You are stalling, and you don't want to stall. There is nothing to be ashamed of here. There is nothing to hide. "Anyway," you say, "I just wanted you to know that James and I—well, we started having sex. I didn't want it to be a secret. That's all."

You take a sip of your soup.

"Ah," Mémé says. Then she reaches across the table to take your hand. "I thought that might be on the horizon." Her fingers squeeze yours. You squeeze back.

Then she pats your hand and goes back to eating her soup.

You clear your throat. There's a lump there, and a stinging in your eyes, even though you're not sad. It's because you are so grateful that she's taken the news like this—so respectfully, so unsurprised, like it's the normal progression of events, which, to you, it is.

She says, "And you'll promise to tell me if you need anything? Condoms, or anything like that?"

This does embarrass you, but you pretend that it doesn't. Birth control is part of being responsible, and you want to have an adult conversation about this. "James has condoms," you say. "We're being careful."

"Of course you are," Mémé says approvingly. "Just making sure. Also, my darling, you do know, don't you, that having sex in the past does not oblige you to have sex in the future. You never have to do anything that you don't want to do. You don't owe James—or anyone—access to your body. Not now. Not ever."

"James isn't like that," you say. "He wouldn't ever try to make me do anything."

"That's good," Mémé says, "but sometimes boys become wolves, you know."

After that first time, you want to try it again—sex with James—but even as cool as Mémé was when you told her, it's not like you're about to just take James into your room and close the door with her at home. And he's got three little siblings at his house, all the time, two sisters in grade school and a new baby brother. And, though James once suggests it, the back of his car doesn't feel like an option to you anymore. So you both count down the days until next Wednesday.

It's Friday when Keisha comes up to you at lunchtime.

You're sitting with James and a couple of the other basketball players, eating a veggie wrap with hummus, when you look up and there she is, staring down at you.

"Hey, Keisha," you say. "What's up?"

"We need to talk," she says.

"Want to sit down?" You ask to be polite, but you really don't have any interest in having a conversation with Keisha at all, let alone in front of James and his teammates.

"*Alone*," Keisha answers.

Alone. You lose your taste for lunch, offer James the second half of your wrap. "I'll see you later, okay?" you tell him, and then follow Keisha out of the lunch room.

She leads you to the library. It's practically empty, just a couple of kids in the good chairs over by the fiction section, one reading a book, the other reading something on his phone. Keisha walks to the far end of the library, to a couple of wooden chairs at a small reading table, its lamp switched on. She sits down; you stay standing. You don't plan to be here long.

"What is it, Keisha?"

"Do you know what's up with Maggie? She's been out of school since Tuesday."

Maggie? Honestly, you haven't paid much attention to Maggie this week, doing your best to let the whole thing go away. Is that true, that she's been out? You think back. You remember seeing Maggie in class . . . but that was Monday.

"Maybe she's got the flu."

"Maybe," Keisha answers. "Maybe not. I've sent her like

five texts and I've tried to call. But no response."

"Why are you so interested in her?"

"I have my reasons," Keisha says. "What I'm wondering is why you're suddenly *not* interested. Since you're, like, her friend and all, going to her house last week just to check up on her." Keisha raises her eyebrow, as if to tell you that she's still not buying that story.

You lower yourself into the chair across from Keisha. "Okay," you say. "I'll give her a call."

"Go by her house," Keisha says, standing up and fishing her phone out of her bag. "And tell her that I showed you this." She flips through some texts, holds the phone out to you so that you can read it, but not close enough that you could take it from her hands.

It's a screenshot of a text from Maggie. It's not clear who she was texting.

I hate Tucker soooo much. I wish he was dead. Maybe I'll kill him myself.

You look up. The reading lamp shines up in Keisha's face, making her glasses glare into unreadable shining discs. "Where did you get this?"

"Doesn't matter," Keisha says, shoving her phone back into her bag. "What matters is that I have it." She turns to leave, then looks back. "Get Maggie to talk to you, Bisou. I don't think she's going to talk to me after the other day."

Why should she? But you don't say this. You don't say anything. Tight-lipped, you nod.

No one answers that afternoon when you ring Maggie's doorbell. You stand scrunched under the small overhang, curled in against the strong, cold wind.

You try knocking. Still nothing. You try the knob; the door is locked.

Keisha isn't going to be satisfied unless you actually make contact with Maggie, so, sighing, you head around the side of the house.

The kitchen door is unlocked. "Hello?" you call as you push it open. It feels weird and awful to go into a house like this, uninvited, but you ignore that feeling and go in anyway. "Anybody home?"

Nothing. No response. The house feels totally empty, though there are a few dishes in the sink, and the coffeepot—cold—is half full.

Maggie's bedroom is upstairs, at the end of the hallway, and that's where you head, your steps soft on the carpeted stairs.

Her door is open, just a crack. You reach out and push it, slowly, and slowly it opens, revealing the side of her desk, a slowly turning ceiling fan, the foot of her bed, and, higher, underneath the covers, a shape.

A body.

iii

the first time
he kissed me
he bunched up my hair
pulled back my head

the first time
he hit me
it made sense
it answered a question

the first time
i kissed you
still warm, wet,
and salty from the womb

i made a promise
he made a promise

it wouldn't happen again

i used to think
mothers left girls
because they deserved to be left

but maybe mothers leave
kicking
and screaming
and bleeding
trying to do anything
but leave

BLOW YOUR HOUSE IN

"Mama?"

She had been sitting in her place by the window that night, just as she always did, looking outside into the softly falling snow, her finger on the bridge of her nose. You had sat by the fire playing with your stuffed dog, making it snuff around under the stack of firewood, searching, you imagined, for a cat.

A soft table lamp and the fire gave the only light, and the room glowed warmly, just like the inside of a storybook, so safe and snug and tight.

But then a flash of light, bright and mean, passed across the room—headlights, you knew—and with the light came the sound of tires crunching on snow.

Mama turned to look at you, her eyes widened so you could see the white all around their dark blue hearts. "Bisou," she said. "Run."

You had made promises. If this moment were ever to come—which, you knew, suddenly and with certainty, was never a question of "if" but rather "when"—you were to run to the ghost room. You were to hide yourself in the skirts of ghosts. You were to close your eyes and plug your ears and stay put, no matter what you heard.

You ran. Up the stairs, past the sleeping room, down the hall, all the way to the end. And you turned the knob, you went inside, you pushed the door closed behind you, you let the ghosts hide you in their skirts, you filled your ears with your fists, you squeezed shut your eyes, and you waited for the world to end.

There were sounds, but you pretended that they were from a movie. At last there was a crash—a loud crash, a window breaking—and then there was nothing more.

Still you waited, shrouded in the skirts of ghosts. Until, at last, you slept.

When you woke, there were no ghosts in the room. Just furniture, draped in sheets, as Mama had told you. It was a boring, dusty bedroom, and you had slept the night underneath a boring, dusty, sheet-draped bed. That was all. Never before had you felt so pleased by the lack of magic in the world. You stood and stretched your arms, and opened the door, and headed to the sleeping room to tell Mama the good news, that the ghosts were gone, and that most likely they had never been there at all.

The door was open, just a crack. You reached out and pushed it, slowly, and slowly it opened, revealing the side of Mama's desk, a slowly turning ceiling fan, the foot of the bed, and, higher, a shape underneath the covers, hair splayed across a white pillowcase, Mama's slack face . . . and blood. So much blood.

You scream. You scream, and scream, and the figure in bed sits bolt upright.

Your head is full of your pounding pulse; your eyes stream tears, and it is Maggie who jumps from her bed, who stumbles in her nightgown across her room.

"Bisou?" she says. "It's okay. Calm down."

But you can't calm down, not for a long time. Your legs feel weak as pudding and you collapse, right there in the doorway to Maggie's room. She goes down to the ground with you, wraps you in her arms, pulls you half into her lap and says, "Shh, shh, it's okay," again and again for as long as it takes you to believe it.

You are in Maggie's house. You are in Maggie's room. You are in Maggie's arms. There is no Mama; there is no blood. There is no shattered window; there is no snow.

You take in a long, jagged breath. You let it out.

"Okay," says Maggie.

You nod. "I'm so sorry," you tell her. "I shouldn't be here."

"It is kinda weird," she says.

You wipe your face on your sleeve. Maggie stands up and offers you her hand. You take it. Together you go to the bed and sit on its edge. You owe Maggie a couple of explanations; you start with the easier one. "Keisha asked me to come check on you. You haven't been at school in a couple of days, and you're not answering your phone."

"Yeah," Maggie says.

"Also," you say, because you might as well tell her everything you know, "Keisha showed me a text you sent to someone. About Tucker."

Maggie shakes her head. "Darcy is such a fucking bitch," she says, more to herself than to you. Then she says, "I was trying to warn her."

"Warn her?"

Maggie sighs. "Look, if I tell you something, will you promise not to tell anyone else? And, you know, I hope you don't think I'm gross or anything once I tell you."

"I won't tell anyone," you say.

"Not even if the secret is that I *did* kill Tucker?" She smiles.

"I am one hundred percent certain that you didn't."

Maggie laughs wryly. "Well, you're *one* person, I guess." Then she looks at you, her face sort of shy, vulnerable. "Look," she says, "I did tell Darcy that I wished Tucker were dead. I was trying to keep her from getting involved with him. Tucker was a really shitty guy. I didn't want anyone else getting hurt by him."

"What did he do?"

Maggie groans, covers her eyes, flops back on her bed. Eyes still covered, she says, "So Tucker told me when we started having sex that it would be totally okay to not use condoms because my mom got me on Norplant way before I was even ready to have sex, just in case, and Tucker said he was a virgin, too, so there was nothing to worry about. But then after we started having sex, I found like, these . . . sores . . . you know, down there? And it burned so bad when I had to pee, it was almost unbearable. And my mom took me to the doctor, and she told me—" Maggie breaks off for a moment, sits up, runs her fingers through her hair. "She told me it was herpes. Okay? There. *Herpes*."

You reach over and take her hand.

She gives you a weak smile. "When I told Tucker, he was like, 'Who else have you been fucking?' and that was so awful. I hadn't ever slept with *anyone* but him. And then he said that he couldn't have given it to me, because he'd never had any of the symptoms I'd been describing. He said once he had, like, a rash, you know, on his dick, but that was it. And then I was all, "But I thought you said you were a virgin, and so why are you saying that the reason you couldn't have given me herpes is because you've never had any sores, not because you've never had any sex before?" And then he grinned and said, like, that girls like it better when they think that boys are virgins, so he'd lied to me. He'd *lied* to me! And then I looked it up online and I found out that some people—guys, especially—they barely have *any* symptoms when they first get herpes, and sometimes it's just like a rash, just like Tucker had described. But when I told him that, he totally denied ever even *having* a rash and called me a liar and a skank, and he told me if I told anyone that he'd given me an STI or whatever, that he'd make sure the whole school thought *I* was the liar, not him. And then he started hooking up with Darcy, you know, that sophomore . . . And that's why I was in his car that night, after the dance. Trying to make him promise to tell Darcy himself about his STI, or at least to get him to promise to wear condoms if they ended up doing it, so she wouldn't end up with herpes, too."

By the time she's done, the words are practically spilling out of Maggie. You're the first person she's told all this to, you can tell by how relieved she seems to be to share it with you. But as soon as she's done talking, another look of worry crosses her face and she screws her mouth into a tight frown.

"I won't tell anyone," you say. "I promise."

Maggie nods. "I believe you. Anyway, I'm getting pretty tired of keeping secrets. I'm just getting over a cold, is all, and that's why I haven't been to school for a couple of days. Plus, someone put something gross into my backpack, and I just didn't feel like being there."

"Something gross? What was it?"

Maggie's mouth forms a tight line, and she shakes her head, and you think she isn't going to answer. But then she blurts, "It was a condom. And it was . . . you know. Used. Tied up at the end and full of . . ." Her voice trails off.

"That is fucking disgusting," you say.

"Hearing it's not nearly as bad as seeing it," she says. "I just, like, reached into my backpack looking for a pencil the other day and there it was. Squishy and fucking gross."

"Oh, God. What did you do with it?"

"What did I *do* with it? I put it under my pillow for the jizz fairy. Jesus, Bisou, I threw it away, of course!"

"No, I mean—did you tell anyone? Like your parents, or a teacher?"

She shakes her head, hard. "There's enough going on, and besides, what was I going to say? And just finding it there . . . in my bag, next to my fucking Hello Kitty pencil holder . . . it made me feel so gross. Anyway," she says, changing the subject, "I just needed a break for a couple of days."

"I get it. I think we should tell Keisha, though, about that text Darcy showed her," you say, thinking about what Keisha does with unanswered questions. "I feel like she'll understand. We don't even have to tell her about the other stuff—about the herpes—if you don't want to."

Maggie shrugs. "I don't know," she says, "I'm getting pretty tired of all of it."

Maggie gets a robe from her closet and the two of you go down to the kitchen. She takes milk out of the fridge and cocoa out of a cabinet and starts heating them up in a saucepan.

You sit at her table and watch her stir. You can see she's had a cold; her nose is red. When the cocoa is steaming, she pours it into two mugs, hands you one.

"So," she says, sitting at the table with you, sipping from her cup, "want to talk about what happened upstairs?"

You don't, actually. It has been nearly a dozen years since you found your mother's body in her bed, her throat ripped, her blood soaking the bed all the way down to the mattress. But Maggie has trusted you with her secret. And you like Maggie, you decide, suddenly and surely. Why have you waited so long to be friends?

Of course, you know why. It's because, even though you always thought Tucker was kind of a dick, when he started saying all those terrible things about Maggie, you didn't bother to fact-check. You basically accepted what he said, assuming he was embellishing a little, as guys sometimes do. This is something to contemplate later—why you believed Tucker, who you never really trusted, instead of Maggie, who had never given you a reason not to.

But now, by way of apologizing, you tell Maggie your story. And the story, you know, is the other part of the reason you have held off being friends with anyone, really, always careful to not be too close with anyone save for Mémé and, more recently, James. Always wary to begin things when you know that things can end.

"When I was four years old, my mom took me to Canada. She was afraid of my father. Really afraid. He beat her up and stuff. I remember the last time, when he gave her two black eyes, broke her nose. That was when she loaded me up in the middle of the night and we hit the road."

The cocoa soothes you, and you stop to take a sip. Such sweetness, and such a bitter story.

"We were living in Canada for a few months, through winter and into early spring, when I guess he found us. I'm not really sure it was him, but who else could it have been? It was a blood moon that night, I remember my mother telling me. Do you know what a blood moon is?"

"Totally," says Maggie, nodding. "It's when there's a full moon and the sun, the moon, and the earth are perfectly lined up. An eclipse that makes the moon look red."

"Exactly," you say, and then you remember the last time you were over, when Maggie mentioned Mercury being in retrograde. "Are you into astrology?"

Maggie nods earnestly. "Very."

"Cool," you answer, though astrology has always seemed to you like a supreme waste of time. "Anyway, it scared me when my mother told me that—the words, blood moon, sounded scary. I was just a little kid. She said it was nothing to be scared of, nothing at all. But later a car pulled up. And my mom made me hide, and I heard things, but it was like I couldn't move. Like I was paralyzed. I fell asleep eventually, and the next morning, when I woke up, I found her dead in her bed."

Maggie takes a sharp breath. This is not the way she expected the story to go, you can tell.

"Yeah," you say, "it was awful. Pretty much the worst scene you can imagine. And the weird thing is, the second-story window was broken, like someone had jumped out of it. The car was still parked in the driveway, keys in the ignition. It had snowed all night, so there weren't any footprints, but whoever killed my mom—my father, I guess—had just disappeared."

You drink some more of the cocoa. You are grateful for it. Maggie reaches across the table to squeeze your hand.

"Mémé—my grandmother—she showed up that morning. Which was also weird, because I hadn't called anyone—the cops or anything, I guess I didn't know how. I don't remember much about what happened."

Maggie leans forward in her chair, toward you, her whole body practically vibrating with compassion. You can feel her wanting to hug you, and your throat thickens with anxiety and emotion.

"I don't think about it often." You hear your own voice as if from a distance. It sounds flat, like you could be talking about anything, or nothing that's important at all. "That happens sometimes, with trauma, early trauma, especially. That's what Mémé says. Your brain will do whatever it needs to do to tamp that shit down. I do my best to help my brain out, you know, in forgetting. But you startled me, I guess, lying in bed like that. You reminded me of my mother." You arrange your face carefully to communicate to Maggie that you do not want to be touched, not now, and look into her eyes, which brim with empathy.

"Anyway, Mémé showed up, and I guess I was sleeping at the foot of the bed where my mother's body was. And then Mémé brought me back here, to her house. I've lived here, with her, ever since."

"Shit," Maggie says, but she doesn't reach across the table, for which you are grateful.

You sit quietly together for a while, sipping cocoa. Your hands, you notice, are steady as they raise the cup to your mouth.

Maggie says, "Did they ever find your dad? Or, like, whoever killed her?"

"The car was stolen, it turned out, so that was a dead end. My father disappeared from his place around that time, so everyone agrees it was probably him, and the Canadian police still haven't shut the case."

"It was lucky your grandmother showed up when she did. Otherwise, who knows how long you might have been there like that . . ."

"Mémé used to say over and over how she wishes she had gotten there sooner. But I don't see how that could have helped. Then he would have just killed them both."

"Yeah. I wonder how she knew where you and your mom were. Do you think she'd been in touch with your mom or something? Could she have known that your dad might do something like this?"

These were good questions, ones you'd asked yourself, of course—not at first, you were too traumatized and too young to question much of anything—but later, in quiet moments here and there, over the years. Those questions, and others, the more you settled into your new home, your new life with Mémé. Like, why were there no pictures of your mother in

Mémé's house? Why did Mémé's phone never seem to ring? Why did you have a grandmother, but no grandfather? But you didn't ask these questions, and Mémé didn't offer answers. It was like you both wanted the same thing, to honor what your mother had asked of you—n'oublie pas d'oublier. Forget, forget, forget. And when you left Quebec, Mémé had not packed your things, perhaps feeling a fresh start, a blank slate, would be the best. You took nothing from the house, not even the skipping stones you and your mother had collected for when the ice would thaw.

"I never really asked," you tell Maggie. "I guess I could tell Mémé didn't want to talk about it, and I didn't want to bring it up again, make her remember."

Maggie nods, then says, "I'm really, really sorry about your mom."

"Thanks," you say, and the word is insignificant and nearly nothing, a paper-thin tissue of a word.

It feels good, to sit together like this. With Maggie.

Maybe she's thinking the same thing, because she says, "I'm glad you came over. I've been lonely." She pulls her phone out of the pocket of her robe and thumbs through it. "None of my friends are texting me back, and the only person who wants to hang out with me is—" Her phone pings. "Oh, speak of the devil." She laughs. "Jesus, this guy doesn't take no for an answer."

She turns the phone toward you, so you can read the text. It's from Graham. **Seriously?** it reads. **Why not? What else are you doing that night?**

Maggie deletes the conversation, shoves her phone back into her pocket. "Anyway," she says, "I'm glad you came."

A WOLF AT THE DOOR

Two more Wednesdays, two more wonderful afternoons with James. Each time the sex feels better than the time before, more natural, though James is embarrassed about how he can only last a few minutes.

"It just feels so *good*," he says, which makes you smile.

That third Wednesday, you decide to try again, after the first time ends quickly. And this time is different—you still don't have an orgasm while he's inside you, but it lasts longer, and you're more able to focus on trying things that feel good for you.

At school, you've invited Maggie to sit with you and James at lunch. The first day she takes you up on the offer, she does so with big, scared eyes, like she's just waiting for someone to say something awful.

But no one does, not even Darcy, who's sitting across from you, on Big Mac's lap. By the end of lunch, Maggie has relaxed and even laughs when James makes a joke about the way Big Mac dances—like an oversize chicken who doesn't know his feathers have all been plucked, he says.

And then, Saturday morning, Halloween morning, you wake to find a streak of blood in your underwear.

It surprises you, even though you knew it must be coming soon; it's been four weeks since that awful night. It seems so . . . odd, that this is something your body does now. That blood is part of your rhythm.

I don't trust anything that bleeds for five days and doesn't die.

You heard some guys at school laughing at that line from an old movie. They thought it was hilarious.

There's a party tonight, of course, because it's Halloween.

When you were little, Mémé would take you trick-or-treating. Your neighborhood was good for that: friendly neighbors, happy porch lights, lots of kids. Since junior high, though, no one trick-or-treats anymore. It's all about the house parties. This year, the party will be at Big Mac's house.

His parents are loaded, and they have a big house on Parkside Drive, backing up to Broadmoor Golf Course, right near the arboretum. James is excited about the party, and though you could take it or leave it, you'll go because it will make James happy.

You spend the day working on homework and helping Mémé with chores around the house. Last time, you barely had any cramps, but today is harder—occasional pains down low, in your uterus, and a persistent sore lower back, just a fragile feeling there, a dull ache. Mémé notices you massaging your back and takes the broom from you. "Why don't you go rest for a while?" she says. "I can finish up in here."

In your room, you lie on your side, curled up in a ball, and consider calling James to cancel. But after lying there for a little while, you feel sort of better. You should go. It'll make James happy, to be with you and his friends together. You text Maggie to see if there's any chance she might want to come— you've been trying to encourage her to get out of the house, and besides, it would be nice to have at least one person there you can talk to besides James—but when she says thanks but no, you understand, and you don't press her.

You haven't planned a costume, so you start pulling open drawers, seeing what you can throw together. There, in the top drawer, you find two necklaces—Maggie's locket, and Mémé's moon.

You remember what Mémé said when she gave the necklace to you—*I liked to imagine that the blade could cut the pain*—and you string it over your forehead, tuck the moon between your breasts.

Maybe it works because you want it to work, like a placebo or something, but your cramps *do* feel lighter; your back *does* feel better.

And then it occurs to you what you can wear tonight.

James picks you up at eight o'clock. You hear the doorbell and you call, "Mémé, can you get the door? I'll be right out!"

You hear the door open, and Mémé says, "Why, hello, James. That's quite a costume."

There is his laugh. Then, "Sorry, Ms. Martel. I thought Bisou would answer the door."

"That's all right," Mémé says. "I've seen worse."

You look at yourself in the long mirror on the back of your bedroom door. You've put your hair back in a low bun, and you've drawn on a beard with brown eyeliner. A gray beanie, red-and-black-checked flannel, jeans, and brown leather work boots complete your lumberjack costume—you'll be warm and comfortable, at least, at Big Mac's party.

Mémé is standing with James in the sitting room waiting for you. He smiles when he sees you, starts to laugh. You don't get the joke at first, until you see what James is holding, scrunched up in his hand: it's a brown, furry mask. He unfolds it, brings it up to his head, puts it on.

"Look at us," he says, his voice slightly muffled by his wolfish visage. "All we're missing is Little Red Riding Hood."

Mémé is watching you, watching James. And you remember what she said to you—*Sometimes boys become wolves.*

Big Mac's house is ridiculous. No one *needs* this much room. And he is an only child. His real name is Mackenzie, named after his maternal grandfather, he likes to tell everyone, who invented some sort of medical device that revolutionized post-op surgical care. No one has ever asked him what exactly the device did; it's clear enough from his address that the most important thing the device did was produce a shitload of money.

James doesn't pull his blue wagon into the long, horseshoe-shaped driveway; he parks on the street. His car leaks oil, so James never parks in driveways. You hold hands as you walk up to the house, weaving through the cars parked there. You can tell who's at the party by the cars. Most of the basketball team, of course.

And there, near the edge of the street, is Keisha's funny little purple Bug.

Though Keisha isn't exactly the party type, *of course* she's here tonight: this party will be a house full of Tucker's friends, loosened up by music and alcohol. The gossip is sure to flow as easily as the beer. Last week, you told her a little about Maggie—nothing specific, just how Tucker had been a major asshole, and you suggested that maybe Keisha could back off, seeing as how Maggie had already gone through plenty. She had been noncommittal, sort of shrugging, but if she's here, maybe she's moving on to new targets.

James stops before he rings the bell, unwinds his fingers from yours, fits the mask over his head.

"How do I look?"

The mask hoods his entire head: thick brown fur; two black-tipped pointed ears; a long, rubbery snout, a shiny black nose, a yawning maw full of teeth. And there, through the eye holes, are James's sweet brown eyes.

"You look great," you tell him.

Inside, the party is exactly as you would expect it to be: dark, loud, cups in hands, a mash-up of costumes that felt exciting and dangerous two years ago, when you were a freshman, but now feel tired, cliché, and actually, pretty boring.

You scan the crowd. There is Graham, circulating among groups, trying to insert himself here, there, anywhere. None of the guys like him, James has told you, but he sometimes shows up anyway, and no one ever has the heart to kick him out. He catches your eye across the crowd and grins, but then he must see James behind you—*with* you—because his smile drops, as if he's tasted something sour, and his eyes flick away. This will be your last house party, you decide, even before you manage to get to the kitchen where you search, in vain, for a bottle of water.

Before you started dating James, your idea of a good Saturday night involved hanging out at home, either alone or with Mémé. Since then, well, it's not that James is a huge partier, just that he has so many friends. And parties fill him up, energize him. They drain you. As much as you love James, you don't love parties. So you decide that if James wants to go to these things on the weekends, that's his call, but after tonight, you're done.

Though you can't find a bottle of water in the kitchen, you do find Keisha, leaning against the counter, talking to Phillip Tang. No costume, just her regular jeans and sweater. It's clear to you that she isn't here to hang out; you recognize her expression. Phillip may think he's flirting, but what is actually happening is an interview.

Phillip Tang was one of Tucker's closest friends. He looks sort of drunk already, the way he keeps running his hands through his thick, short dark hair, the way he goes to lean against the counter but misjudges exactly how far away it is, stumbling a little. He's dressed up as Spider-Man, largely, you suspect, because he looks so good in the costume, with his wide shoulders, small waist, and an ass the girls are always giggling about.

"So how come I never see you at parties?" Phillip says to Keisha. You watch him lean into her; one of her twists has come loose from her bun, and he winds it around his finger, tugs on it. "You could be pretty if you tried a little," he adds, but with a smile that softens it.

You stare at them, unblinking. Phillip is one of those guys who is great at everything—straight As, all APs, never late, makes the female teachers giggle, first-string tight end on the football team, first-chair violin.

But.

There have been rumors. Like the whole thing with Cara Lee, who went out with him freshman year for a while and then abruptly dropped out of school. She transferred to a private high school on the other side of town, and it was weird the way Phillip and his friends never talked about her after that, the way she never showed up for any parties or games or dances. On a Friday she was in school, and on Monday she wasn't. You'd texted her once or twice, because you'd been partners in science lab, but she didn't ever respond and then someone told you that she'd changed her number.

And then there was the time over spring break last year when Phillip went to visit his brother at Berkeley. James told you about some girl, a freshman there, who'd accused Phillip and his brother of doing something to her while she was passed out. But then the charges were dropped for some reason, maybe because it hadn't been true, maybe because all of

Phillip's brother's fraternity friends had sworn it wasn't.

You angle your way behind Phillip to look for a cup in the cabinet near Keisha's head.

"Maybe we should go outside where we can hear each other better," Phillip suggests to Keisha, even though it's not all that loud in the kitchen.

"I can hear you fine," Keisha says to Phillip as she scoots over so that you can open the cabinet. She shoots you a quick glance—annoyed. "Anyway," she continues, "it's strange that they couldn't identify it."

"There's all kinds of weird shit out there," Phillip says, one hand on the back of his neck, the other holding his red cup. "That's why I stay away from it. Who the fuck knows what they cut it with?"

"Mm-hmm," Keisha says. "Definitely safer to stick with alcohol. And I thought Tucker usually did, too?" She lifts her voice at the end of the sentence, so it becomes a question.

Phillip shrugs, takes a sip. "I guess," he says, "but he must have decided to try something new that night."

You have a glass, you've filled it with water from the sink, and now you have no good reason to be standing there, a point Keisha emphasizes with her piercing stare.

Phillip sees her looking at you, and he grins. You can tell that he thinks she wants you to leave them alone for a different reason. "Hey, Bisou," he says.

"Hey, Phillip."

You leave Keisha to her interrogation.

James isn't in the living room. The music is loud in here, too loud, it seems to you, and it's like the blood in your veins is vibrating with the rhythm of it. It's super crowded, shoulder to shoulder, that weird mix of masks and tutus and glitter and gore that Halloween always brings, so it could be that James is somewhere in the crowd, somewhere in the middle, but somehow you know he's not. You skirt the crowd, making your way toward the back door so that you can get to the porch; even if James isn't there, at least you'll be able to breathe.

Another group has gathered here outside, backs forming a tight circle with a joint at its center, glowing red each time the next person takes it and inhales.

You don't smoke very often, and you don't feel like it tonight, but the joint still smells good the way pot can, earthy and stinky. You smell the particular scent of James, too, even though he's on the far side of the circle—the wind must be blowing just right to carry the smell of him, his wintergreen-and-anise deodorant, the crisp lemon of his soap, to you.

Except there is no wind.

"Bisou," James says, and his voice is honey. "Baby."

You smell them all—James, his wintergreen and anise, his lemon; Big Mac next to him, sour, like he hasn't bathed, but dripped over with Drakkar Noir; Darcy, thick in baby pow-der; Graham, the orange Tic Tacs he's always sucking on; Lorraine, lots of hair spray, the chemicals in it make your nose itch, and something else . . . you close your eyes, focus delib-erately, breathe in deep through your nose. Blood. She has her period.

Layered over all of it—the menstrual blood, the breath mints, the hair spray, the body spray, the soap, the sweat, all the things that reveal these people as human bodies even as they fight to mask that humanity—is the smoky drift of mar-ijuana.

You open your eyes. James is taking the joint being passed to him, saying, "I'm good, I'm driving." He holds it out in your direction.

You shake your head. "It's okay, you can if you want, I can drive."

"You sure?"

You nod. And then you look up, into the wide white eye of the full moon.

The party happens all around you. The joint is ashed, and another replaces it. Drinks are downed, cups refilled. James takes your hand and leads you back inside, and he pulls his mask back on as you go to the living room, where people have pushed the furniture to the walls, where in dark corners bodies shadow into each other, where in the center the crowd pulses with a shared rhythm.

You see that Keisha has moved her interrogation to another subject; she's cornered Caleb—literally cornered him, he's wedged between the room's massive fireplace and a chair, with Keisha blocking his path out of the room. You can't hear their words, but you feel their energy—Keisha, leaning forward, insistent, and Caleb, clearly wanting to get back to the party but too polite to push past her.

And, a little way away, Phillip, red cup still in hand, watching them both, his jaw tense.

James is a good dancer. He takes you to the middle of the room and spins you around, then pulls you close until the long, lean plane of him fits right up against you, his leg parting your thighs, and you wind your arms up and around his neck, the polyester fur of his mask brushing against your hands. He nuzzles the cold rubber nose into your throat, and you grab the mask, pull it off.

"I like *your* face," you tell him.

"The better to kiss you with," he says, stoned, grinning, and then his warm, wet mouth is on yours, and you are reminded yet again that James is an even better kisser than he is a dancer.

You kiss and you dance and you wonder, untroubled, at the fact that you can smell everything, all around you, even things you shouldn't be able to smell, like what brand of beer

Graham, dancing nearby, has on his breath (Keystone Light, layered over those orange Tic Tacs), or that Marcella and her ex-boyfriend Marco, across the room, have definitely reunited tonight, the twinned scent of their sex thick on both of them.

You press yourself more firmly into James, you pull his sweater away from his back and run your fingers up and down his warm skin, you tangle your tongue with his and take his lower lip between your teeth. He makes a sound only you can hear, a soft moan, and you feel all the ways his body responds to you.

The song ends, but you're not done kissing him yet, and you don't want to open your eyes, you don't want to see what's around you, you want it to be Wednesday afternoon again.

"Damn, Keisha, what do I have to do to get you to dance like *that*?" It's Phillip's voice, but you ignore it, squeeze James's hips, and, on your own time, step back, just one step.

"You don't have enough roofies and your dad doesn't have enough lawyers to make *that* happen," Keisha answers, so quick, so smart, so cuttingly mean.

The room goes dead quiet for half a beat, and then Big Mac roars, "Holy shit, man! *Burned!*"

Laughter blisters the room. You turn and find Keisha and Phillip; Caleb has disappeared, probably relieved to be away from the weight of Keisha's intensity, and Phillip has slid next to her, too close. Now Keisha is the one who is cornered, by him. But Keisha isn't as polite as Caleb, and you watch Phillip's face turn an ugly reddish-purple, you watch as he backs away from Keisha, and his hands are fists.

James laughs, too, almost everyone is laughing, maybe for different reasons, some because they've been on the butt end of a Phillip barb and it feels good to watch him take it for a change, some because they've heard the rumors about Berkeley and always wondered what went down; a couple because they were friends with Cara Lee and maybe they know more than you do.

The sound of laughter at his back, Phillip turns and leaves.

"I fucking hate these parties," Keisha says, and you shouldn't be able to hear her across the sound of laughter, across the ramping-up bass beat of the next song.

But you do.

The party shifts not long after that, like the night has turned a corner. It's winding down, and kids start to head home, peeling off in groups of twos and threes. Keisha leaves, too; maybe she figures that whoever is still here is too drunk to be worth interrogating at this point. You watch her say goodbye to Big Mac; "Thank you for the hospitality, Mackenzie," she says, and he bows in acknowledgment with a drunk and delighted smile. Then she heads to the front door, her back stiff and straight in that formal way she carries herself, like she holds herself to a different standard or something. She's annoying as hell and dangerous, too, with all her questions, but you can't help but admire her. *Like* her, even.

You are ready to go home, too, but James says, "My mom will lose her shit if she sees me like this. Do you mind if just I crash here? You can take my car." There are just a few people left, all guys from James's team, and they're settling in to watch some kung fu movie on Big Mac's enormous TV. "You can come get me tomorrow," James says, "or one of the guys can drive me over to pick it up in the morning."

"Are you sure? I could take you home."

"Totally sure," James says, kissing your head. "I'm just going to crash."

"Okay," you say, and you lean in to kiss his neck. Before you leave, you want to use the bathroom; James waits outside the door to make sure no one bothers you. You pee and change your tampon, and then go to the sink to wash your hands. You catch sight of yourself in the mirror—your face is still smeared with the eyeliner beard, which makes you laugh. You wash it off, dry your face and hands, and rebraid your hair.

There is James, patiently leaning against the wall in the hallway. "Nice shave," he says, and he laces his fingers through yours, walking with you out into the driveway and down to the street. A thick, wet fog has crept in, and you breathe in heavy, damp air. It's the kind of air that cuts right through, to the core of you, and when James lets go of your hand to loop his arm up over your shoulders, you lean into him.

James watches as you slide behind the wheel of his long blue wagon, as you turn the key. He leans over and cranks the heat all the way to high, flips on the defrost button. "Be care-ful," he says, and he kisses you, then slams shut the door and watches as you pull away from the curb.

The streets are quiet as the fog. You drive carefully, head-lights caught as if in spider's webs.

Perhaps it is because you are driving so carefully, so slowly, that you notice, pulled to the side of the road in the shadows of the arboretum's entrance, Keisha's purple Bug.

iv

people break things, my girl
that is the truth

promises
hearts
families
bones

not everything is broken

the velvet black sky
your steady, sleeping breaths
the path, thick with snow
my promise to you

but the dawn will break
your sleep will break
the path
the path
the path will break

i cannot stop the breaking

LONE WOLF

You pull James's wagon behind Keisha's Bug.

It is empty; you can see this from here, and that it is listing slightly to the right.

You leave James's headlights on and step out of his car. Every hair on your body feels erect, as if each hair is a tiny antenna, gathering information.

The right rear tire has a bad flat. Maybe Keisha ran over something sharp, you try to tell yourself, but the hairs on your body say otherwise.

Hers is one of the really old Bugs, the kind with the engine in the back, and when you rest your hand on the car's tail end, you can tell that it's been parked for a little while, but not too long, from the warmth that still radiates from it.

Even though you know Keisha isn't in her car, you look carefully into each window. The car is neat, just the way Keisha *would* keep her car: a stack of books on the floor behind the passenger seat; a little reusable trash bin tucked between the two front bucket seats; a few hair ties looped over the stick shift, all black; an I Support Planned Parenthood sticker in the lower right corner of the windshield.

And, on the passenger seat, her cell phone.

You try the driver's side door; it's unlocked. No keys.

No Keisha.

You scan the fog, the murky air lit up by James's headlights and the dark, damp nothingness beyond, the brace of trees.

"Keisha," you say loudly, not a question but a command.

She does not answer. You walk beyond the halo thrown by headlights, stare into the yawning maw of the arboretum. Your hand goes to your throat, finds the chain of the necklace Mémé gave to you.

"Keisha!" you say again, this time even louder, and into the trees.

There is still no answer.

You feel the tight squeeze of your uterus as it cramps, you feel the swell of your tampon as it fills with your blood, and you sniff the air. Beyond the smells of your own body, of the car's warm engine, of the fog, you smell something else.

Rusted metal, singed hair, the stink of animal breath, all mingled together into a specific braid of scent you have smelled twice before, but until this moment, had not connected. You smelled this last month, alone in the forest with the pewter wolf. And you smelled it long before that, when you hid in the skirts of ghosts waiting for your mother to come for you.

"Keisha," you say again, but this time it's just a whisper. She cannot come to you; you will have to go to her. You pull the necklace from beneath your shirt; you unloop it from your neck, pull the metal claw from its sheath, and wrap the chain around your fist.

Leaving the light of the car behind you, leaving the road, you step into the trees.

It's impossible to know which direction she went. Eyes narrowed, adjusting to the dark, you scan the ground. At first, you see nothing but pine needles and fallen leaves, but then— there. Up ahead, and to the path that branches left. Something red.

You crouch to pick it up. It's a piece of fabric. Red, with black lines, like . . . spiderwebs.

You run.

The trees are tall, dark shadows that whoosh into shape as you pass; your face is wet from fog; you run.

Your hand grips the long, mean claw; your boots are sure

and steady beneath you; you run.

There is the rest of Phillip's costume, shed like a snakeskin; you run.

And then you are deep in the forest, encircled by trees and fog, and you taste in the back of your throat your own fear mixed with adrenaline, the burn of acid.

You hear her scream—Keisha, high-pitched, scared, not a word but a sound, a desperate, last-chance alarm.

You roar in response as you run, so that if he kills her before you get to them, Keisha will not die thinking that no one tried to save her, and so that he will know that there will be a price paid for her spilled blood.

And then the fog pulls back like a curtain, and you see them: Keisha, forced up against a tall fir tree, a slash in the thigh of her jeans revealing a deep red wound, her empty hands thrusting out in front of her, and, back on his haunches, ready to leap, lips curled, eyes narrowed, ears forward—a wolf.

"Hey!" you yell, and the wolf turns his heavy, dark head. His eyes glow gold, and he snarls.

You spread your arms wide, taking up space, offering your chest, daring the wolf to come at you.

And he turns in your direction, but he doesn't attack; he watches you, measuring you, reading you.

The wolf takes two slow steps forward, and you hold your ground. You like it just where you are; the earth is even, and there is space to maneuver. The animal is ten slow steps away from you, maybe just two quick bounds, if he decides to leap.

Your weight is even over your heels, and you've got your claw, sharper than his, longer than his, in your dominant hand.

There are things you know now, in this moment, among these trees: the moon is full. It has been one full cycle since last you faced a wolf. You are stronger than you were, and faster than you were, and you, in this moment, are made for this moment.

The animal confronting you is both a wolf and not a wolf. And you—you are both a girl and not a girl. You are a hunter, and this wolf, though he thinks he is the predator, is your prey.

You scan the wolf for weaknesses and strengths. He's big, much larger than a wolf should be, and thick with muscle under his dull black pelt. His black lips are snarled back, his teeth are shiny with spit. His eyes are narrowed and cunning. He is young and strong and ready to kill.

You know the wolf is about to spring when he shifts his weight farther back on his haunches, when his front paws spread and claw into the earth. You shift your left foot behind your right, your dominant hand forward, elbow tight and close to your body. Your knees are soft; your grip is hard.

The wolf growls, snarls, and then moves.

You are aware of Keisha, still backed up against the tree, and you see her in your peripheral vision, face twisted in pain and fear. You hope she stays where she is, out of the way, and doesn't try to help. But hope is all you have time for as the wolf bounds once, twice, and then he is in the air and almost upon you, claws and teeth and fur, and if the wolf lands on you, he will flatten you, you will be pinned beneath him on the forest floor, and he will tear your throat with his fangs.

Your heart beats steady and strong, your limbs vibrate with anticipation. As the wolf flies toward you, all teeth and claws, you see your target—the pulse of his throat—and you know you have one chance to land the first strike. You lunge forward, springing off your back foot, and you meet the wolf in the air. He has ten claws, but you have one, your sickle-shaped gift from Mémé.

You meet the wolf's flesh just above the collarbones, and you are fast and sure as you stick the wolf, plunging your claw into his body until your fingers meet bloody fur, and then you yank up, hard, a quick solid slit, and then the wolf is upon you, his weight throwing you back onto the forest floor, and you cross your left arm over your face, and the hot jet of blood pulses from within.

Now Keisha cries out. She rushes to you, and she grabs the wolf by its pelt and grunts as she tries to pull him off you, but he is deadweight, and not until you push up against him are the two of you able to roll it away from your body.

You are red with blood; in your hand, your claw is thick with gore; your eyes see through a haze of wolf blood that coats your face; but you are alive, and so is Keisha.

She sobs, stifles it, and gives you her hand. You grab it, and then you are standing together over the wolf's body. Minutes pass as you stand there, holding each other. You should move. You should run. But instead you stay. You wait. And together, you watch as the wolf's eyes glaze dead, as the bloody wound stops weeping, and then as the creature transforms from dead wolf to dead boy—Phillip, naked, cut from sternum to chin.

"Oh God oh God oh God," Keisha says.

You pant from adrenaline and exertion, but now is not the time to rest. When Keisha moves toward Phillip's body to touch him, to see if he is real, if *this* is real, you reach out and grab her arm.

"Don't," you say. "Don't touch anything."

She stops. Nods. You release her arm, leaving a bloody print on her sweater.

"Did you drop anything?" you ask. "Is there anything here that we need to find?"

Keisha draws a deep, shaking breath. She pats her pockets, pulls out her car keys. Then, "My phone."

"It's in your car."

She nods. "Nothing."

"Okay," you say. "Let's go."

Together you turn back toward the road, where your cars are parked, conspicuously, you realize now, and—*shit*—you've left James's headlights on. If anyone has come down that road, they've seen the cars, the headlights, and they'll remember that, for sure.

"Hurry," you tell Keisha, and she tries, but she's limping, and the faster she goes, the more her thigh wound bleeds. You stop for her, sheathe the bloody claw and shove it into the pocket of your jeans, wrap Keisha's arm over your shoulders and grab her around the waist. "Lean on me," you tell her, and she does. She slows you down, but there's nothing to be done about that. Her face is ashen from exertion and pain, and with each step her expression tightens more and more.

At last you come to the woods' edge. James's headlights are still glowing, and it's a relief now, at least, because it means you haven't killed his battery. You open the passenger side door of Keisha's car and sit her down in it; she cry-moans when she's able to take her weight off her injured leg.

"Stay here," you tell her. "I'm going to turn on the wagon's engine to keep it alive."

Keisha nods, closes her eyes. She does not ask questions, which is a first.

You jog over to James's car, fit the key into the ignition, turn. For a second it sounds like it's too dead to catch; the lights flicker like maybe the battery is too drained to get the job done, but then the engine roars and you nearly cry with relief.

"Okay," you say out loud. You take your hand off the keys and leave them red with blood. You survey yourself. Blood everywhere: dark on your jeans, sticky on your arms in places where it's thick, drying and cracking other places where it's splattered more thinly. Your whole shirt is wet with blood, soaked through.

You've seen enough crime dramas to know that if anyone ever investigates James's car, they'll find this blood in it somewhere. You will never get it clean enough.

You have to be fast, and you have to be thorough. You need to get your story straight with Keisha, and you need to get off the road.

You are careful to touch as little as possible as you get out of James's car, leaving the engine running. You go back over to Keisha, who has her head in her hands. She's vomited, you see, onto the gravel. You kick dirt over the acrid sick, and then you kneel down in front of her. "Keisha," you say. "There's no time."

She tightens her fingers in her hair, and for a moment you're shot through with fear, that she won't be able to pull it together, that's she won't be able to help. But then her fingers relax, her head lifts slowly, and she looks you right in the eyes.

"Okay," she says. "What do we do?"

"Text your mom and tell her you're sleeping over at my house because you have a flat. I don't live far from here."

Keisha fishes her phone out from beneath her legs—she's sat on it—and she sends the message. Her fingers are steady. A moment later a text pings back: **OK**.

"Good," you say. "We need to get out of here. There's no time to change your tire. You're just going to have to drive on

155

the flat. It'll wreck your rim, there's nothing we can do about that."

Keisha nods. She gets to her feet, and you help her around to the driver's side. "I'll follow you," you say. "Do you know where I live?"

She shakes her head.

"Over on Thirty-Seventh. Number Sixteen-Ten."

She nods. "Okay."

When she's got her car started, you go back to the wagon. You wish you had a plastic sheet or something to lay down—you're going to get blood everywhere, it seems like—and you check the back of the wagon for the blanket, but it's gone, James has moved it.

At least no one has gone by, and there's no indication that anyone's stopped while you were in the arboretum. Maybe you got really lucky and no one has been by this whole time. You are struck by the absurdity that anything about this entire night could be viewed as "lucky."

"People can get used to most anything," Mémé sometimes says, and you guess she is right.

Now you are grateful for the heavy fog; maybe it's kept drivers off the road. Maybe no one saw the cars parked by the arboretum entrance, and maybe no one will see you now, following Keisha's slow, off-kilter Bug home.

A few minutes later, you pull up to your house; James would never park in your driveway because of his oil leak, but the car has bigger problems right now than a leaky engine. Keisha parks at the curb while you pull up the driveway, and you leave the car running while you open the garage door. Then you maneuver the wagon inside.

When the engine and the headlights are off, you relax, just a little. You've been holding yourself so tense, every muscle tight, and now, at least, you are home.

"Do you have any first-aid stuff?" Keisha asks. She's limped up the driveway and stands in the open garage doorway.

"Yeah, of course, come inside."

Keisha steps into the garage, and you close the door behind her.

Safe. You are covered in Phillip's blood, and there is a body in the arboretum, and Maggie's rim is definitely ruined, and she's got a deep gash in her thigh, but, for now, you are safe in the pitch-dark garage.

Then the door that connects the garage to the kitchen squeaks open, bringing with it a stream of warm honey light and the shape of Mémé.

"Bisou," she says. "You're home."

V

who's afraid of the big bad wolf

i am afraid

of everything

THE BETTER TO SEE YOU

There is a fraction of a second between Mémé opening the
door to the house and Mémé flicking on the overhead
light. In that moment, you reel through possible stories—you
hit a deer on the road, and you tried to save it, and it bled
all over you. There was an accident at the party, one of the
kids got cut by a broken bottle, but you applied pressure, and
everything is fine.

Then the light is on and the lies stick in your throat.

Mémé scans the scene—you, thick with blood; Keisha,
leg slashed, looking now like she might pass out; James's car,

159

parked in her garage.

"Did anyone see you?"

Her voice is sharp, but not scared. Not surprised, even.

"I—I don't think so."

"You don't *think* so?"

You nod.

"All right," she says. "Both of you. Take off all your clothes."

Keisha obeys without question, pulling her sweater and T-shirt off together. Mémé steps forward and takes them. Keisha's unbuttoned her jeans but she can't get them off over her boots, and her leg is too hurt for her to bend down and untie them, so Mémé tosses the sweater and shirt into the sink beside the workbench in the garage, kneels down, and undoes Keisha's shoes for her. Then, as gentle as she once was with you when she helped you change at night, she helps Keisha shimmy out of her jeans, doing her best to keep the rough fabric from rubbing against her injured thigh.

Keisha whimpers a little but doesn't cry out, and then she's standing in her underwear and bra. You are still fully dressed, blood-soaked, watching.

"You too, Bisou," Mémé says, and you kneel down to unknot your laces and strip out of your clothes. Even your bra is stained red; the wolf—the boy—has bled so much that you're soaked all the way to the skin, so you unhook your bra and toss it along with the rest of your clothes into the washbasin.

You grab a T-shirt from the clean-laundry basket near the machine and pull it on.

Mémé disappears back into the house. You have no idea what the hell is going on. Keisha is beside you, and she is trembling.

Mémé returns with lighter fluid, a pack of long kitchen matches, a bunch of rags, and a gallon of bleach. "Bisou," she says, "help your friend into the shower and stay with her in case she passes out. You wash off, too. I'll take care of this."

She indicates the car, the clothes, maybe the whole garage.

"Okay." Your voice sounds normal, like this is a normal conversation about normal things. "Come on," you say to Keisha, but she just stands there, arms folded across her stomach, in a gray sports bra and white underwear, staring at Mémé. And her expression—it's her investigative reporter expression.

"Later." You reach out and take her by the arm, pull her toward the door to the kitchen.

She follows, but she looks back over her shoulder at Mémé, who is pouring lighter fluid over your clothes in the laundry sink.

Keisha almost slips as she steps over the bathtub rim. She's shaking again, all over, and she looks like she could pass out at any moment.

There's a little metal stool in the corner of the bathroom that you sometimes sit on when you blow-dry your hair, and you put it into the bathtub. You help Keisha step out of her underwear and pull off her bra, and then you put them into the sink.

Keisha sits naked, shivering, on the stool. Gently, you take her glasses from her face and set them on the counter.

Now, without her glasses, Keisha looks truly naked. Her eyes seem smaller without them, a bit unfocused, and she blinks several times. It's her eyes you avoid as you get the water going. You wait until it's the right temperature coming out of the bath nozzle and then take down the shower head and flip the bypass knob. Keisha sits, grasping the stool with both hands, while you run the water up her legs, trying not to spray directly into the wound on her left thigh.

It's two wounds, actually, you see now. One is bigger and deeper, and then, just below, where a second claw must have caught her, is a shallower wound, this one crusted over with clotted blood.

You pick up the bottle of body wash and flip open the lid. "Sorry," you say, and then you squirt it right at her wound.

Keisha hisses with the sting of it. You've got a clean washcloth that was hanging on the towel bar, and you use it to lather the soap into and around the wound. Keisha's grip on the stool tightens but she doesn't try to pull away.

You scrub for a full minute and then spray her down—her leg, which is bleeding harder, and the rest of her, too. Then you crank off the water and drape a towel over her shoulders.

There's some first-aid stuff—gauze and some useless Band-Aids—under the sink. None of it really looks big enough to deal with Keisha's injury. Then you see the maxi pads, and think, why not, they're supposed to soak up blood, and you unwrap one and place it facedown on Keisha's wound. She snorts a laugh at the absurdity of it.

There's some medical tape, and you wind that a few times over the pad and Keisha's thigh.

"Okay." You help Keisha stand and hold her hand as she steps out of the tub. Then you leave her to dry off and go to your room to get her some clothes—a pair of loose sweatpants and a T-shirt. You grab her a pair of your underwear, too.

When she's dressed, you walk her to your bed and help her get in. You pull up the covers and hope she'll stop shivering soon. She's left her glasses behind, on the bathroom counter, as if she has seen enough this night. It's your turn for a shower, and you rifle through your drawers for another set of clothes.

But before you leave: "Bisou."

You turn back.

"Did that really happen?"

"I think so," you say. "I'm pretty sure."

"Is that . . . what happened to Tucker?"

This question was answered for you back in the woods, but you do not answer Keisha now. Is this Keisha the girl or Keisha the reporter asking? "Let me take a shower," you say. "We'll talk later."

Keisha rests her head against the pillow and closes her eyes.

You pee and pull out your tampon before you climb into the shower. You let the water pour over your head, washing your hair forward, and you watch the blood rinse from you, inside and out, wolf blood and womb blood, both.

It's many minutes before the water runs clean, and then you scrub yourself with soap, and then you turn off the water, put in a fresh tampon, and dry your body.

There are Keisha's glasses. You pick them up; a smear of blood streaks across one lens. Gently, you wash them, then hold them up to the light to make sure they are clean. Through the lenses, the world blurs for you. Strange how a thing can strengthen one person and weaken another.

Keisha is asleep. You switch off the bedside lamp.

Mémé is still in the garage. The air stings with the smell of bleach. There's an orange bucket next to the open driver's side door of James's car, and a plastic trash bag beside it; the bucket is half full of soapy water, and Mémé is leaning into the car, scrubbing.

She is methodical. Already the dashboard has been wiped down, and the steering wheel, and the ignition. She's wiped down the gear shift and the center console, and now she's working on the driver's seat.

She's started at the top, the headrest, and has wiped down

the seat back; it's damp and shiny clean.

She's working on the seat now, and she has her glasses on, and she's found a headlamp among the camping gear, which she shines down on her work.

"It's a good thing he has vinyl seats," Mémé says, "or we'd have to arrange a car fire."

She looks up and smiles, and you wonder if maybe she's joking, though you don't know how she could joke right now about anything. You don't smile back. You don't do anything—you don't offer to help, you just watch as she puts a damp, bloody rag into the plastic bag and then dips her hand into the bucket of soapy water, fishes out a new rag, squeezes it, and goes back to work.

At last she is done. You have never seen James's car look so clean. It gleams, and you can't see any evidence of how it looked before.

Mémé takes the bucket of soapy water and the bag of used rags over to the laundry sink, where she burned your clothes; the sink is empty, and there's no sign of what she did with the remains, though the smell of smoke lingers. She pours the soapy water down the drain, and then she spreads another plastic bag on the floor near the washing machine; one by one she pulls out the used rags from the bag, rinses them as clean as she can, squeezes the excess water from them, and spreads them on the plastic bag.

"We'll burn them when they're dry," she says.

Then she washes her hands and forearms, the water from the sink steaming hot, and scrubs with soap. She dries off with another rag and adds this one to the pile on the floor. You go back to your bathroom to retrieve the T-shirt and underwear, then drop them onto the pile as well.

Mémé is still wearing the headlamp, and not until her hands are clean and dry does she pull it from her head, press the button to turn it off.

She turns to you; her long gray hair is barely disordered from its braid. "Now," she says. "Perhaps we should move James's car to the street, and then how about a cup of tea?"

You back the car out of the garage and park it next to the curb in front of your house. Mémé stands silhouetted against the light of the garage and watches. It's raining now, which is good; it'll wash away Keisha's vomit and obscure any footprints you and she might have left behind. You shut off the engine, close the car door quietly, lock it, and walk back up the driveway to where Mémé waits.

You are tired. So, so tired. More tired, perhaps, than you have ever been.

Mémé pulls closed the garage door. You follow her into the kitchen. She fills the kettle and puts it to heat on the stove. You fill the pot with tea—Earl Grey, because you doubt either of you will sleep tonight anyway.

"Bergamot," Mémé says when she pours hot water over the leaves in the pot. "Excellent choice."

You can't smile. The unasked, unanswered questions seem to form a haze between you, a scrim.

You sit at the round wooden table, in the same chair you always sit in. Mémé unwraps a loaf of her bread from its blue checked cloth, cuts thick slices, and brings them to the table with butter and honey.

You are, you realize, starving.

You take a slice of the bread and slather it thick with butter, drizzle the honey across it, tear a bite with your teeth. You chew, swallow, and take a deep sip of the steaming mug of tea Mémé has poured for you. She sits, holding her cup, watching you.

"It made me hungry, too," she says. "The hunting."

She reaches into the pocket of her sweater, pulls out the sickle-moon necklace. She turns it over in her hands; it's clean, the gore gone.

Then she reaches across the table and, for the second time, gives it to you.

You take it again. You loop it back around your neck. You tuck it beneath your T-shirt.

And then your eyes fill with tears, your hands begin to tremble, and you cry.

"Oh, Bisou," Mémé says, and the deep sadness in her voice ratchets up your own emotions, and you set down the bread and put your elbows on the table, your head in your hands, and you cry and cry and cry.

Mémé moves to the seat next to you, and she pulls you close, pulls you to her chest, tucks your head beneath her chin, and she holds you tight as you tremble. She holds you and rocks you and you are a child again, just arrived at Mémé's house, and behind your eyes is a wash of red and death. There is Phillip's body, and the wolf he was, and the pewter wolf, and Mama, too, with her throat torn, asleep forever in her blood-soaked bed.

"I am sorry," Mémé says, arms tight, rocking you. "I am so, so sorry."

Your tea is cold before you have finished with tears. You wipe your face with a cloth napkin. Mémé dumps your tea in the sink and pours you a fresh cup, pressing it into your hands.

"Drink," she says, and you do, though the tea is black and bitter.

Finally, you are able to ask the question you have wanted to ask for a month, since the night of the pewter wolf. "Mémé," you say, "what is happening?"

She sighs. "I should have prepared you, I suppose, but I hoped—I thought perhaps—that it would not happen to you. Why should it? It never happened to your mother. Though other things did."

"What never happened?"

"This," Mémé says, waving her hand toward the garage, and, you suppose, toward the bloodied rags, the ashes of your burned clothes, James's car, the woods beyond, the woods everywhere.

"But . . . it happened to you?"

"Indeed it did." Mémé looks beyond you, her hands encircling her cup. You see some of yourself in the set of her eyes, the shape of her nose. You have only vague memories of your mother's face, and only of the very end of her life, when you had been together in the old, empty farmhouse, in the snow. But Mémé, it seems, has looked the same as far back as you can remember, to that terrible day when she came to you, to Mama's bloody bed.

Her hair is steel gray now, with shots of white; then, it had been streaked brown and gray, but other than its color, it is still the same, long and smooth in a thick braid. Her face is lined, the skin looser around her jaw than it must have been that day. But something about her has always seemed unchanging. Mémé is reliable in her steadfastness; always she has baked bread on the same two days every week. Always she drinks tea in the morning and late in the afternoon. Always she has worn pants—corduroys, jeans—always she has been plain-faced and keen-eyed.

And now you are forced to shift your perception of her. It is as if you have always seen her from one angle, and now she has turned, rotated, and you are confronted with another facet. Mémé, it seems, is a killer, too. A killer, like you.

Her eyes return to you, from whatever—from whenever—she had been. Her eyes, green-gray and serious, stare into yours.

Then, "It is far past the time I should have told you," she says. And Mémé begins.

II

WHAT SYBIL SAYS

Who's Afraid?

All right, my child. All right.

I have spent many nights—many, many nights—wondering if I would ever tell this story. To be true, I hoped I never would. I hoped, dear one, that you would not need to hear it. For this is not a story for just anyone, you know. This is not a story most ears could hear, not a tale most girls would believe. But you will believe it. You will, because it is already your story. I am just filling in the blanks for you.

I could not know for certain if we would share this story. I suspected, of course, when I heard about the first boy, the night of your dance—but you did not confide in me. Oh, I don't blame you for that, not at all—it is the same as I would have done. I thought, maybe it is someone else out there in the woods. Maybe it isn't my girl, my Bisou.

But maybe it *was* you. I couldn't know, not without asking—and that is not a question one asks. So I gave you the blade, and I waited, and now I know.

I am getting ahead of myself. It's been so long, you see, since I spoke of any of these things, though I've often wondered . . . all right. I will start at the beginning, my love.

I was my mother's second child. First came my brother, John. When he was three years old, I was born, but not into a happy home. Not a healthy home. Our home was sick, darling. It was sick and dark and by the time I was five years old, my mother was dead, my father, disappeared.

My brother John and I—we were just eight and five—were sent to live with Mother's aunt Gennie and her husband, Frank, on their farm outside Montreal. It was a fine place to grow up, I suppose—there were sheep all the year round and lambs each spring. There was blood, too, each winter, when the lambs went to slaughter, and sheep milk to drink, white as snow, until the next rutting season.

Farm life, dear one, is beautiful and terrible all mixed together. Much like life off the farm, I suppose.

I lived on that farm for a dozen years, mostly happy. I was

never really very close to any of them—not my brother, nor Aunt Gennie or her husband, Frank, though they were kind to us, and I think, looking back, that they must have hoped that John and I would become, with time, the children they themselves were unable to bear.

I was a disappointment, I know that. John, though, did grow close to them. He was good boy, a loyal boy, and the farm was a good fit for him. He never had the urge to leave, and after he finished school, he stayed right there on that farm for the rest of his days, even after Frank's heart gave out, even after Gennie was gone, he stayed on that farm until he died, right there on the farm, in his bed, they told me, in an upstairs room at the end of the hall.

But I'm getting ahead of myself, dear girl.

Frank stayed on the farm. I did not. I didn't fit there. At school, I did my work well enough, but always felt as if I was going through the motions, nothing more. And I know I made Gennie . . . uncomfortable. I made her sad.

They didn't neglect me. They did not. They did the best they could, with what they had. For John, that was enough. He was an easy child to love. He remembered our parents much more clearly than I did, but even so, Mother's death and Father's disappearance didn't do to him what they did to me, I suppose.

This is what John was like: He was the kind of boy who would rejoice over the birth of the lambs each spring, and cry over their slaughter each winter, and hum over the lamb chops on his plate that same night. He was a boy who took exactly what life gave him.

I suppose that is a good kind of a child for a farm, and that kind of boy grows into a good farmer. I was not like that; I was secretive, often hostile. I was brittle, and angry, and solitary even when I most longed for connection. I refused to eat the meat my aunt and uncle provided. I would not drink the milk the mother sheep gave.

That—my diet, my refusal to eat such things—was why I didn't get my monthly cycle the way other girls did. At least, that was Gennie's theory. For even after all the other girls at school had begun to bleed, still I was dry, and I stayed dry all through high school.

When I was accepted to the university here in Seattle, I think we were all relieved. The scholarship meant that Gennie and Frank wouldn't have to support me, and it meant I would not be beholden to them more than I already was.

Don't misunderstand me. I was grateful to them, truly I was. They had taken me in, they had sheltered and fed me the best they could, they had tried to love me, though perhaps that had proven to be too great a hurdle. No matter—they loved John, and he loved them, and I, eighteen, could leave them all behind with a clear conscience and start a life for myself.

So I boarded a plane—the first time I'd ever left the ground—in the fall of 1976, landing not far from where I had been born, not far from where you and I live today. But I returned to the region with no real memories of it, having been so young when John and I moved away. I unpacked my few things into a dorm room, I began my classes, I lived modestly and enjoyed myself more than I ever had before.

Here, my work made sense. It was work mostly of my choosing, in areas that interested me—physics and philosophy and poetry. It was in my first poetry course, you know—didn't you know?—that I met Garland. Your grandfather.

But that was later.

Those first few weeks at university were the best of my life. If there was an Eden, I had found it, I was certain. But Eden didn't last. It never does. Not more than a month into the school year, something terrible happened. I didn't know the girl—she was an upperclassman, a junior, some sort of science major. The obituary they ran said she had planned to teach after graduation.

But of course, she wouldn't get to do that. They found her in the woods not far from campus.

Before she was even in the ground, there were whispers about how she wasn't a very good girl—not that she *deserved* what happened to her, of course, no one was saying *that*, but that if she hadn't been out so late, way past curfew, and if she hadn't been known to be so free and loose with boys, with men, then she would have been perfectly safe in her own bed that night.

I was sorry to hear about what had happened, of course, but I hadn't known the girl and it seemed like a freak event, to be honest. And I was busy; aside from classes, I had finally begun to make friends, real friends, for the first time.

My closest friend was my roommate. Laura. She was a local girl, the first in her family to go to college. And she was absolutely darling—these enormous dark eyes, the sweetest smile, those curls. And smart. Smarter than anyone I'd ever met. Smarter than me, that's certain. Smart, charming, funny— and somehow, she wanted to be my friend! *Me*, who'd never felt close to . . . well, anyone, I suppose, not a single soul, since Mother died.

Maybe it was sharing a room with Laura that finally started my cycle. They say that can happen, don't they, that women who live together bleed together? Well, it happened, much to my shock. Honestly, I had stopped expecting it to ever come and then, in November, just before Thanksgiving, there it was.

Laura was so kind about it. I didn't have any pads, naturally, and so I had to ask her for help. "You can have all the pads you want," she told me, "but if you want my advice, go straight to tampons." She told me that her mother had forbidden her to use tampons at home—"They'll take your virginity," her mother had told her—and Laura hadn't had the heart to confess that that job had already been done by her junior high school boyfriend!

In any case, she gave me what I needed, and she didn't laugh at me for being so late. She said I was lucky, even, for managing to put it off this long, as if I had any control in the matter.

So you can imagine how I felt later that same night when I woke up to moonlight pouring through our bare window, flooding Laura's still-made, empty bed. She had gone to a party to meet a boy, someone she used to date in high school. She'd been excited, and a little nervous, when she'd been getting ready to go out. Laura went out a lot, but she never stayed out this late. And she always came home. There was something wrong. I knew it. I could feel it, and every part of me itched with it. It was almost as if I could *smell* the trouble. It was coming, I was sure, from the woods.

Our dorm room was on the ground floor, and it was easy enough to open the window, to climb outside. It was a dry night, and I remember how cold it was—my breath huffed a cloud in front of me as I crossed the campus, making my way toward the trees.

When had I ever been this aware of the world around me? Never. There had been a small fire on our campus several weeks before. Nothing major—an old outbuilding had caught fire. A prank, maybe, by drunk students? No one knew. The structure had been unimportant, the incident largely forgotten. I hadn't given it a thought since the day after it had burned. But this night, creeping across campus under the wide, white moon, I smelled the char of burned wood. What's more, trees that dogs had visited seemed to glow with the scent of their urine. I passed an overfull trash can and smelled the sticky sweetness of an unfinished soda stuffed inside it, among the rot.

At the edge of the forest, it was clear to me that I wasn't alone. Night birds, skittering rats and skunks—the woods were full of life. Most of it felt innocuous, but there was more . . . there was something terrible out there, too.

I felt pulled toward it as if by a hook in my chest, and as I went deeper into the forest, the canopy of trees blocked out the moon.

My hands clenched in empty fists; my heart thudded into my chest.

And then I heard a howl, a triumphant, screaming sound, and I began to run.

The wolf behowls the moon.

—*A MIDSUMMER-NIGHT'S DREAM*

As I ran, the hook in my chest pulled tighter, as if the line that pulled me reeled in. And though it was dark, and though I did not know the path I took, I did not stumble. I did not fall.

I ran, my throat thick with fear. And then I heard a scream, and then I heard it end. I knew it was Laura, and I knew I was too late to save her.

A wolf hunched over her, its pelt as white as moonlight. Its hips shuddered as it feasted on her throat, as it tore her breast.

I smelled the iron of her blood. I smelled the heat of the wolf's breath. And then it turned its head toward where I stood, underneath a tall fir tree, and it pinned me with its eyes—blue, mean, smart.

And when it turned back to its feast as if I was of no consequence, no concern, my fear shifted to anger. I stormed toward the wolf, I screamed as I ran, but then it was off, so fast, and though I chased it, though I ran faster and harder than I ever had, it disappeared.

There was nothing to do but return to Laura's body, and pick her up, and carry her home.

A girl in my dorm heard me calling from outside, and she turned on the lights to find me standing with Laura in my arms. She screamed and woke up the others, and someone called an ambulance, and someone called the police, and then we were swarmed by men—police officers and emergency responders. Someone must have called the dean because soon he was there, too, in striped pajamas and a dark blue robe.

They took Laura to the hospital, for an autopsy, I supposed, as no one there could save her. And they took me to the police station, still in blood-soaked clothes.

At one point, Laura's family came in—her father, mother, a redheaded little boy who was maybe ten years old. They were shuttled right past me, into a room with a closed door. The boy looked at me until the door was shut, and I couldn't help but feel that I had failed him. That, somehow, I had failed them all.

The officers' questions became an interrogation.

Why hadn't Laura been in her bed?

I didn't know.

Why had I woken in the night?

I couldn't recall . . . the moonlight, perhaps?

How had I found her there, in the forest?

I heard her scream.

But why had I gone in that direction? How had I known which way to go?

I didn't know. Maybe because another girl had been found dead there just a month before?

It was a white wolf? With blue eyes? That sounds strange.

Yes, I told them. It *was* strange.

The questions carried through the night, and finally someone thought to offer me different clothes, though all they had were men's sweatpants and a worn shirt, which I changed into. My bloodstained clothes disappeared in a plastic bag and were taken—where? A lab where the blood would be tested? A garbage can? An incinerator?

They returned me to campus late the next morning, near to noon. By then I had bled through the tampon I was wearing, too embarrassed to ask the all-male police force for sanitary supplies.

There were two more rounds of interrogation in the days that followed, and a write-up both in the student paper and the city press. There were looks from other students; there were questions unasked in their eyes and on their screwed-tight lips.

Then the rumors began: Laura, who had seemed to be such a good girl, was actually not so good after all, people began to say. Two boys from WSU told a reporter that they had seen Laura the weekend before, drunker than any girl should allow herself to get, at a mixer. She was flirting outrageously with all the guys, and the skirt she was wearing . . . well, it didn't leave a lot to the imagination. A girl who had been in one of Laura's classes said that sometimes she'd show up late to their study sessions, wearing sunglasses inside, probably hungover. A teacher from Laura's high school said that Laura was one of the most talented students he'd worked with in his entire career, but, he said, there was "something about her." The kind of girl who was asking for trouble.

And so, before the next full moon, that story had become Laura's legacy—she was a girl who didn't keep her knees closed, who played too fast, too hard. A morality tale for the rest of us. A warning.

The wolf is not always a wolf.
—*ITALIAN PROVERB*

I was not assigned a new roommate. I suppose it was bad luck, to sleep in the bed of a girl who had been killed. Or maybe the other girls harbored suspicions that I had had something to do with what happened to Laura, even though the police seemed satisfied by my answers.

After Laura's death, there were only a few weeks left before winter break. The last day of classes, the clouds produced a dusting of snow, and everyone—the students, the faculty, the staff—left for home in fine spirits. There weren't many students on campus over the holidays, just those of us without money for travel and those for whom home was a worse place to be on Christmas morning than an empty dormitory. I would have been welcome back on the farm, I know that, but I had no desire to go. I had a stack of books; I had a stash of chocolate bars; I was content to nest, doing my best to ignore the bare mattress and empty shelves on the other side of the room.

Eventually, though, I had to venture out to the grocery store. The dining commons were closed for the holidays, so that meant I was fixing food on a hot plate in my room. Also, with the full moon came my menses, and I needed supplies. It was on my way home from the store that a young man caught up with me. I had seen him around campus, and everyone knew who he was—tall, blond, very handsome, Dennis Cartwright had been voted Big Man on Campus three years in a row.

You've never heard of that award? That's for the best—it's a silly thing. Well, this was a different time, in some ways. Much has changed, my darling, though too much has stayed the same.

In any case, Dennis jogged up behind me. It was the middle of the day, two days after Christmas. He was wearing sweats and running shoes, training for some sport or other.

"You're Sybil, right?" he said.

I didn't deny it. He jogged slowly beside me as I walked, hefting my bag of groceries down the path to my dorm. He asked why I hadn't gone home for the holidays and didn't press me when I was vague in my response.

I was . . . lonely. And I wasn't used to attention from a boy like Dennis—so handsome, so popular, the kind of boy the world was built for. So that must have been why I agreed to go out with him that night, why I returned to my dorm flustered and excited, why I spent twice the time I usually would spend on my hair and face.

He said he would pick me up at seven. I was waiting for him in the front hallway of my dorm, watching though the door's glass inset for him to arrive, half expecting him to stand me up. But he arrived right on time, a few minutes early, even, and we went out for pizza and then a movie. He paid for both, which made me uncomfortable, but I didn't have a lot of spending money, so I didn't stop him when he insisted. He took me to see *Carrie*, that film about the telekinetic girl, the one who does such terrible things to her classmates after they treat her so poorly. I'll admit, I was excited to be sitting in the dark with Dennis, sharing popcorn with him, and when the lights went down and he took my hand, it was like a dream.

But then the film began, and we watched the opening scene—when Carrie gets her period in the locker room shower. Have you seen it? And all the other girls laugh at her and pelt her with tampons and pads? Oh, it was awful, just terrible, and I felt so sad and sick for her. And Dennis—he *laughed*. A loud, mean laugh. Like he really thought it was funny. A joke. And from that moment on, I was counting down the moments until the film was over and I could go back to my dorm room and be done with Dennis and our date.

The movie ended, finally, at last, and the theater emptied out onto the street. The moon was out, it was a beautiful night, I remember. Dennis and I walked to his car and he opened the passenger door for me, a perfect gentleman. But I couldn't get the sound of his laugh out of my head. I couldn't stop hearing it.

And Dennis didn't take the turn to my dorm that he should have taken. He rolled right past it, and when I pointed it out, I said, "Dennis, you missed your turn," he said, "That's not my turn," and he kept going.

He drove us to a quiet parking lot and he turned into a spot, he put the car in park and twisted off the ignition. And then he smiled at me, and leaned across the front seat, and kissed me.

I did not want to kiss Dennis. I told him to stop, pretending like it was a big joke at first—I laughed loudly, as if it was preposterous that he could think this thing might happen between us, but my laugh, my protestations, seemed only to anger him. He kissed me harder, and the hand he'd been running down my arm stopped at my wrist, circled it, held it in my lap.

Oh, darling, I wish I didn't have to tell you stories like this. I really do. I suppose that's why I've waited all this time. But there's nothing to do but go forward, I suppose.

He got rough with me, dear one. He tore the neck of my

blouse, and he bruised my wrist, but as soon as I could manage it, I found the door handle with my other hand and pried it open. I yanked up with my arm and broke his grip, and I landed hard on the asphalt, hard enough to bruise my tailbone, hard enough to rip the skin from both of my elbows.

And then Dennis laughed, as he had during the movie—he laughed at me on the ground. "Come on, Sybil," he said. "Don't play hard to get."

I wasn't playing. He knew I wasn't playing; he knew because he wasn't playing, either. I stumbled to my feet and took off running.

Well, dear, he chased, and I am sure you know where this story goes. It's your story, too, after all.

I ran, and he chased, and soon I became aware that it was no longer a man who followed me—it was a beast, a wolf. A white wolf with blue eyes, I saw, when I decided the time for running had passed.

I am sure you have discovered, as I did that night, that sometimes we are made of different stuff than we imagined.

The wolf was in no hurry to attack now that I had stopped running, now that I had turned to stand my ground. His thick white tail pendulumed back and forth, slowly, and he took slow steps forward, and I swear to you that he smiled.

It was the smile that did it to me. I roared like a beast, and though I had nothing in my hands to defend me, no weapons, just my own ten fingers and nails, I attacked.

I was fast and keen and ruthless—things I never knew I could be, but suddenly was, as if some different blood, some stronger blood, flowed through my veins. The white wolf snarled and leaped toward me, ears forward, and though he was swift, I was swifter. I went for his eyes—those blue eyes— and, fingers clenched like claws, I dug at them, the hot-wet squish of them against my palms. The wolf yelped and collapsed, his right eye half out of its socket, the left awash in a scrim of blood. I stood, panting, my left arm bleeding badly above my elbow where he'd gotten me with teeth or claws, I didn't know which. Then the wolf shook his head and righted himself, and though his vision was compromised, his nose could still track me, and he growled and snarled and came at me with a face full of teeth and blood.

When he leaped this time, though his fierceness was not dampened by his injuries, his precision was, and his speed, and I was able to anticipate where he would land and where he would strike. I got my arms up and ready, and when he made contact, my right hand went up and over his muzzle, my left around the back of his scruff, and I yanked, hard, and felt the crack of his neck.

He fell dead at my feet, darling, and you know what happened after that, moments later—how the wolf shivered and changed and became a man.

It was Dennis, naked and dead.

That, dear heart, was the first time I ever saw a man without any clothes on his body. I had that thought, staring down at him, frozen, I suppose, in shock. Here was a man who had been with me just hours before, who had paid for my dinner. Here was man who had taken me against my wishes to an empty parking lot. Here was a man who had bruised my wrist and torn my blouse.

Here was a man who had become a wolf, a man who had killed my friend.

I was not sorry he was dead.

It is better to be torn to pieces
than to become a wolf's prey.
—RUSSIAN PROVERB

A dead boy—especially a dead Big Man on Campus, a dead star athlete—seemed to make a much bigger impression on just about everyone than two dead girls.

Dennis's death made the national newspapers, and I heard that later some novelist even wrote a book "inspired by the murder that shocked a college town," though I never read it. I doubt it was anything like the truth of that night.

This time, no one tsked about how Dennis shouldn't have been alone in the woods, no one reported having seen him drunk and disorderly in the days and weeks before his death.

Everyone mourned.

I did not mourn, but I stayed quiet. Head down, avoiding conversations about his death. Someone in town reported having seen Dennis with "an ordinary-looking brunette" at the movies that night, but no one thought she might be me, and I didn't offer up that information.

Life went on, as life does, and though I took care to keep to myself, even this was not all that different from how things had been before he died—before Laura died, too.

School resumed, a new year began—1977—and as winter faded and spring bloomed, with no more awful encounters, I began to reconstruct the events of the previous winter not as a dream, exactly, but as something that might as well have happened in a different world, or to a different person. The wound on my arm healed before T-shirt season, and there were no more deaths on campus. It was easy to believe—it was comfortable to believe—that whatever may have happened, it was over and done with, and I could safely put it out of my mind for good.

It was true that with each cycle—of the moon and my blood—I felt a heightened sense of awareness. It was as if colors were more saturated; as if smells were sharper and more immediate; the whole world, turned up. But I felt no pull to the woods, and so it was easy enough to lie to myself and say nothing had changed. That *I* had not changed.

That semester, I enrolled in Feminist Poetry, two words I hadn't given much thought to, to be honest. The class fit my schedule and filled a prerequisite. I wasn't expecting much. I wasn't expecting *anything*.

Even without expectations, however, I was surprised when I met Garland. The course was taught by a woman and, with the exception of Garland, it was populated entirely by female students.

Walking into class that first day, I saw Garland at once. He sat in the third row, a head higher than any of the fifteen young women in the seats around him. His books were stacked neatly in the top right corner of his desk; he had a notebook folded open; he held a pencil in his left hand, and he twirled it, with nervous energy, around his fingers.

He wasn't handsome. That's not to say that he wasn't attractive; he *was* attractive, to me, though the other girls didn't seem to pay him much attention. He was too skinny, and too tall; he was too white, as if he'd spent all his life indoors; and he wore glasses that didn't sit quite straight on his face, lenses smudged with fingerprints. He wore his hair shorn unfashionably short, and it was clear he pressed his shirts. He was . . . unthreatening. That's what he was, more than anything else. When I walked in, he looked up and smiled, almost apologetically, as if he was in a space that might have preferred if he hadn't been there at all.

The course was taught by Professor Lane, a young black woman not much older than us students. All that spring, I read the words of women—Lola Ridge, and Sylvia Plath, and Qiu Jin, and Adrienne Rich, and Gertrude Stein, and Maya Angelou, and Margaret Atwood, and Lucille Clifton, and Djuna Barnes, and Anne Sexton . . . I never had known that there were so many ways to be a woman, that there were so many voices.

I read poetry, and I fell in love with Garland Wright. He came to my dorm almost every evening, though he had to leave by curfew. In every way I was closed, he was open. For every secret I kept, he offered up a vulnerability. He loved to talk about his mother, Clara, who had been a computer programmer at MIT. He told me that his mother had loved her work more than she loved her children, but he didn't say it like he was upset; he said it with pride, and affection. He was so proud of his mother, so proud to be her son. She had died the summer before, Garland told me, and he was taking this course, Feminist Poetry, as a way to feel close to her. He said that if he could learn to understand the poets that she loved, then it would be like he could be close to her again. Even though she was gone.

That was probably when I fell in love with him. That night, in my dorm room, when he confessed to me why he was in the poetry class, even though he was a computer science student. That night was also the second time I saw a naked man, and this time it was much, much better.

Oh, don't blush like that, darling girl! Love is a beautiful thing, after all.

And that is what we did, all through that spring—we loved. Each other, and poetry, and each blossom that burst open. When school was out for the summer, I decided not to return to the farm. I rented a room in town from a rising senior whose roommate was going abroad, but I mostly used it to store my things. Almost every night, I was with Garland. He had a room in a house with three other young men, all serious, like him, all earnest. Two of them had girlfriends, like Garland, and the third had an on-again, off-again romance with a teaching assistant, a very good-looking young man named George.

And all that spring, and all that summer, with all the love, I did my best to forget the white wolf, the dead boy, even Laura, for I couldn't think of her without thinking of the other.

It was during that summer that I received a small package from the farm, from Gennie. In it was a letter, which told me that Frank had had a minor heart attack, but was recovering well, and that John had taken over most of the heavy duties. "We don't know what we would do without him," the letter said, which would have wounded me if I had been in a different place, if I hadn't had Garland. As it was, I was glad for the three of them, that they had each other.

Gennie also wrote that she had come across some of my mother's possessions while doing some spring cleaning, and that she found a necklace she thought I'd like. "I don't think your mother ever wore it," she wrote. She'd found it, she said, in an old yellowed envelope tucked among some papers. The envelope said "Frannie's things." Frannie, you know, was my mother's mother.

"I'm sorry it took me all these years to go through your mother's things," Gennie wrote, "but this necklace, I think, would suit you."

It was the necklace you are wearing right now. My grandmother's, and then your grandmother's, and now yours. Isn't life strange, my darling? I discovered, as you did, the necklace's sharp-tipped secret, and because it did suit me, I wore it, from time to time.

When the leaves began to crisp and darken that next September, rather than returning to the dorms, I moved with Garland into a tiny studio apartment up above a Chinese restaurant and developed a keen appreciation for Asian cuisine. I began a class in writing poetry, which scared me deeply. It was one thing to read and appreciate the words of other women; it was another thing entirely, so naked-feeling, to write my own. Garland was a dear and listened to me read any of the poems I was willing to share with him, which weren't many. And everything seemed just lovely.

It did until five weeks after school had started back up— Wednesday, October 26, 1977. The night of a full moon.

A wolf sheds his coat every year,
but his nature never changes.
—*RUSSIAN PROVERB*

Garland was asleep in our bed next to me, glasses still on, the book he'd been reading splayed open on his chest. I was hot, and then cold, and uncomfortable, done reading the book of poems I'd brought to bed with me, back tender with the beginning of my monthly flow.

I leaned over and took Garland's glasses from his face and his book from his chest, and I put them on the bedside table. I flipped off the lamp and stared toward the window across from me, through its clean, clear rectangle and out at the wide, white moon.

I was hot again. I threw the covers back, walked to the window, stared outside. There was a reason I should be out there. I didn't know what the reason was, but I was certain there *was* a reason, and I felt trapped like a caged animal by the four walls of our tiny apartment, walls I usually so loved. But I *wasn't* trapped, of course. I was free to go, anytime.

And so I went. I dressed, tied tight my shoelaces, and unlocked our door. Just before I passed through it, I decided that I'd like to have my grandmother's necklace with me, and so I took it from the dresser where it lay and strung it around my neck.

Our door opened to a tiny balcony that led down behind the Chinese restaurant to the alley. It was raining, but not badly, and I had my hair tucked up into a cap. I stood at the base of the stairs in the rain, hesitant. Then I decided that I would just go where my feet took me, without thinking too much about it.

My feet took me, of course, to the woods. Always the woods, yes, my love?

And since this is a night of truth telling, let me tell you this as well: I loved it. Being outside, alone, in the night. The moon gazing down on me, a benevolent goddess. The strength I felt. The smells, the sensations, all of it.

When I was upon the path of pins, I began to run. There wasn't much time, I knew, though I didn't know how I knew it.

Here, trees broke the moonlight into shadow. I felt aware of everything—of the distance between trees; of the rustle of nocturnal animals in the undergrowth; of the smell of bird droppings. I felt so *alive*, dearest, alive like I felt when I read a particularly wonderful poem, or when I managed to write a line that felt perfectly true, or when I laid in Garland's arms. And, for the first time in many years, I imagined Mother's face, my mother, who was not alive, who would never be alive again, because of the man who killed her. And I felt angry, dear one. Oh, the rage was thick enough to choke. But I swallowed it, for this was no time to be distracted. Now, out here, somewhere, there was a wolf who hunted. I knew it. And it was my duty to hunt the wolf.

I saw the animal before I saw his prey. He was bigger even than the white wolf had been, his pelt a dark brown. He stood still in a beam of moonlight, ears forward like an eager dog that was about to get a treat.

The treat, I saw then, was a girl.

She was crouched down in the roots of a tree, her hands on either side of her knees. She wasn't making any sounds, though her face was wet with tears.

She was a black girl, young, too young to be a student at my school. She was your age, dear one, maybe even younger. The raindrops caught in her hair. In the moonlight the raindrops sparkled. Here was a girl who would be dead in two minutes, maybe less, if I had not risen from the safety of my bed, if I had not left the apartment.

I didn't want the girl to see me. That would be a complication later. I was glad I wore a hat, and I turned up the collar of my vest, and I crouched and found a rock. I stood, aimed for the wolf, and threw the rock as hard as I could. It struck him on his left hip and he yelped in surprise and pain. He swiveled his head to find me, and though the dark obscured me from the girl, it was nothing to the wolf. He pinned me with his gaze. He narrowed his eyes.

And then he swiveled in my direction, and I turned, too, and ran.

I tore through the forest, the thrumming rush of the wolf's pace behind me. I hoped that the girl would get up, I willed her to get up and run toward home. Why she had been in the forest, what lies she would tell others and herself to explain her muddied shoes, her midnight absence, I did not know. She could meet with more or different trouble on her way, but that was beyond my reach. Now, I had two jobs: to lead this wolf far away, and to kill him.

As I ran, I found the sickle moon at my throat and I scanned the terrain for the most advantageous position. This wolf was fast, faster than the white wolf had been, faster than me. I felt the distance between his teeth and my back closing, and I knew that we would meet, either on his terms or on mine.

There is only one way to kill a wolf, dear heart. Quickly.

No time for second-guessing, or hesitation, or misplaced guilt. No room for any of that.

He leaped, I knew he did from the grunt he released and then the absence of his footfalls. He was too close not to land on me; I had nowhere to go but down, and so I dropped my right shoulder and tucked my head and rolled.

The wolf landed as I turned faceup, and he was greeted with my claw. Your claw now, dear one. His neck was unprotected, an easy target, and I slashed through it, opening his pelt and loosing his blood.

He twitched as he died, drowning in his own blood. I waited for him to become a man—tall, white, naked—before heading home.

I was so glad that the rain had stopped. I imagined the trail of blood I would have left if there had been rain to wash it from me as I walked. The streets were empty, and I made it to the alley behind my building unseen. I stripped naked right there, in the alley, and I shoved my bloodied clothes, even my socks, my shoes, my bra, my underwear, deep into a trash bag in the Chinese restaurant's dumpster.

I tiptoed up the stairs and into our apartment where Garland still slept, his arm thrown across his eyes. I locked the bathroom door behind me and climbed gratefully into the shower. I was naked except for the necklace—your necklace—which I took with me under the water, scrubbing it clean as I scrubbed myself.

Garland and I stayed in that apartment above the restaurant for three years, until I graduated. He was older than I was and following in his mother's footsteps of working with computers, and he had no problem finding a job after he graduated, the year before me. We stayed in the tiny apartment anyway, even though his salary meant we could afford more, in part because it was convenient for me to be close to campus during my last year, and also because we loved our tiny nest and would be sad to say goodbye to it.

There were other wolves—not many, but a few, always pulling me out of bed and to the trees in the light of a full moon. I was good at it, killing them, and it was satisfying, ending them. The last year we lived in the apartment, though, there were no wolves. I don't know why, I still do not—sometimes there are wolves, and sometimes there are no wolves. That year, there were none. There was only love, and poetry, and beauty.

After I graduated with a dual degree in women's studies and literature, there was really no reason to keep living there. Especially because I was newly pregnant with your mother. That was a busy summer. I graduated, we married, we bought a house—this house—and I fell into the beautiful trance of pregnancy, of falling in love with those first kicks, admiring and appreciating my body's amazing capacity to grow life and shift to fit it. We didn't spend much time worrying about names; if the baby was a girl, her name would be Clara, after Garland's mother. If it was a boy . . . well, we both felt certain she would be a girl.

And of course, we were right.

Clara Constance Wright, born on the first of February.

Oh, what a darling girl. You know some of the end of her story, but you don't know who your mother was in those first years.

Such a fairy-tale life: me, married to a prince of a man, all the wolves banished to distant memory, to nightmares, and this sweet babe in my arms, all of us living together—well, not in a castle, but we weren't castle people. In a charming cottage on the edge of the forest. Garland had to go back to work almost as soon as we were home from the hospital—fathers didn't get much time off in those days—and then it was just me and dear Clara, in the dreamy haze of nursing, our bodies perfectly synched, my breasts swelling and aching the moment before she stirred for a feeding.

She was two months old when the killings began again.

It was a teenage girl, a student at the public high school nearby. She was fifteen. Later I learned that she had a bad reputation—she was a drinker, they said, and had a liking for short skirts and halter tops. She liked *men*, they said— emphasis on "men," not boys. Nothing was said of the fact that "men" obviously liked her, too.

Her name was Leila. I would have saved her if I could have.

But I had felt no pull to leave the house, none of the tingling urgency I had felt during my college years. And anyway, I had a baby to protect now.

I began to look down at my daughter, asleep in my arms, with a terrible feeling of complicity. It wasn't my fault that this girl had died. Of course it wasn't. But still.

I racked my brain, wondering what I could possibly do, if there was anything I *could* do. And it came to me, during a middle-of-the-night feeding, just a week after Leila had died. I looked down at my daughter, her mouth a cupid's bow at my breast, and I realized that one thing was different between this wolf attack and those that came before. Do you know what the difference was, my dear one? Have you worked it out?

Yes. That is right. During each of the other attacks—even the night of my own attack by the white wolf—I had been bleeding. With the full moon came my menses, and with the full moon came the wolves.

One who is not willing to risk
her child will not catch the wolf.
—*CHINESE PROVERB*

All right, my darling. All right. Every story has its sad parts, and we have reached that point in mine.

You know what I had to do: I had to wean my child to bottle, and though my breasts ached and leaked milk as she cried, as her sweet mouth searched for my flesh but found only rubber, I denied her. I bound my breasts and I refused to give her what she begged for, even when her screams became angry, even when she rejected the bottle again and again.

This was the first fight between me and Garland. "I just don't understand," he said the second night after I'd made my choice. He said it again and again, his distress mimicking Clara's—first confused, and then anxious, and then mournful. Then angry. "Why won't you just give her what she wants?" he demanded, pacing, watching me try to fit the rubber nipple into her furious mouth. "You have it! She needs it! Give it to her."

I shook my head, I ignored my own tears, and it must have seemed to him that I ignored Clara's tears, too, and his. Of course, I did not ignore them. How could I? These were my people, my two people in the big wide world. They were all I had. Beneath the cloth that bound my breasts, I felt my heart break from the pain of denying my child.

Eventually Garland took Clara and the bottle from me. He walked her outside, to the front porch, and he paced with her, back and forth, until she resigned herself to her new reality. They both did. And she took the bottle at last.

And with the next moon came my blood, and with my blood came my senses, and with my senses came the hunt, and a kill, swift and merciless, the wolf who had killed the month before and had come to kill again. I took no joy in any of it, but there was the grim satisfaction of knowing I was doing a job that needed to be done, and there would be girls saved by my actions, by my daughter's unwilling sacrifice.

How many girls might have died if a wolf had been prowling at the start of my pregnancy? I thought about this, awake at night in bed next to Garland, a chasm between us. Nine. Nine women, plus another three for the months I breastfed, the months before I forced Clara's weaning and began my menses again. A dozen women.

One was dead—Leila—and I began to say her name in my head all the time, Leila, Leila, Leila, it thrummed in my veins and my chest, I barely noticed I was still saying it, thinking other thoughts over her name, going about my day, tending to Clara, straightening the house, cooking a meal. But always it was there, beneath the other thoughts, a baseline of regret and shame. Leila, Leila, Leila.

I would never get pregnant again. That was clear. In the first months after weaning Clara, that seemed like something I didn't need to worry about, as Garland would barely look at me, let alone touch me. But Clara grew, thrived even, learning to laugh and sit up on her own. And before she was crawling, Garland was smiling at me again, taking my hand on our evening walks, reaching for me in the night.

"It's too soon," I told him, and he waited.

But it wasn't just my fear of pregnancy that kept me from sleeping with my husband—it was the knowledge that he could pull away from me, like he had. He could withhold his love. He hadn't trusted that what I was doing, I did for a good reason. He hadn't trusted me.

We wouldn't be celibate forever, I knew that. I could have

gotten on the pill, but I didn't know how that might affect my cycle, my awareness of the forest and the wolves. My instinct told me it would dampen my senses, maybe overpower them entirely, to allow something other than the moon to regulate my flow. And by the time Clara was five months old, pulling herself to standing, making noises that sounded like "Mama" and "Dada" even if she didn't yet mean them, I found myself needing the connection with Garland as much as he needed it with me.

I bought some condoms, and when I offered one to Garland, he took it. But the next day, he asked me when I might be ready to try for another baby. He was an only child, and he wanted Clara to be raised with a sibling. This was something I had known before we married. At the time, it was an easy thing to agree to.

But now, when Garland asked when I'd be ready for a second pregnancy, I answered, "Never." There could never be another child.

Well, dearest, I'll spare you the details of the cycle of arguments this caused. I *will* tell you that though I had bought a pack of a dozen condoms, I had no pressing need to buy a second.

We loved our baby. That seemed like perhaps enough. We slept like strangers most nights, backs to one another, and we spent our days together like very polite acquaintances.

Clara crawled, then walked, then babbled and talked, and

soon she was a beautiful big girl of three years old. There were no wolves, not then. Not in the forest, though they began to appear in my poetry, again and again.

One night, Garland and I had a rare evening out together. We'd hired a sitter, a neighbor girl, to stay with Clara. He and I went to dinner, and then stayed in the restaurant bar for another drink, and then a third. We were well and truly drunk when he asked me:

"What is it with all the wolves?"

We were drinking whiskey, and I took a long drink before answering. "They haunt me," I told him. "Ever since the white wolf took Laura and I didn't stop it, they haunt me."

Of course, Garland was talking about the wolves in my poems, not the wolves in the woods, and I am certain that deep down I was aware of that. How long can a person keep such a secret from her partner? For me, it turned out that the answer was ten years—from the time I met Garland until the ice knocked about the empty glass of my fourth drink that night.

Ten years, dearest, is a long time for a secret. In ten years, a secret grows deep roots. It works its way into every crevice of the relationship. Sometimes, when you expose the secret to the light, when you untwist its limbs and pull it away, the relationship can grow stronger. But other times, dear one, this is not possible.

Garland pressed me. What did I mean, a white wolf had

killed Laura? He knew who she was, of course; he'd been a student at the university when she died.

I didn't want to carry my truth alone anymore. Our daughter was four. I wanted my marriage back, I wanted my husband back, I wanted my family back. And so I told him everything—about killing the white wolf, and about the wolves that followed.

Garland listened, his drink growing warm in his hands, and when I finished, he put his drink on the bar, he put one hand in my lap, the other in my hair, and he kissed me. He kissed me, and I kissed him, whiskey and truth on our lips between us.

I was dizzy with all of it—the alcohol, the relief of speaking the truth, at long last, of spilling my secret to him, and with the passion of our kiss, the heat it created.

Well, sometimes people do the things they swear they will never do. And so it was that two weeks later, when the moon was full and my blood was due, it did not come.

Darling dear, I could not have another pregnancy. You must understand. That would mean at least nine months, more likely ten, even if I didn't breastfeed a single time, that I would be without my menses. There could be nine lives lost, maybe ten, because of my foolish mistake, my selfish passion.

I found that I was not willing to trade potential life for potential deaths. And so, I made the necessary arrangements, much as it pained me to do so.

And my mistake, dear one, was not the abortion. My mistake was leaving a phone number with the clinic.

When they called to check on me the next day, I was resting in bed. The second I heard the ringing of the phone, before Garland even answered, I knew who was calling. There was nothing I could do; the house had only one phone, and it hung in the kitchen where Garland was cooking dinner.

I lay in bed, eyes tightly shut, and imagined his face as he answered the phone—quickly, not wanting its ring to wake me—his dear face, the face I loved so much. His smudged glasses. His hair, less tidy now, in messy waves pushed back from his forehead. Those lips that had loved me saying "Hello?" into the receiver. And then I pictured his face shifting as the nurse on the other end of the line asked for me, then refused to answer when he asked who was calling, said only that she'd call back. I saw his face crinkle in confusion, I imagined a flash of fear in his eyes as he wondered if—no, it couldn't be—and then I heard him place the phone, gently, back on the cradle.

I heard his steps coming down the hall. I heard him turn the handle to our bedroom door.

Though I wanted to keep my eyes shut, though I considered pretending to be asleep, I opened my eyes. Garland deserved the truth. And, I told myself, he had listened when I had told him about the wolves. He had understood that. He would understand this, too.

I sat up. Still tender, my abdomen cramped, and my hand went to my stomach.

Garland's eyes grew wide and round with fear. "Sybil," he said, "what have you done?"

I thought he had understood me, that night. But I had been wrong. He thought that I had been telling him a story. Speaking in metaphors. Being poetic. But he had been wrong, too.

When he understood, that day as I bled after my abortion, that I meant everything I had said—that there were actual wolves in the forest, and that they killed girls, and that one of them had tried to kill me, and that under their wolf skins they were really boys and men—then he took two steps away from the bed.

"You're telling me you've killed six men," he said.

"Six wolves," I told him. "I've killed six wolves."

"Six men," he said, "and now our child."

Semantically speaking, I had terminated my pregnancy, not killed our child. Our child was Clara, playing in the next room with her dolls.

That was the day our marriage died. And when Garland backed out of our room and then drove away from our house, he took Clara with him.

It was a week before I heard anything from him. A week of barely sleeping, of no recourse. What could I do? There was no one I could call, no one I could ask for help.

Then the letter came. The letter from Garland. There was

no return address, but I recognized the handwriting, and I recognized the name he'd written in script above our address— Sybil Martel, my maiden name, not Sybil Wright, the name I'd taken when we'd married. And I knew what the letter inside would say, though I read it anyway. He had taken another job in another city. If I was wise, he wrote, I would not try to find them. If I did, he would tell the police what I had told him, and I would end up either in jail or in an institution.

My daughter was gone. My husband was gone. I was alone, in this house, in this cottage on the edge of the trees. All I had left were my poems, and my duty. And that necklace, dear one. My only inheritance.

*Wolves will pay dearly
for the tears of the sheep.*

—RUSSIAN PROVERB

The years that followed were laced with death. There were wolves to kill, yes, but also other deaths—I got news first that Frank had died, and then Gennie, and then, a few years later, my brother John died, too.

The farm was mine, but what did I need with a farm? I hired a private detective to find Garland, and I wrote to him to say that our daughter, Clara, was now, at twelve—for that was how old she was by then—the owner of a sheep farm in Canada. Of course, the sheep were sold off and the house closed up, but it was Clara's. I signed it over to her.

My letter got no response. I did not expect one. And that, dearest, was the end of the story as far as I knew.

Now, of course, there is much more that I know—I know your mother's story, though, as you know, that chapter is not a happy one, either. The first I heard of Clara again, a dozen years after John died, was from a phone call. The number had a Canadian area code; it was a doctor, Laurence Waterman, who sounded very old, and I realized almost immediately that he must have been—he had seemed an old man years ago when I had known him, before leaving the farm, over thirty years ago. He must have been at least ninety that evening when he called. He said that he was sorry to bother me, but he had gone through some trouble finding my phone number, and did I know that a young woman and a small child were living in my family's farmhouse? He thought they might be squatters, but he didn't want to call the police until he checked with me.

"Describe them," I asked.

He told me that the young woman was in her early twenties, maybe twenty-five. The child seemed to be her daughter, no more than four or five years old, and they both had long brown curls. "Like yours used to be, come to think of it," he said.

I told him that it sounded as though Clara, my daughter, had decided to make use of her early inheritance, and I didn't let on my surprise at hearing that she was a mother, and I, a grandmother.

"Oh, I see," Dr. Waterhouse said, but he didn't sound settled, and I didn't remember him to be a busybody.

"What is it?" I asked.

And that is when he said, "Well, I don't mean to upset you, Sybil, but your daughter's face looks . . . pretty bad. It's getting better now, but it looks to me like either she was in an accident, or maybe someone beat her." And he told me that he'd only seen them leave the house once or twice in the months they'd been there.

He didn't need to say more to get me to my car, to send me on the road to the airport. It was the end of February, my darling, nearly dusk. And it was a full moon—I remember that moon well. It was a blood moon that night. Have I told you that before? I was in an airplane, you know, on my way to her—to both of you—and I saw it when we took off, huge and strange in the sky. I felt ill, and nervous, like I should be on the ground, not trapped and jittery on a plane. I told myself that I had no reason to fear that she was in any sort of immediate danger. I tried to calm myself with thoughts of what you might be like, the granddaughter I hadn't known existed until that very day. I decided, on that long plane ride, that if Clara allowed me to be part of your life, I'd ask you to call me Mémé. But I was restless. I had no cause to worry, not exactly. Just . . . I needed to be there. Suddenly, and certainly. And the moon was so huge, and so red.

I did everything I could. I need you to know that. I took

the first available flight. I booked a rental car and ran straight from the gate to the rental lot. I drove as fast as I could, dear one, faster than was safe on those unfamiliar Quebec roads.

But still, when I got to the farm, I saw both a long green car and a brown sedan parked in the driveway, the sedan dusted in snow as if it hadn't been driven in days, the green car parked at an angle, boxing it in.

I knew, even before I found the front door ajar, that I was too late. I knew.

But what I found in that room, your mother . . . and you, curled at the foot of the bed, her blood everywhere . . . I thought I had lost you both, I was sure you were dead, too, and then, when I stepped toward you, you moved—oh, thank goodness, you moved. It was your mother's blood everywhere. Not a drop of yours.

It's all right, darling, you can cry. Don't hold it in. You can cry. Ah, my dear girl.

We stayed at Dr. Waterhouse's home for two nights before I brought you here. Do you remember? No? Well, that's no surprise. Sometimes it's a blessing, the things a mind can forget . . . though I think the body never does.

I hated to leave you that first night, dear one, but the moon, you see, is only full for two nights in a cycle, and there was hunting to be done.

I wandered in the wood that edged the farmland. Snow fell, but softly. I crashed through bushes, I whacked my arms against the sides of trees, I cleared my throat and whistled and hummed. I made myself a target—and I drew the wolf.

Dun brown. Black eyes. I had seen bigger wolves. I had *killed* bigger wolves.

I had my claw in my fist. I had never wanted it more, to kill. I wanted it so intensely, so much, so passionately—to tell the truth, I wanted that kill more than I had ever wanted anything before, more than I have wanted anything since.

And perhaps that is why I failed.

He attacked, and I parried with a thrust of my claw. I caught him in his face—his left cheek—and flayed it open. He yelped and fell back. The fur split; yellow fat and red blood oozed out, and he shook his head, spraying red across the white snow.

His eyes narrowed and he stepped forward, and I did, too, tasting the kill on the back of my tongue.

He recognized it, I think—my desire. My need. And so, he turned and ran.

This, I had not expected. I chased, but he was faster. There were droplets of his blood and there were his tracks, and I followed until the snowfall thickened and he was lost to me.

I searched until the moon was gone and the sun about to rise. The next night, the moon began to wane, and I knew he was gone.

I had no choice but to bundle you up and to bring you back

here, to my house, to our home, and here I have kept you and loved you the best I know how.

It had been years, so many years, that I had lived alone. I had accepted it, the loneliness. But then, you were here. It broke my heart open, Bisou. And I kept watch by the moon, and I hunted when hunting needed to be done, and always I have kept special watch for the wolf who killed your mother, always I have been tortured by my failure to find him. Then, last summer, in July, with my birthday, the thing I had worried about for many years—since first I'd realized that my strengths were tied to my moon flow—it happened. I am lucky, I suppose. I bled longer than most women, until I was sixty-one.

I saved many lives, dear girl, but I could not save them all. I could not save your mother's.

Later, after I'd brought you home, I learned that Garland had died, too, when your mother was just eighteen, of leukemia. I learned about your father as well—not much, just a few details about their relationship. Neighbors told me they had suspicions that he didn't treat her well. That he hit her. One said there had been yelling once, not long before you and your mother disappeared, that he had said he would make her pay if she ever left him.

And he did. He made her pay. I wanted to make him pay, too, but even if I had caught and killed him, his life would not be worth a fraction of hers, and his debts could never be canceled, never, never. Some debts, dearest, cannot be paid.

I watched you grow, and heal as best you could, and I waited as you changed from girl to woman, and I wondered if you might be like me, if you too might cycle with the moon. And, to be honest, I didn't know whether to hope that you would or pray that you wouldn't. Can one wish for two opposing things at the same time?

Now, here we are, the truth between us plain and bare.

Tell me, Bisou. Tell me. What do you make of it?

OVER AND THROUGH

TO HEAR YOU WITH

Sunrise pinkens the sky as Mémé finishes telling her story. You watch it through the window above the kitchen sink.

Mémé asks, "Tell me, Bisou. Tell me. What do you make of it?"

You close your eyes. You blink them open. There is Mémé, across from you, her empty tea cup between her hands. Her hands look like your hands will look in forty years. Her hair, over her shoulder, steely gray and white around the temples, looks like your hair will look in forty years. Her face, thoughtful, lined, serious, concerned—it is the face you will see one day, in forty years, in a mirror. Her eyes, brown and green, have seen the same things your eyes have seen. Wolves, and their blood. Mothers, and their daughters. Moons, and love.

You close your eyes again. The story Mémé has told you beats against the backs of your eyelids. You open them. There is Mémé, waiting for you to speak.

What do you make of it?

"I'm so tired," you say, and Mémé holds her face almost perfectly still. If you did not know her face so well, if you were someone else, you would not recognize the flash of disappointment that appears, then disappears. You *do* recognize it, both her disappointment and her attempt to mask it. You recognize it because you mirror both the disappointment and its mask, though you are disappointed in different things. Mémé is disappointed at your reaction to her story, shared finally after all this time, and you are disappointed to learn that Mémé has failed to kill your father.

"Of course you're tired," Mémé says. She stands and piles together dishes to take to the sink. She turns on the water and rinses them. "There's one more thing," she says, and she goes from the kitchen. You close your eyes and listen as she walks to her room—then silence—then the sound of her returning to you.

You open your eyes. She is holding your mother's poems.

"I found these, among your mother's things, in the farmhouse. I should have given them to you long ago."

There are five poems. Just five, no matter how many times you have read them, always when Mémé was gone from the house, always slipping them from the back of her bedside table drawer, underneath the envelope of cash, always returning them just as you found them.

"Your mother never knew," Mémé says, "that poetry was something we shared."

You take the poems from Mémé's hand. It seems she is reluctant to loosen them, but she does, and then you stand, and you turn, and you take the poems to your room, you tuck them in the drawer of your own bedside table. You do not need to read the poems; you know every word by heart. You have known them for years.

You have tried to piece together a mother who is gone from those few words, scattered across pages. You have wanted to see her, to bring her back, to reshape the black letters into a living breathing person, a mother. Mémé, it seems, wanted the same.

Keisha is in your bed. She is awake, hands behind her head, staring up at the ceiling.

"Hey," she says.

"Hey."

Keisha wants to talk, of course, she wants explanations.

But she seems to understand that you're not yet ready for conversation.

She flips back the covers, and you climb into your bed, next to her. It's a double bed, so there is room, and you find yourself feeling grateful that you are not alone in it.

Alone. That is the word. That is what pressed on you, heavily, with every word of Mémé's story. How many years did Mémé spend solitary, cut off from her family, from people she could have loved, if she hadn't had such a secret to bear?

It's the word your mother's poems echo, too—alone.

You don't want to be alone. You shiver, cold suddenly beneath the covers, and you imagine your life unspooling before you in a series of full moons and new moons, of hunts and kills.

You roll onto your side so that Keisha can't see your face when the tears come.

When you wake, you are alone. Even before you open your eyes, you can tell from the light outside your window that it is late morning, and that the rain has stopped. The house is fragrant with rosemary and garlic; Mémé is making soup.

In the kitchen, the big red stockpot is simmering over a low flame. You lift the lid, breathe in the savory steam. There's a wooden spoon on a rest next to the stove, and you stir the soup before replacing the lid. This stockpot has lived in this house since before you did. This spoon, with the black scorch mark across the handle from the day, years ago, when it fell into the flame, is something you can count on to always be the same. The smell of the soup. The quiet ticking of the kitchen clock. All so normal, so reliable.

Mémé and Keisha are together in the front room. They are sitting in the low armchairs on either side of the fireplace; between them, the cracking orange flames. Keisha sits forward in her seat, hands palm-up on her thighs. Mémé leans back, arms folded.

Keisha, you determine, has been asking questions. Mémé, you guess, has been deflecting them.

"The soup smells good," you say from the doorway.

Both Keisha and Mémé turn in your direction.

"Bisou," Mémé says.

"Hey, Bisou." Keisha looks better. Her glasses are back on.

"Hey." You join them by the fire, pulling the ottoman that's between them back a little before sitting on it.

"You grandmother was just telling me a little bit about her life," Keisha says, and your eyes go to Mémé's face. Her expression is impassive. "I didn't know your grandmother is a poet. I write poetry sometimes, too."

"Huh. I thought your writing was all nonfiction. Like, for the paper."

"Poetry tells the truth, too," Keisha says. "Just in a different way."

Now Mémé smiles, but she does not unfold her arms. She

likes Keisha, you can tell, but you'd bet money that no matter how much Mémé likes her, she hasn't told Keisha *that* much about her past. After all, you're sixteen years old, you've lived with Mémé for a dozen years, and she's just now filled you in on her story. But, you wonder, if she'd told it to you sooner, before you had experienced the wolves for yourself, would you have believed her?

"I'm going to make a salad to go with the soup," Mémé says, rising. "Here, Bisou, you can have my chair."

Keisha watches Mémé disappear into the kitchen. Then she turns to you. "She didn't ask me *anything* about last night," she whispers to you. "Not about the blood, or my leg, or the flat tire, *nothing*." She raises her eyebrows and waits impatiently for you to explain what the hell is happening.

"Mémé's pretty good at minding her own business," you offer, and you slide into her seat.

Keisha tightens her lips, shakes her head. "What's going on, Bisou? Last night, after I left the party, I could tell almost as soon as I started driving that there was something wrong with my tire. I wanted to make it home, but the air went out of it fast and I had to pull over. When I got out to look at it, I saw that it was slashed—I hadn't run over a nail or anything like that. It was *slashed*. And then I heard something growling at me, and I don't know, I was filled with dread and felt more afraid than I've ever been in my entire life. And I started running, into the forest, and that thing chased me, and then it had me up against a tree, and it clawed my leg, Bisou. It would have killed me if you hadn't seen my car and stopped, if you hadn't screamed and distracted it, if you hadn't shown up like some sort of . . . I don't know, like a warrior queen, and killed it."

You let Keisha talk, even though she's not telling you anything you didn't already know. She needs to work through it. She needs to say it out loud.

"And then," she says, her voice dropping still lower, "then it *changed*, and it wasn't a wolf anymore. It was Phillip. And he was dead."

Her cheeks are flushed now, red with remembering.

You just sit there for a moment, feeling the warmth of the fire on the right side of your body. You could lie. You could tell her she's remembered it wrong, you could make her question her own brain. But—

"Yes," you say. "All that happened."

There's another moment that passes, and then Keisha lets out a long, held breath. "Okay," she says, sounding relieved. "Okay."

She feels better, you can tell, with the facts of the matter laid out between you. You think of Mémé, how she spent ten years alone with her secret before she told Garland, and how she lost him anyway. You imagine the long, lonely years between the day Garland took your mother away from Mémé and the day she came to you, the day she found you at the foot of your mother's bed.

And then you think of yourself—how all your life, you've held yourself to the periphery. You've been friendly, but not friends, with the kids at school. You've watched others play sports, or form clubs, but never joined. Was it truly your choice to hold yourself apart, or were you acting on Mémé's unspoken rules?

Both, you decide, and probably you had other reasons you can't understand from this moment, this place.

Keisha is not your friend. Not yet. And if Keisha's going to bail over this, if she's going to run to the cops or figure out a way to make this whole thing about you being crazy or whatever, you'd rather know that sooner than later.

"There's more," you say, and Keisha listens.

You tell her about Tucker—about how you had been running in the woods, and how you heard an animal behind you, and how your body told you not to run, but to turn, to fight. You tell her about driving toward home from Big Mac's party, and seeing her car, and knowing that something awful was happening. You tell her that you are stronger and better when you're bleeding. She listens without asking questions as you tell her about the blood and the wolves. But when you've finished, she goes straight for the part of the story you've omitted, the detail you've skipped over.

"What were you doing in the woods that night, anyway? After homecoming?"

You can tell her about killing wolf boys. But telling her about the blood on James's chin . . . you can't tell her that.

"James and I had a fight. I got out of the car and cut through the woods toward home."

"What was the fight about?"

"It was . . . personal."

Keisha isn't satisfied. "Did he say something? Did he *do* something? Do you think *he* might be a wolf, too? Do you think they *all* might be wolves?"

"No," you say quickly. "James isn't a wolf. He couldn't be."

"He must have done something pretty bad to make you get out of the car. To get you to go through the woods alone."

Keisha is persistent, always.

"It doesn't matter." You make your voice firm, your expression flat. You worry if, by not telling her why you left James that night in the car, she'll harbor suspicions about him; but even so, this topic is a closed door. You want to make sure she knows that.

Keisha doesn't know that. You know her well enough to suspect she doesn't believe in closed doors.

But she lets it go, for now.

"Did you tell anyone else?"

You shake your head. "Who would believe me? Would *you* have believed me, if you hadn't seen it for yourself?"

Keisha takes a minute, considering the question. "I don't know. I mean, probably not. I tend not to believe things I can't verify." She tilts her head as she stares at you, evaluating. "You're what they call a credible source. So I'd wonder: What motivation could you have for lying? If I couldn't dig one up, then I'd consider the next most likely answer: that you simply *believed* that boys turn into wolves. I'd explore that possibility thoroughly before I considered accepting that boys *actually* turned into wolves. It's definitely more likely that you were hallucinating or unstable in some way than . . ."

"Than what actually happened."

She nods. "So, I guess that's the problem, huh?"

"Yeah," you say. "Now there's another body in the woods. They'll find Phillip and they'll start asking questions."

"Yes," Keisha says. "Well, we'll just have to make sure we have our story straight. And, Bisou, that means you're going to have to trust me. Your grandmother will, too. I'm not an idiot, you know."

"I know." Keisha is one of the smartest people you have ever met.

"You'll both have to trust me," she says. "You *and* your grandmother."

You consider this. Keisha is better than you at figuring stuff out; she is a clear thinker, methodical, smart. Two dead boys in the span of two months . . . maybe the cops were able to explain Tucker's death as an accident, but a broken neck is probably different from a slashed throat.

"Wait here." You leave Keisha by the fire and go into the kitchen.

Mémé has finished making the salad and is rinsing the cutting board and knife. The woman who told you an extraordinary story of death and wolves is gone; she looks, by all accounts, like a normal woman who has lived a normal life. That makes you wonder, what kinds of secrets might other people be carrying around? What histories? What fears? What complicities?

"Lunch is ready," Mémé says. She wipes down the cutting board with a red striped cloth. "Will you set the table?"

You take three bowls and three plates from the cabinet, and three spoons, three forks, and three butter knives from the drawer, and three napkins from the basket on the countertop. "Mémé," you begin, "the authorities are going to find Phillip's body. They're going to be asking questions."

"Will you get the butter dish?"

You take the covered dish from the shelf near the stove and bring it to the table, set it next to the bread bowl.

"They'll want to interview everyone who was at the party," you continue. "That will include me and Keisha. And it's pretty unlikely that no one drove by the whole time our cars were parked by the side of the road. And I left the headlights on—did I tell you that?—someone's bound to remember passing our cars."

"Water or tea?" Mémé asks.

"I don't know. Water." You take the pitcher Mémé fills to the table; some of it sloshes out, and your grandmother returns to the counter for a towel. "Keisha and I are going to have to have the same story."

"Of course," Mémé says. She brings three glasses to the table and sets one next to each plate.

"So maybe we should talk about it?"

The table is set. The soup tureen is between the bread bowl and the salad bowl. Lunch looks delicious. It smells delicious.

"Mémé," you say, "Keisha is smart. Really smart."

"I'm not much in the habit of sharing my secrets," Mémé says. "It hasn't . . . gone well for me."

"*Not* sharing them hasn't gone all that well for you, either, has it?" Your voice is sharp, and it cuts, you can tell, from the way Mémé stiffens, just for a moment. You try again, this time more gently. "Like it or not, Keisha's part of this. She's still here; she hasn't run off yet."

Mémé is still, then shakes her head. "I don't like it."

"Well," you say, and your voice sharpens again, "it's too late, anyway. Keisha was there, she *saw*. That's just the way it is."

There is a twitch of tightened muscle in Mémé's jaw. Her knuckles are white as they grip the edge of the table. She closes her eyes. When she opens them, she turns to look at you. "For forty-three years, I bled. For forty-three years, I hunted. All that time, it was up to me, and me alone, to keep this place safe. I was not perfect. But I did my best, with what I had."

You're sure she's going to tell you that you need to defer to her. That you need to follow her lead, trust her wisdom, stay on her path.

But she doesn't.

"Now you bleed," she says. "The burden is yours. For that, I am sorry. It's a lonely life. You are not alone in the way I was. You have me. But the choice is yours, darling girl, and you alone must make it."

"I love you," you say.

This surprises her, if only for its suddenness, and her eyes widen, and then shine. "I love you, too, my dear one," Mémé says. "You are my shining star."

You go to her, and her arms are wide, and she folds you into them. You rest your head upon her shoulder and close your eyes, and you breathe in her cocoa butter, her patchouli, her Mémé-ness.

It's a long time before you pull away, and even then, Mémé releases you with reluctance.

She wipes her face, one cheek and then the other. This is the first time you have seen her cry.

"I say we tell her everything. She's smart, Mémé, and I can tell you that if Keisha doesn't have answers, she's going to keep asking questions until she does. And anyway, what else can we do?"

Mémé says, resigned, "I can't think of any other options. We'll have to trust her."

"I'm glad to hear it." It's Keisha, from the kitchen doorway. "Anyway, I'm pretty clear already, I think, on the main parts. You're like Bisou, aren't you? You're a hunter, too."

238

IN SHEEP'S CLOTHING

K eisha has been busy since Tucker's death—that quickly becomes obvious. Over lunch, Mémé sketches the outline of her story, the parts relevant to what's happening, not going into all the details she shared with you about Garland and your mother. Keisha nods, listens, and eats two bowls of soup.

When Mémé tells Keisha about the first wolf she encountered at college, Keisha says, "Dennis Cartwright."

Mémé's eyes widen in surprise, an expression you don't

often see her wear. "How did you know that?"

"I'm a reporter," Keisha says, a little too pleased with herself. "It's what I do. After Tucker died, I started digging around in old newspapers at the library. Just to see if I could find anything similar having happened around here. I had to go a long way back, but there it was. Dennis Cartwright, found naked in the woods, with a broken neck. It seemed like an awfully odd coincidence. But sometimes life is just weirdly cyclical, and so I left Dennis Cartwright out of my article about Tucker because I wasn't sure how it connected, or if it did at all."

Mémé looks at Keisha differently now. Appraising. Perhaps, even, approving. And when she returns to her story, she offers a bit more detail. She respects Keisha, you can tell.

"I have questions," Keisha says after Mémé has finished, which almost makes you laugh. "In my research, I found that there had been a few men found in the woods, like Phillip and Tucker, but not many, and not for a long time. And you're saying you've had to hunt wolves all your life."

"There isn't always a wolf," Mémé says. "Sometimes years go by without a predator in the woods."

"Yes, but even so, you must have killed more wolves than there were bodies of men in the woods."

"Well," Mémé says, "I knew that what I was doing was good. But there was no guarantee that everyone would see the situation as clearly."

"You disposed of the bodies."

Mémé nods.

"How many wolves?" you ask.

Mémé's jaw clenches, like she doesn't want to answer. At last, she does. "Dozens."

"And no one ever caught you?"

"There was a girl, once. About twenty years ago. I know she saw my face in the moonlight. I'd tried to lead the wolf away—that was what I always did first, get the wolf away from its target, as far away as I could—then, kill. It was the safest for everyone. But this wolf didn't want to leave his prey. I could tell that he wanted to deal with me and then go back to finish her off. So I had no choice but to fight him there, in front of her. When he was dead, she stepped forward, and we stood together and watched the wolf shiver back into human form. Then she said, 'Thank you.' She told me this wasn't the first time the man had assaulted her, but the other times, though he'd done terrible things, he hadn't become a wolf. 'At least,' she said, 'he didn't look like one.' She was so grateful, and she looked me straight in my eyes, and then she embraced me."

Mémé is quiet for a moment, remembering. "I told her to leave, and she did, promising she wouldn't tell anyone what she'd seen."

"Maybe she would have helped you, if you had asked," Keisha says. "Maybe she could have been a friend."

Mémé laughs softly. "I don't know. Maybe. I didn't think in those terms. It was after Garland, and I wasn't looking for friends. I was focused on doing what had to be done."

Mémé hasn't told Keisha about Garland, but Keisha doesn't ask. She gets the gist of it, probably, just from the expression on Mémé's face, the fact that Mémé hadn't recognized a potential friend or wanted one.

"It sounds lonely," Keisha says, "hunting wolves. Being a hunter. I wonder if that's the only way."

"It was the only way I knew," Mémé says brusquely—this is the second time she has had to explain her choices today, and you can tell that it pains her. "I never thought I could save everyone. There are too many terrible things that can happen, and not just because of wolves. For whatever reason, I could do this thing—the thing Bisou can do now. I could go into these woods, here in Washington. I could challenge a wolf. But I was not blind to the facts of the world. Wolves are not the whole danger, yes? Terrible things happen every day, all the time, all across the globe, to women and to girls. I could not stop them all from happening. I could barely stop a fraction of them from happening. Whatever I did, whatever power I had, it was just a drop. But it was *my* drop, do you see? It was not nothing. To the people I saved, to the wolves I killed—it was everything. And, for many years, it was my everything, as well." She is quiet. And then, "I didn't want anyone else to be in danger. I didn't *want* any of it. I'm sure Bisou doesn't either."

You don't. You don't want it.

You wonder if they have found Phillip's body yet.

"Do you think there are others?" Keisha asks. "Other hunters?"

"It's possible," Mémé says. "There could be, I suppose, any number of us. I haven't ever looked. How would I go about such a task? Would I take out an advertisement in the classified ads, or start an online group? And even if I were to find another hunter, what then?"

"You could compare notes," Keisha says. "Support each other."

"If the others were anything like I am, they wouldn't welcome such support," Mémé says. "If they were anything like me, they would have also learned how dangerous it can be to speak of this aloud."

"Even so," Keisha pushes, "maybe there's a way to teach what you know." She has that earnest, enthusiastic tone again, that Keisha tone. "Maybe there could be more of you. More fighters."

"It's not that we need more wolf hunters," you say. "It's that we need men to stop becoming wolves."

"What we need right *now*," Mémé says, her voice a cautious warning, "is to get through these next few days. Heads down. Eyes up. The world is not kind to women who cry wolf," she cautions. "It never has been."

You look at Mémé's face. You look at Keisha's. One old; one young. One bare; one spectacled. And, both, fiercely determined.

At last, Keisha nods. "First things first," she agrees. "Triage. Like in an emergency room. First, we stop the bleeding. Then, later—"

"First things first," Mémé interrupts, and that is the end of the discussion.

By the time the evening news announces the discovery of Phillip Tang's body, Keisha's tire has been changed, James has been by to collect his car—"Aw, Bisou, you didn't have to wash it!"—and you have your story straight.

"I had a flat," Keisha says, as you run through it together one more time before she goes home. "I pulled over and checked it out, looked in my trunk for a spare, figured out I didn't have a jack. I would have called for help, but my phone was dead, so I was waiting for it to charge enough to make a call."

"That's when I came by in James's wagon," you say. "We looked together at the tire and decided maybe it would just be better to go home to my place, since it looked like it was getting ready to rain."

"I followed you home. We came inside and slept. This morning, your grandmother helped us reshape the rim in her garage and then taught us how to change a tire."

"Because every girl should know how to take care of herself," you add.

"Exactly. We hung out at your house all day, and then I headed home at . . ." Keisha checks the time on her phone. "At around eight o'clock. Just after hearing the news about Phillip from the news station your grandmother was watching."

"Okay," you say, and you follow Keisha out onto the porch. Her car is parked in the driveway, rim a little worse for the wear but not as bad as you'd thought it would be.

"Bisou," Keisha says, her voice dropping a little, "I know your grandmother thinks the safest thing to do is to keep all of this to ourselves. And I know it's her story, too. I get that. But things don't change unless people change them."

"I don't know what you want us to do, Keisha."

"I don't either. But, just . . . think about it. Okay?"

This girl doesn't know how to be chill. Not even a little. Maybe she's right, that things could turn out okay if you told your story. But maybe she's wrong. And she doesn't have anything to lose, compared to you and Mémé. To get her to leave, you say, "Okay. But don't do *anything* until you talk to me first."

"Of course not," Keisha says. Then, "And Bisou? Thank you."

After Keisha has gone, you go to your room and shut the door. You sit on the edge of the bed; you pull open the drawer of the bedside table. You take out your mother's poems, unfold them, and spread them across the quilt.

You read them through. They feel like sacred documents. You have always been so careful not to leave a mark on them, to refold them right along the crease. But now they are yours.

You stack the poems again, with the poem marked "i" on the top. You find a pencil in your drawer, then cast it aside and dig until you find a pen. You yank off the cap with your teeth. You answer her, scrawling your words next to hers.

i

I know now
that mothers leave

But I know more

I know they try to stay

You read her poem, and then yours. You're no poet—you don't even know what makes something a poem instead of a bunch of sentences just randomly broken into different lines. But it's better this way—answering her, taking the poems out of the drawer, not turning them into relics.

When you close your eyes, you see the farmhouse. You remember each room; the pond; the skipping stones.

"It's totally a serial killer." Lorraine is practically foaming with excitement.

"Both of them were naked." Darcy takes a loud bite of her apple, and says, chewing, "*Totally* naked."

"Do you want to hear something weird?"

Darcy leans in closer to Lorraine.

"I heard that Maggie used to have a thing with Phillip. A couple of years ago. Before high school. Like, they were each other's first girlfriend and boyfriend. Isn't that *bizarre*? That she's, like, the common denominator?"

The lunchroom is abuzz with the news as if it's the plot-line from a TV show, or something they've read online, not like they're talking about real people who actually went to this school.

You don't have much of an appetite. You have a sandwich and an orange in front of you, and a little thermos of soup left over from the weekend, but mostly you're just moving it around. Lorraine and Darcy are sitting at the table behind you, and you are doing your best to ignore them, reading the school paper on your phone. It's hard, though. Their blood-thirsty glee is so gross.

There's an article, of course, about Phillip's death—Keisha's written it, and you're pretty impressed how dispassionate she managed to keep it.

There's another letter to the editor, too.

A hundred years ago, by the time people were our age, they were paired up. That meant they didn't have to worry about the sexual marketplace the way that young people do today. Thanks to the rise of feminism and the "sexual revolution," so-called alpha males get their pick of the girls, and the rest of us are left out in the cold, no matter how smart or talented we are.

Back in the day, men were pretty much guaranteed a wife, and this meant their sexual desires were met on a regular basis, which, let's face it, is good for society as a whole. Who wants a horde of horny guys wandering around? But now that's pretty much what we have, as women are choosing their mates and competing for (or sharing) the top men. Some psychologists are arguing that the cure for our societal problems is a return to forced monogamy, and I, for one, think that's a great idea. A girl for every guy—isn't that fairer than one guy getting all the girls, and the rest of us left alone on Saturday nights?

It's signed, "It's No Crime to Expect Love."

The letter manages to be both idiotically stupid and remarkably creepy at the same time. You push away your sandwich, appetite gone.

James isn't eating much, either. He didn't like Tucker or Phillip, but the first was a teammate, and the second was a guy he'd known since kindergarten, and maybe he's thinking that either of them could have been him.

As if James knows what you're thinking, he says, "I think we should stay out of the woods for a while." He's picking at the skin of his thumb, near his nail bed, a nervous habit he has. You rest your hand on top of his to quiet it.

"You're scared."

"Aren't you?" James asks. "I mean, anyone could be next. It could be me. It could be you."

"Nobody's going to be next," you say, but your voice is unconvincing. You don't really know that. You try again. "You won't be next. Neither will I."

"That's because we're going to stay out of the woods." James flips over his hand, laces his fingers with yours, squeezes. "Okay?"

You think about Mémé, about everything she sacrificed, about all the times she went back into the woods. You think about the girls she saved.

And then you squeeze James's hand, and you lie to him. "Okay."

"So, I've been doing some research." It's after school. James is working out today, and Keisha has offered to drive you home.

"Of course you have."

"Have you ever heard of Pierre Burgot and Michel Verdun? Or Gilles Garnier, or Peter Stumpp?"

"Should I have?"

Keisha checks her rearview mirror and then looks over her shoulder before she changes lanes. "They were executed back in the fifteen hundreds for crimes of lycanthropy."

"Lycanthropy?"

"Being werewolves, basically. And killing people."

"Really?"

"Yep. The first two, Burgot and Verdun, were a team, I guess. Like, serial killer buddies. They were French. Garnier was a French guy, too, called the "Werewolf of Dole." He confessed to serial killings before he was executed. There was another man—that's Stumpp, he was German. He confessed to murder, rape, and cannibalism, all while under the spell of full moons. His daughter and his girlfriend were both executed along with him."

"Were Stumpp's daughter and girlfriend werewolves, too? Or murderers?"

"Nope. They were killed for 'knowledge of his crimes' and for having sex with him."

"His *daughter* had sex with him?"

"Not willingly. Maybe no one cared if it was rape or consensual. Either way, she was guilty."

Keisha is a careful follower of traffic laws. She uses her blinkers every time she changes lanes, and she comes to a full stop at each stop sign. When a light ahead turns yellow, she slows to a stop, even though she probably would have had time to make it through.

"Do you know what's interesting?" Keisha asks. "People used to believe that werewolves were created by witches. So, even way back in the fourteenth century, women were being blamed for men's bad behavior."

You don't say anything to this. You think of Mémé, of the girls she saved, how everyone wondered what those girls were doing out alone at night. You think of your mother. You think of your father, still out there somewhere. And the other women who might have crossed his path in the years between then and now. It's too much to think about, and so you focus your attention on just one thing.

"Hey," you say, "what's up with the letters to the editor lately?"

"Yeah, I know," Keisha says, eyes on the road. "They're awful."

"So why are you running them? Aren't you, like, the editor?"

"I ran the first one because it was gross but nonthreatening, and I wasn't in the mood for another round of emails from dude-bros complaining about how biased the school paper is," Keisha says. "I ran the second one, though, so I could write a response to it." Here, she smiles, but it's more like a baring of teeth than a sign of happiness. "I'm going to eviscerate him tomorrow. Fucking incel."

It occurs to you that Keisha may enjoy a fight as much as you do.

"An incel?" you ask. "What's that?"

"Oh, my friend, that's a dark deep dive for sure," Keisha says, pulling up in front of your house. "Don't google before bedtime unless you like nightmares."

Incel. You tuck the word away for later. "Thanks for the ride," you say.

"Anytime."

Since it's a Monday, you expect to be greeted by the wafting yeasty smell of fresh bread, and Mémé does not disappoint you. You stop just inside the door, close your eyes, breathe the fresh hot scent.

You sit down on the bench to untie your shoes, and that is when you notice the footprint—big, a man's print—on the entry rug.

And then you hear two voices in the kitchen: Mémé's, and a man's.

"Are you sure about that?" says the man.

"Yes, Alan, though I will let you know if I change my mind."

You walk in your socks, silently, to the kitchen doorway. Mémé is standing by the sink, leaning against the counter, holding a mug. On the counter is a slip of paper with something written on it. Even from this distance, you can tell the writing is not hers. Sitting at the table, a cup of coffee in his hand, is the plainclothes officer you encountered in the forest when you went looking for the wolf's body and found instead a taped-off crime scene. His back is to you, but you recognize him by the slope of his shoulders, the way he takes up space. He is wearing his boots in the house, even though they are muddy, even though there is a rule against shoes past the entry hall.

Mémé makes eye contact with you briefly over the officer's head. Her eyes, you think, are warning you.

"Well," the officer says, "if you change your mind . . ."

"I'll have your number." She sets her cup down on the counter and taps the slip of paper, as if to indicate that the conversation has reached its end. You can read his name, above the number: Alan Scott.

To his credit, the officer takes the hint. He finishes his coffee in a quick slurp, wipes his mouth with the back of his hand. He gets up—a bit awkwardly, like his knees give him some trouble—and then walks over to put his cup in the sink. His badge, strung around his neck like jewelry, catches the light and shines. He is standing just inches from Mémé, who straightens herself from leaning, taking up space of her own.

"Thanks for the coffee," he says, and then he turns toward the doorway. "Oh," he says, surprised. "I didn't hear you come in. Sybil, she looks just like you."

"There is a resemblance," Mémé says. "I'll walk you to the door."

You step to the side, giving the officer wide berth to pass. Mémé follows him into the hallway and opens the door for him to leave.

"All right, girls," he says to both of you. "Stay safe, now. Don't go into the woods."

You bristle at this, but Mémé laughs. "Good advice," she says. "You stay safe, too."

When he's outside, Mémé waits until he's gone down the stairs from the porch before she closes the door.

"What was that about?"

"It was odd," Mémé says.

"What was he doing here?"

"He said he wanted to ask me on a date."

"Really?"

Mémé smiles. "Don't act so surprised. It happens, from time to time."

"That's not what I meant," you say. "Just—why *now*?"

"Apparently you ran into him in the woods last month?"

You nod.

"I guess meeting you . . . jogged his memory. He says we met once, many years ago, though I can't recall when that might have been . . . I suppose seeing you—our resemblance . . ."

Mémé's expression is inscrutable.

Anxiety tightens your stomach. "Did he say anything about Phillip?"

"Nothing specific. He did mention that there were a couple of incidents with girls, one here in Seattle, another in Berkeley, where Phillip's brother is a student? Problems that might have made either of the young women perhaps less than sorry to see Phillip dead. Not, he said, that the girls were under investigation."

"Why would he tell you that?"

"I don't know, actually."

"Do you think he suspects something? Do you think he knows?"

Mémé leans against the counter again, taps her fingers against it. "He didn't give any indication that he did," she says at last. "Though it is strange that he volunteered information about the investigation."

"It's my fault," you say. "You never left bodies . . . I've left two in two months."

Mémé waves her hand, shushes you. "Don't be silly," she says. "You couldn't have known."

"We should have gone back and moved it."

"I considered it. But it seemed the greater risk."

"But the cops—"

"Yes, the cops," Mémé says, "it's true, and there could be others, too, whose unwanted attention this could attract. But it's no use crying over spilled milk, my darling. If there is blame, it is mine, for not giving you information you could have used. Knowledge, as they say, is power. And I kept you in the dark for too long. For that, I hope you'll forgive me. As for the bodies . . . well, if any problems arise as a result, I shall resolve them."

"*We*," you say, and you take her hand. "If there are any problems, Mémé, *we'll* fix them. Together."

Mémé smiles, squeezes your fingers in her warm strong grip. "Of course, my girl, of course."

Then she slices you a thick, warm slice of bread, and butters it for you as if you were a child.

You take the bread to your room. You close your door, and then you pull your mother's poems from the bedside drawer. You trace your finger up and down each letter, following the path she took all those years ago.

She was a whole person once. A living person. A daughter, then a wife, and then a mother—but aside from that, aside from those roles, she was a person.

You wonder what your mother would be like now, if she were alive instead of dead. Would she have written other poems? Would she have had other children? Would she have rehabilitated the farm? Would she have sold it and used the money to travel with you abroad?

She would have lived to see the thaw, if he had not come. She would have watched your little hands as they gripped stones, as you learned to skip them across the pond.

You write.

II

I was alone
in the ghost room
waiting for it to end
alone
hoping he wouldn't find me

he came
and blew down everything
the moon was made of blood
your bed was full of blood

when he touched you
with his fists and fangs
he could have kept you safe
but he didn't want to

ALPHA AND OMEGA

A Response to "It's No Crime to Expect Love"
By Keisha Montgomery, Editor in Chief

A hundred years ago, antibiotics hadn't been invented yet and you could die from an infected zit.

And as much as I would like to invent a time machine and send you back to such a fine era, time machines are as much of a fantasy as those psychologists you're talking about—the ones who would force girls to be in your sexual service as some sort of magical cure for social ills.

Because you seem to like science so much, let me tell you about natural selection. This is the theory where undesirable traits are bred out because they're undesirable. This happens to every single living creature. Roosters who can't get laid don't flap off to Mother Nature demanding a chicken sex slave. They work on their crow.

You talk about how smart and talented you are, but then you go and reveal that you think "forced monogamy" is a good idea. That right there makes you a complete dodo. Forcing anything when it comes to sex is completely unacceptable. It's an idea that, like the dodo, has died out except in the most primordial of post-pubescent-boy swamps.

Come out of the swamp. Cleanse yourself of the ooze. It's not going to guarantee you a partner, but it's a start. I'd offer you a hand, but you presumably have two of those. You can use one to pull yourself out of the muck and the other—well, use your imagination on that one the next time you're alone on Saturday night.

"It's got more comments than any other post this year," Keisha says, a little smug, the day after her response goes live. "Almost all positive." She looks up from her phone, grins. "And Mackenzie asked me out."

"Big Mac?"

She nods.

"What did you say?"

"I told him I'd think about it," Keisha says. "We're pretty busy right now." You are together in your bedroom. You are supposed to be studying for the chemistry test (Keisha's idea, and one you took her up on since she's currently setting the curve), but though your books are open, no real studying has been done. First Keisha had to show you all the comments to her editorial response, and now she's moved on to something else.

"Maybe we should sync our cycles," she says.

Since you rescued her in the woods, Keisha has made your business her business. You aren't sure if it's because she feels grateful to you or if it's because she views you like a real-life research project, but your suspicions lean toward the latter.

"What are you talking about?"

"I read somewhere that if women spend a lot of time together, they can get their menstrual cycles to align. I'll bet you're an alpha."

"An alpha?"

"Mm-hmm." Keisha grabs her laptop, flips it open. "An alpha female stays on her cycle. Everyone else syncs up with her. It can take a long time, though, like months." Keisha is eager now, doing what she does best—research—but after a minute, her face falls. "Oh."

"What is it?" You scoot over to look at her screen, intrigued now in spite of yourself.

"I guess maybe it isn't true. It's confirmation bias, this says. There's new research—they had all these women, room-mates and teammates and stuff—track their periods with an app. And they found out that women who spend a lot of time together usually move further apart in their cycles, not closer together." She knits her brow. "I wonder why that is." She begins typing again, her fingers hitting the keys hard.

"Why would you even *want* to sync up with my . . . cycle?"

Keisha doesn't answer. Her lips are tight and behind her glasses, her eyes narrow in concentration. "That's interesting," she says after a minute of reading, but she's not talking to you. She is lost in her own little world.

It's annoying. You guys have work to do, and if she is going to ignore you, she should just go home. "*What's* interesting?"

"Oh," Keisha says, looking up and snapping back into the present. "Sorry." She turns her laptop around and hands it over so you can read the article she's found. The first part recaps what she's already said—that even though women often believe their periods are syncing up, when their experiential evidence is tracked as data, there's no true correlation, maybe even a slight reverse correlation.

The article goes on:

In large-mammal studies, researchers found that among groups that spent most of their time together (great apes, other primates, etc.), menses did not occur in sync. Researchers postulate that this may be because it does not provide an evolutionary advantage for all potential mating partners to be unavailable for insemination during the same period. Indeed, it is much more advantageous for there to always be a female who is "ready and willing" for mating behavior to occur.

You hand the laptop back to Keisha. "Ew."

"Totally," she says. "It's super gross to think about it that way—that it's better for the males if females don't sync." She sighs, clicks away from the article and onto something else. "So much for that theory."

You ask her again. "Why would you want to try to sync cycles, anyway?"

"Oh. I just thought, like, maybe if we were on the same schedule, then maybe, you know, when you need to go into the forest to . . . hunt . . . then I could go with you. Maybe if we had our periods together, I would be like you. You know. Maybe I'd get, like, strong and tough, when you did." She shrugs, looking sort of embarrassed, and pushes her glasses up the bridge of her nose—the tortoiseshell ones today.

You laugh. "That's not a very scientific line of reasoning."

"It was just an idea!"

"Anyway, if I were the alpha, wouldn't that make you, like, my omega?"

"Your beta," Keisha corrects. "It would be funny, actually, because those terms usually apply to pack animals. Like dogs. And wolves."

"I'm not a wolf."

"Oh, I know." Keisha skims another article on her laptop while she talks to you. It's amazing, how she can do both things at the same time. "But it would be an advantage for you not to be alone out there. Like your grandmother. I still think that's sad."

"It's not sad," you say. "It's brave."

"Things can be more than one thing at a time," says Keisha, and she's right. Brave and sad. Boys and wolves.

"Anyway," you say, "I'd rather not have to fight wolves than just have more company while I fought them."

Keisha doesn't argue with you, but she gazes frankly into your eyes, and you look away first. This too, is more than one thing—true, but also not true.

There's something uniquely satisfying about ending a wolf. The quick hard twist of the neck. The stab-and-pull of the blade through fur and flesh. The gush of blood. The letting.

"Here's another fun fact," Keisha says, showing you her laptop again. "Did you know that humans are the only land mammals that go through menopause?"

"Keisha, why on earth would I know that?"

"Because it's fascinating. Most mammals keep reproducing until they die—of old age, or because of a predator, or whatever. But humans don't."

In spite of yourself, you are interested. "Why?"

"It's evolutionarily advantageous for there to be female elders to help with the babies while not distracted by babies of their own. You know about hunters and gatherers, right?"

"Of course."

"We really should say *gatherers and hunters*. Because, like, almost all the time, early humans survived on what was gathered, *not* what was hunted. I read this article on NPR's website. It turns out that hunters were only successful three percent of the time."

"Really?"

"Yes," says Keisha, and now she's on a roll. "If early human tribes depended on the hunters, they would have all starved."

"So most of the food came from the gatherers."

"Uh-huh. But when women have babies, that slows them down."

"So the grandmothers took care of the kids?"

"That's the hypothesis. And it could be because the grandmothers weren't having kids themselves anymore that they were able to take care of their grandchildren, freeing up the younger women for foraging." She shuts her laptop and sets it aside.

You thumb through her chemistry flash cards. Some of the terms are familiar, but you don't remember most of them. "If that's true," you say, setting down the cards, "then why do we always hear so much about the hunters?"

"Because," says Keisha, the word practically dripping with derision, "until recently, history has been written almost exclusively by *men*."

You snort a little.

"It's true!" She's picked up the flash cards and begins separating them quickly into two piles, those she knows well and those she needs to memorize. The pile of terms she knows is much bigger. "Imagine how different our whole understanding of the world could be if women were reporting what had happened instead of men. History is recorded by those in charge, and in the Western world, that means almost exclusively by white men. That's why I'm going to be a reporter."

"You're going to single-handedly change the world by telling it like it is," you say with a laugh.

"No," Keisha says, one word, firm. "Not single-handedly. No one changes the world by themselves."

"Well," you say, "Mémé sort of has."

Keisha shrugs. "Your grandmother is amazing. And she's saved lives, that's for sure. But the world is the same as it was, Bisou. Now she's stopped bleeding, and hunting, and you've started. Anyway," she says, "if I can't help you with the hunting, there have to be other things I can do."

Maybe not in a fight, but definitely in other ways, it's good to have Keisha on your side. "Here's something you can do," you say, scooping up the larger stack of flash cards, the ones Keisha knows. "Let's add all the ones I don't know to the study pile, too."

Even before the teacher hands back your chemistry test, you know it will be your highest score of the year. Keisha is smart and thorough, and she doesn't take shortcuts. Together, you studied three times longer for this test than you ever have studied for a test on your own.

"How are you so good at this?" you ask Keisha when you get back your test and see the red "92%" at the top.

"At studying?" Keisha smirks. "It isn't that hard. I just don't give up until I've solved the problem. Whatever the problem is—figuring out an equation or how to memorize a list or what I think the poet really means when he writes about a red wheelbarrow. I'm good at eliminating the wrong answers and accepting that whatever is left, no matter how improbable, must be true."

You're leaving chem together. At the back table, with tears in her eyes, Maggie is shoving her test into her backpack.

She's got her hair pulled up into a rough ponytail, but she's missed one long strand. Her face is scrubbed bare, and her whole body seems to radiate stress.

You stop at her desk. "Maggie? Are you okay?"

She wipes her eyes, zips shut her backpack. "You two sure are peas in a pod these days," she says, and she doesn't look at your face as she stands up and heads out of the class, her shoulder hitting yours as she passes.

She's gone before you can answer. "What's with her?" you ask Keisha.

"We're shitheads, that's what's the matter," Keisha says, groaning.

And then you realize that the last time you really talked to Maggie was before the party at Big Mac's, and that actually she texted you a couple of times and you never wrote her back.

"Have *you* called her?"

Keisha shakes her head. "I meant to call her after . . . you know . . . to tell her I was sorry, but I never did. We hurt her feelings."

"We should go visit her," you say. "After school?"

But when you go to the parking lot after the last bell to meet Keisha, you see James waiting for you. He's standing on the top step in a rare ray of sunshine. When you emerge from the building, his face breaks into a smile.

"Hey, Bisou." He leans in and kisses you. "Happy Wednesday."

Is it Wednesday? Shit. It is. "Hey," you say, and you kiss him back. The air is cold, but his lips are warm, and you'd way rather take him to your house, to your bedroom, to your bed, than go with Keisha to check on Maggie.

But you remember the look on Maggie's face—hurt, angry, maybe even a little ashamed, like there was something wrong with *her* that was why you hadn't called or texted her back, and you pull your lips away from James's.

"I'm so sorry, but I can't today."

He moans, runs his hands up and down your arms, says, "Don't tease me like that, Bisou."

You laugh. "I wish I were teasing," you say, and you kiss him again before stepping away. "But I'm not. I've got something I've got to do this afternoon with Keisha. See?" you say, pointing to the parking lot, where she's standing by her Bug. "She's waiting for me."

He groans. "Really? Can't it wait till tomorrow?"

You shake your head. "No."

His shoulders soften in acceptance. "Okay," he says. "But call me later?"

You nod, stand on your toes to kiss him again. "Later."

Maggie opens the door, but not right away. Her eyes are narrowed, her face suspicious.

"What do you want?"

"We were worried about you," Keisha says. "Can we come in?"

Maggie looks like maybe she's going to say no, but then she sighs in resignation and she pulls wide the door.

Keisha pushes through first, and you follow, giving Maggie an apologetic smile that she does not return.

"You looked miserable today in chem," Keisha says, sitting down on the couch in the front room. You take the armchair near the window, and Maggie slumps to the floor, crosses her legs, leans against the wall underneath the TV. She doesn't say anything at first. She looks like she's thinking about something, like she is deciding whether or not to trust you. And your heart aches for her. She's always deciding whether to trust people, and then trusting them, and then regretting it. You don't want her to regret trusting you, not again. You almost want her *not* to confide in you so that there is no chance of letting her down.

Then she says, "I hate everything about high school. I'm done. I'm out."

She sets her mouth resolutely, lips tight, like she's ready to defend this decision if you and Keisha start telling her it's a dumb idea. But Keisha doesn't do that; instead, she asks, "What are you going to do instead?"

"I've already got a job at my aunt's nursery. Sweeping up, watering, not exactly sexy, but it pays more than minimum wage. And, I don't know. I'll take classes or something. At the community college." She shrugs. "Anything but high school."

"Wow," says Keisha. Then she's quiet, for a change.

"I'd hate to see you leave, Maggie," you say. You know that you haven't been acting in a way that makes that seem like the truth, though it is.

"I fucking *hate* it there. I hate the gossip. I hate the guys. Half the time, I even hate the two of you."

First there's tension, the pain of a bandage ripped off, and then there's relief, the particular relief of an ugly truth said out loud.

"Maggie," you say, "I'm really sorry. I'm so sorry. We've been—busy. But that's no excuse to disappear."

Her mouth twists, and you can tell she's trying not to cry.

"It's not just you," she says. "I found this fucking picture in my locker this morning when I got to school." She reaches for her backpack and unzips it, fumbles through it until she finds what she was looking for—a piece of paper, folded in half. She thrusts it out, and Keisha takes it.

She unfolds it. You can't see it clearly from where you're sitting, but you can tell it's a photo, low-quality, printed on regular computer paper rather than shiny photo paper.

"Maggie," breathes Keisha, "someone put this in your *locker*?"

Maggie nods, and you scoot around closer to Keisha to see the picture. It's a dick pic, sort of blurry, erect, pinkish and pale with a puff of brown pubes, and next to it—maybe for size comparison, maybe as a threat—is an unsheathed knife.

"Who would send something like that?" Maggie says. "What did I ever do to deserve this shit?"

"You didn't do *anything*," Keisha says firmly, and she refolds the image. "Maggie, this is a *crime*. Guys can't just give pictures like this to people. At the very least, it's harassment. Plus, you're a minor. That makes giving you this picture a *felony*, I think, even without the creepy knife. We should show this to someone. Like, the police."

Maggie shakes her head, wipes her eyes. "If I tell the police, then my parents will find out, and I don't want them worrying about me. Anyway," she says, "I feel better just telling you guys."

For a minute, Keisha looks like she's going to argue, like

she's going to insist that Maggie go to the authorities, but then she sighs and hands the paper back. "I'm really sorry, Maggie," she says.

"I am too," you say. "I'm sorry."

Maggie smiles, kind of shy, and says, "I'm glad you guys came over."

Then Maggie gets snacks from the kitchen and Keisha throws pillows on the floor and the three of you form a cozy triangle, legs crossed, a bag of chips between you and each with a glass of lemonade.

"So," Maggie says. "Phillip, huh?"

You look over to Keisha to make sure that you're still in agreement about keeping the truth of that night between the two of you, but Keisha either doesn't notice that you're looking at her, or she ignores you.

"Nobody can shut up about it. Did you see the rotating police patrols at school this week? And I guess they're talking to everyone who was close to Phillip or was hanging out with him at the party. They came to my house last night."

This is news to you. Now Keisha looks at you, shrugs. "It was no big deal. They just wanted to know what Phillip and I talked about that night, how he seemed, if I noticed anything that might link him and Tucker."

"But Tucker's death was an accident, right? Phillip—he was killed. His throat was cut."

When Maggie says this—*His throat was cut*—you see it

again, on the backs of your eyes: the dark wolf, leaping, the red that gushed from him in a hot pulsing fountain of gore.

"Yeah," Keisha says, "but they were both in the woods. And they were both naked."

You look up to find Maggie staring at you, suddenly and with wide eyes. A shock of dread hits you. But when she speaks, Maggie says, "Oh, Bisou, I didn't even *think* about your mom. This must be hard on you, the way Phillip died."

"Your mom?" asks Keisha, but you ignore her.

"Yeah, thanks, Maggie," you say. "I appreciate that, but I'm okay."

Maggie leans over anyway and hugs you, and as you breathe in the sweetness of her shampoo, you have to fight back tears. Maggie, with all those kids at school gossiping about her, and some creep leaving condoms and dick pics for her to find, and probably still dealing with the fallout from Tucker's little STI gift . . . still, she's worried about *you*, whether it's hard for *you* to be hearing about a violent death.

If Maggie wants to be your friend, that's a gift you'd be a fucking fool to refuse. So you wrap your arms around Maggie and hug her back.

When you release each other, Keisha is watching. You can see her brain churning behind her eyes. You know she's working out what Maggie meant about your mom, and you know she's going to have plenty of questions later.

But for now, she keeps the conversation on Phillip and Tucker. "The police are looking for common threads," she says. "They're doing an autopsy. They'll look for the same drugs they found in Tucker. And honestly, I won't be surprised if they find them."

"You really think some drug made them do this?" Maggie asks.

"I'll bet they had the same toxins in their bodies," Keisha answers.

Maggie considers this before speaking. "I wouldn't figure Phillip for the kind to put anything in his body. No chemicals or anything like that. He was one of those 'my body is my temple' kind of guys. But," she says, "he wasn't above putting things in *other* people's bodies."

"You mean that girl at Berkeley?" you ask.

"Her," Maggie says, taking a sip of lemonade, "and Cara Lee, that girl who dropped out of school freshman year. I ran into her, you know, a couple of days ago. Our moms are still friends kinda."

"Really?" Keisha says. You know her well enough now that you recognize her tone, that trying-to-sound-casual-but-actually-terribly-interested tone. "Had she heard about Phillip?"

"Mm-hmm. She said that maybe there is a God after all."

* * *

Driving away from Maggie's house, Keisha is quiet, and even though her eyes are on the road and she's as careful a driver as ever, you can tell she is far away in her mind. She doesn't bring up what Maggie said about your mother, and you're grateful. It's not that it's a secret; it's just that it hurts to talk about. Still, you can't stop yourself from asking, "What are you thinking?"

"Hmm?" Keisha's gaze flicks from the road, to you in the passenger seat, and then back to traffic. "Oh," she says, "it's just strange. You know me. Verify, fact-check, double-check."

"Yeah?"

The light ahead turns red, and Keisha slows and stops.

"And with Tucker and Phillip, I know the truth of the end of their stories. I know how they died, and why. But I don't know what made them that way. What made them into wolves. Do you think they were just . . . born that way? Like, a genetic anomaly?"

"I don't know what makes a wolf," you say.

Keisha nods, but her hands tighten on the steering wheel, and you can tell it's not enough for her. And when the light turns green again, Keisha, who always pays attention to everything, is lost in thought and doesn't step on the gas until the driver behind her honks his horn.

Outside, the sun has disappeared. The sky is aglow with evening, and all around you, one by one, drivers switch on their headlights. Keisha reaches over and turns hers on, too.

* * *

The toxicology report is back by the third week of November. Blood alcohol concentration: .13. Unusual compounds discovered: methylone and cathinone. Same as Tucker.

The cops pivot their investigation away from the high school and toward local drug dealers. Channel 4 News does a special report on designer drugs and the kids who use them.

And by the time Thanksgiving break rolls around, talk about the story at school has faded. You know this is in part because Keisha has let the story die; if she hadn't been in the woods that night—if she hadn't seen it for herself—she wouldn't have ever stopped digging. And it occurs to you how interesting that is—how people follow the stories that they are led to, and how quickly most people will fade away from a topic that they're not repeatedly, consistently reminded about.

People, you suppose, can get used to pretty much anything. After all, when the moon is full near the end of November and you bleed again, you are not surprised when its light, flooding through your bedroom window, keeps you wide awake. You are not surprised when you slip from your blankets, pull on your jeans, your boots, when you drape your claw around your neck and tuck it into your shirt before you zip up your red sweatshirt and tuck your hair into its hood. The forest waits, and as you close the door silently behind you, you breathe in the night's damp air, you flex your fingers and tighten them to fists, and you go into the trees to roam and hunt.

TALK OF THE WOLF

Fall becomes winter, and winter stretches into the new year, and all the while the forest is barren of wolves. Each month with your flow, you go into the woods, no matter the weather, and you prowl under the full-bellied moon. Is the forest safe because you roam it? Or is it simply that there are no wolves, and your presence is neither a deterrent nor a provocation? You cannot know.

"There isn't always a wolf," Mémé reminds you, "but there is always the threat of one."

Aside from the threat of wolves and the monthly appearance of your menses, your life moves through the seasons the same as it ever has. Since late November, James has been busy with basketball, and most afternoons he's at practice or a game—even Wednesdays. You still see him at school and on weekends. When you are together, in stolen moments between classes, on weekend mornings when you accompany him on rainy jogs—he's training for basketball, and you are training now, too—your desire for him is insistent, demanding. You wonder, one Saturday afternoon, your chin rubbed red from his weekend stubble, your vulva swollen with desire, if this is because you have seen death, and you have wrought it. It is no wonder you crave the aliveness of his mouth and hands so very much.

When you are not with James, you find yourself spending more and more time in an odd little trinity—you, Keisha, and Maggie, who, you are coming to find out, is one of the funniest people you have ever met.

Maggie's parents are allowing her to do spring semester through a homeschool program, with the agreement that they'll discuss over the summer whether she'll return to Garfield for senior year. Other than working at her aunt's nursery a few days a week, Maggie is a total homebody. She reads a lot, and she's started getting into manga. She says her parents think it's a good idea for her to just unwind and remember what sort of stuff she actually *likes*.

"It's weird," Maggie says. "I've been in school since I was four, and before that I was in day care, since I was a baby. Other than weekends and holidays, or when I was sick, I can't remember a time when I had a day on my own schedule, you know? Just, wake up when I wake up, no alarm or anything, and eat when I'm actually hungry instead of when it's time to eat? It's super luxurious, and I love it."

Maggie likes to lip-synch and she thinks bowling is way better with bumpers and she is obsessed with astrology and she says people who dip everything in ranch dressing are "monsters." She pulls her hair up into a bun and lets it down at least three times in an afternoon and she likes yoga and she thinks queefing is "hilarious."

She comes over to hang out at your house, walking over two miles from her place to get there. Sometimes when you get home from school, you find her in the kitchen with Mémé, munching on cookies and the two of them laughing together over some video Maggie has pulled up on her phone.

This, more than anything, is what surprises you. The friendship between Mémé and Maggie. You've barely ever seen Mémé with someone else—in a way, Mémé has always been yours alone.

Maggie starts volunteering with Mémé at the library on Wednesdays, and she takes home some of Mémé's sourdough starter to try making bread of her own. She knows where you keep your tea strainers and the little teaspoons Mémé likes to use to stir in cream. Mémé even tells Maggie about her alter ego, the pen name she uses as a romance novelist. "A novelist's job," you hear her telling Maggie one afternoon, "is to be a careful student of human nature. Of power. Of attraction and repulsion. The writer's job is to pay attention. And to not shy away from the best and the worst. To reveal truth, in lies."

You could be jealous. You could resent this sharing of Mémé—after all, it's not like you have relatives to spare—but you don't. She has new stories to share with you, funny little things about what Maggie said or the new Ethiopian coffee place they tried together after their shift at the library. But this is only part of it. It's as if the more Mémé expands into her friendship with Maggie, the more Mémé there is for you.

People aren't pastries, divisible only into quantifiable sections. Maybe they are more like sourdough—indefinitely full of potential, able to share again and again, only to rise and grow and fill each space.

One day after school, you find Maggie and Mémé sitting on the floor of the front room, legs crossed, eyes closed, meditating. When you come through the door, Maggie's eyes snap open and she grins. "I'm so glad you're home," she says, untwisting her legs and standing. "Meditating is boring as *shit*."

Keisha comes over a lot, too, and she keeps up a pretty steady stream of questions when it's just you and her, wanting to know more and more about everything—about what your strength feels like when it comes with your period, and how fast do you think you can run, and how did you know how to fight a wolf, anyway? They're questions you don't have satisfying answers for. But when Maggie is there, the three of you could be any three friends hanging out together, laughing and making jokes about each other and having fun.

And when it's the four of you—when Keisha, Maggie, and Mémé fill all the other seats at the round kitchen table, when dinner is before you and candles are lit, when their faces glow in the quivering light, you feel this electric hum of energy circling the table, you feel yourself bigger and brighter in their reflections of you.

"We're like a coven," Maggie says one night.

"I'm the crone," says Mémé.

"No," says Maggie. "Don't say that."

"It's not a bad word," Keisha says. "A crone is an elder woman. She's the keeper of wisdom. Crones used to be revered and respected above everyone else. But when the church grew powerful during the Inquisition, they started to distrust the old women. Crones were tortured and killed, the stories people told about them changed. Instead of being powerfully wise, old women in stories became powerfully evil."

"Like wicked witches," Maggie says.

"Exactly."

"Well," Maggie says to Mémé, "you're not wicked. But you *are* a witch. We all are."

You can tell this pleases Mémé, who offers her left hand to Maggie, and her right hand to you. Across from her, Keisha links hands with you and Maggie, too, and the four of you form a circle.

"Our coven," Mémé says. And then, "I see you here, my sweet girls, and I know that you are more together than you are apart. Bisou, you're the hands. Keisha is the head. And Maggie, the heart." She says, to you, "Can you forgive me, dearest one? For keeping you to myself for so long?"

Tears prick your eyes as you nod, and the four of you squeeze hands, an electric pulse that circles around and around again. It's in your kitchen, and with these women, that you have something you didn't know was possible, something you didn't know you needed.

That is how it goes, with more evenings spent together than apart, as the days grow longer, stretching toward spring.

///

The first time James kissed me
he asked me first
if he could
and I said yes

The last time
you kissed me
I don't remember
I was so young when he took you
I used to pretend
That I didn't remember anything
I used to pretend that the past
Was in the past

But each month
The moon grows
And I grow with it

And I'm making a promise
I'm making you a promise

I can kick
And scream
And bleed

And stay right where I fucking am.

Everything cycles. The moon; your own rhythm; the seasons.
Luck, too.

Since the day that Maggie found the picture in her locker

and decided to leave school, it seemed her luck had improved. There have been no more "gifts," and no more texts, either, from Graham, who, as Keisha pointed out and you and Maggie both agreed, was probably the owner of the dick in the picture.

And there have been no more letters to the editor, either, which makes Keisha think that probably Graham was the anonymous writer of these, too. Maybe her response shook him, or shut him up. You have gone online to research "incel," and Keisha wasn't wrong about it being the stuff of nightmares. Page after page of entitled, whiny diatribes written by men—mostly young, mostly white—who call themselves "involuntary celibates," "incels" for short. Basically, guys who can't get laid and are really, really angry about it. Guys who feel entitled to sex. Young men who feel cheated and wronged by their sexless lives and the girls who aren't interested in them, and who won't shut up about it. But the one in your school has, it seems. For the moment.

It's March when Maggie's good luck ends. Turning the corner to your street, hood up against the frigid air, you find her sitting on the porch. Her eyes are red and swollen, and she clutches an envelope in her mittened hands.

It is cold, and you've walked as swiftly as you could from the bus stop. Just past four in the afternoon, the sky, heavy and gray, is turning. She shivers, sitting there on your porch, and when she sees you coming up the path and stands, it is as if her bones are stiff with cold.

"Hey," you say, "what's wrong?"

"There was something in my mailbox," she says miserably.

This is the same Maggie who, just days ago, laughed endlessly at a video of an orangutan kissing and cuddling a kitten. She made you watch it seven times. Today, Maggie looks as though she has never laughed, and like she will never laugh again.

"Do you think it's from Graham?"

Maggie shrugs, a halfhearted, empty shrug, as if it takes too much energy even to lift and drop her shoulders.

"Come inside."

She waits as you twist the key in the lock, she follows you into the house. You feel the weight of her behind you, just standing there, as you squat to loosen your boots, then kick them off.

You hate Graham. That's all you can think, all you can feel. How much you hate him, even before you see what he's sent.

Turning, you hold your hand out for Maggie to give you the envelope. It's large, light brown with a little brass clasp. There's no stamp, or address; just her name, Maggie Williams, written in a blockish script.

"This was mailed to you?" you ask, handing it back to her.

"It was in my mailbox," Maggie says. "Hand delivered, I guess."

Imagining Graham pulling up to Maggie's mailbox and slipping the envelope inside feels like an extra level of violation.

Maggie follows you into the kitchen. She's still shivering, so you set the envelope on the table and start the kettle. Maggie watches as you spoon loose tea into the pot and pull cups from the cabinet. When the kettle screams, Maggie pulls her mittens from her hands and brings it to the table. She pours a stream of steaming water into the pot over the fragrant tea leaves. You clamp down the lid, she returns the kettle to the stove, and you slip a trivet beneath the pot. She and you move so smoothly in the kitchen, no words needed, a pas de deux, and you can feel her relaxing—not all the way, but it's a start, as you go through the familiar motions together.

Maggie brings the sugar bowl from the counter, then slips into her regular seat at the table. Thunder growls, deep and menacing. You pour tea, amber and steaming.

Sometimes it takes Maggie a while before she's ready to talk. You know this. After a few sips of tea, she pushes the envelope across to you.

With something like dread, you fold up the arms of the envelope's brass clasp and pull open the flap. There's a big, folded-up piece of paper inside, and as you pull it out you see it's riddled with rough little holes. Unfolded, it's a green-shaded woman dressed in shorts and a tank, pointing a handgun, and marked all over with numbers: an "8" on her forehead; a "7" on each of her breasts; a "10" on her stomach; a "6" on each hip. Her lips are tilted up in a smile. She is shattered by bullet holes. Scrawled across the top is one word: MAGGIE.

You trace your fingers across the front of the target. From this side, the edges of the holes are smooth; underneath, on the plain-white backside, they petal out, rough and jagged.

"We're calling Keisha," you decide, and you don't wait for Maggie to agree before you find your phone.

Keisha doesn't answer, but she texts right back. **Studying. Call later?**

You respond, **No. Come over now.**

A moment passes, no more, before she answers, **Okay.**

It is as if the downpour brings a flood of people: first Keisha joins you and Maggie. She listens as Maggie explains about the envelope, and you notice that she doesn't touch it—your prints, and Maggie's, too, are all over it, probably fucking up any prints Graham might have left—and she asks Maggie, "Do you still have that photo?"

Maggie shakes her head. "I threw it away that first day. I didn't want it in my house."

Keisha sighs, but she doesn't say anything else about it, just, "Maggie, I think we need to tell the police about this."

"About what?" It's Mémé, coming through the garage door into the kitchen, arms full of groceries.

"Hey, Sybil," Maggie says, and you all move to help Mémé with the bags.

"Maggie's stalker is rearing his head again," you tell Mémé. Maggie has told Mémé in general terms why she left school—the way the other students treated her, and that a boy was sort of tormenting her. She hasn't gone into specifics beyond this, probably seeing her relationship with Mémé as separate from all of that. But now, as Mémé stares down at the shooting target, unblinking, Maggie tells her story backward—the target, and before that, the picture, and before that, the condom, and all through, texts and calls from Graham, asking for a date, pushing for a date, angrily *demanding* a date.

"It was stupid of me not to save the photo," Maggie says, her fingers tracing the table's wood grain. "I just—I didn't want it in my house."

"Do your parents know about all this?" Mémé asks.

"I told them some of it," Maggie says, "a while ago. They knew I wasn't happy—that's why they let me do this semester as homeschool, because of all the gossip, because I was so stressed all the time. But I didn't tell them the specifics. I didn't want them to worry," she says. "And also—because it was just so *gross*. And I felt—I don't know, I guess I felt ashamed." And she's crying, and Mémé takes her in her arms, and you watch, helpless, as this person you have grown to love suffers, and there is nothing you can do.

When Maggie has calmed, Mémé says, "Maggie, we need to call your parents. You need to let them in. Let's not keep the secrets of bad men. What do you say?"

And Maggie nods, and pulls out her phone.

As you all wait for Maggie's parents, you put together a meal—reheated squash soup, arugula salad, fresh bread. By the time they arrive, it is full dark, and the rain has nearly stopped. You hear the doorbell and watch from the hallway as Maggie answers it.

Their names are Renée and Richard. They are dressed in suits, and they each have a straight crease, as if from worry, between their eyes. His hairline is receding; her hair is worn flattened against her head and pulled straight back into a low bun. When they see the shooting target on the kitchen table, Richard's eyes fill with tears, and Renée's hands tighten to fists.

Mémé insists everyone eats, and everyone insists they are not hungry, but still Mémé serves up bowls of soup and passes around the bread and salad, and everyone but Renée has something. Renée cannot stop pacing, her high-heeled shoes tapping an angry rhythm into the floor.

"Renée, honey, please," Richard says, but she ignores him.

They are divided about whether or not to call the police. Richard wants to; Renée is not so sure. "They'll find a way to say it's Maggie's fault. Maggie doesn't need that kind of help."

"There's one officer I know," Mémé offers. "Not well, but

well enough that I think we can at least count on him to listen. And I have his direct line."

At last, Renée nods. Mémé pulls a slip of paper from the drawer by the fridge, and she dials the phone hanging on the wall. You can see from where you sit that the paper has his first name—Alan—printed neatly in block letters—above the number.

He answers on the first ring. You can't hear his side of the conversation, but you hear the up and down of his voice— the warm, surprised tone with which he answers her call; the pivoting into receptive listening when she explains why she is calling; an abrupt goodbye, and then Mémé replaces the receiver on its hook.

"He's coming right over," Mémé says, and not twenty minutes pass before there is a knock on the door, and Officer Scott comes into the kitchen followed by a younger, female officer, the one from that day in the woods. Her badge reads VASQUEZ.

And everyone is gentle, and kind, and also angry with the heat of a thousand fires. Officer Scott takes the target as evidence, and Officer Vasquez writes down everything Maggie shares—it spills now like a fountain from her on this retelling, the envelope in her mailbox, the picture in her locker, the condom—and as she speaks, she chokes, and cries, and Officer Vasquez waits while Maggie's parents embrace her, their faces full of sorrow and rage in equal measure. Maggie tells them too about the texts she's been getting from Graham, and Keisha pulls up digital copies of the letters to the editor the school paper has printed, points out to the officers that the first letters of the words in the signatures spell *incel*.

"We take this sort of thing very seriously," Officer Vasquez tells Maggie and her parents.

"We're sorry this happened to you," Officer Scott says. "We promise we'll be on top of this."

Finally, they take their notes and the target, and they ask Maggie and her parents to come to the police station the next day to fill out a report.

Mémé walks the officers to the door; Officer Vasquez goes out first, but the other one—the cop with the crush—hangs back. He says something to Mémé. You strain to hear him, but the kitchen is still full, the atmosphere more relaxed now, with Maggie and her parents laughing at something Keisha has said.

It looks serious, though, whatever Officer Scott is telling Mémé, maybe something about Maggie and what's going on with her . . . or maybe not. Maybe they are talking about something else.

And then, they leave. First the officers, then Maggie and her parents, and then Keisha. After you've shut the door behind Keisha, you turn to Mémé. "That policeman," you begin.

"Mm-hmm," she says, and she pushes her thumb against her forehead, in the place Maggie has called "the third eye."

"What did he say to you before he left?"

"Oh, nothing, dearest, nothing. He just wanted to thank me for convincing Maggie to reach out. That's all."

Her hand returns to her side. She looks tired in a way you are not used to seeing. It unsettles you. Then she smiles, but she is far away. Leaning in, Mémé kisses you good night. You return her kisses, first on one cheek, and then the other.

"Des bisous de ma Bisou," she says, then turns for her room.

Then you are alone, and you look out the kitchen window, above the sink. The rain has stopped; the sky has cleared; the moon, waxing gibbous, spies down.

KEEP THE WOLF FROM THE DOOR

"What do you *mean* there's not enough evidence?"

"That's what they said. They were really nice about it, but that's what they said."

Maggie's voice sounds tinny and far away, even though she's sitting right next to you on the couch in her front room. Her arms are folded across her chest.

"What about the target?" You don't mean it to come out like an attack, like an accusation, but Maggie recoils from your words as if she's been struck.

"Babe," James says, his hand on your arm, "give her a minute. Let her talk."

You had been in James's car on the way home from school when Maggie had called, and instead of taking you home, James navigated the car here, to Maggie's house. Her parents aren't yet home from work, and Maggie pulled back the curtain of the window near the front door to see who was there before she let you in. There was another window that was peered through, another time. You blinked, and you saw your mother stroke the broken ridge of her nose. You blinked again, and she was gone.

"It's my own fault," Maggie says. "I threw away the condom and the picture. I should have kept them, they said."

"Jeez, Mags, who would have held on to a nasty used *condom*?" James wrinkles up his face. "I would have thrown it away, too."

Nine days. That's how much time has passed since Maggie appeared at your house with the shooting target, and in that time the police have collected her statement, visited Graham and his parents to hear what he had to say, referred the issue to the prosecutor, and have decided there isn't "enough cause" to move forward.

You have told James about the condom, and the photo, and the target. You have told him about the letters to the editor, and all the times Graham had pushed Maggie for a date since

Tucker died. You told him about incels, but he didn't need the term defined; he'd heard it already.

"Like that guy out in California, in Santa Barbara, who killed those girls and left behind, like, a manifesto," he said.

"It's not your *fault*, Maggie," you say. "It's *his* fault, for doing all that shitty stuff to you."

"I don't have the condom or the picture, and it turned out the target wasn't really shot at. The holes had graphite around the edges, not gunpowder."

"Like, from a pencil?" James asks.

She nods. "It *was* illegal to put the target in the mailbox, because only mail is supposed to go in the mailbox, so that's actually a federal crime, and the other things were against the law, too—but there's no proof that Graham did it, and none of the texts he sent were 'explicitly threatening,' they said, and Officer Vasquez said that there was no way the prosecutor could build a case. And she said that an officer would talk to Graham and his parents, but probably they'd 'lawyer up,' and until he did something—violent—there was nothing they could do."

"Officer Vasquez *said* that?"

She nods, miserable. "She corrected herself pretty fast. Said she'd meant to say 'unless,' not 'until,' but that doesn't make it that much better anyway, does it?" Maggie shrugs.

"Did they give you *any* helpful advice?" James asks.

"They said we can apply for a restraining order." Maggie dabs the corners of her eyes with the sleeve of her sweatshirt. "Oh, and they told us that maybe we should get a dog."

"Let *me* do something, Mags," James says. He is holding your hand, and you can tell by how tight he is squeezing it that he is white-hot mad. "Me and Big Mac can go over to his place and have words."

Maggie shakes her head, vehement. "No," she says. "I don't want you to do that."

"But Mags," James says, "it'll be okay. Just let me—"

Her mouth is a tight line, and she shakes her head again.

You can feel James ready to push, and you know his intentions are good. But you tell him, "James, she says no."

And he deflates a little, and leans back, and his grip on your hand grows softer. "I just can't believe we can't do anything," he says.

"You can keep being my friend," Maggie says.

"Of course, Mags," James says. "I'm just so sorry that you have to deal with this shit. I never knew . . ." He pauses, and you see a storm behind his eyes. "I'm sorry."

"They told her to get a dog," James says. You are back in his car. His eyes are on the road, but he grips the wheel tightly and shakes his head. "A fucking *dog*."

"Maggie doesn't need a dog," you tell James.

That night, just past ten, after Mémé has gone to bed, you pull out your mother's poems. You read her words again, and yours. Then you turn to the fourth poem. You take up your pen.

IV

Maybe people break things
Maybe that's the truth

But they make things, too

Promises
Bread
Friendships
Families
Love

I can break things
I can make things, too.

I stand
On two strong legs
I kill
With two strong hands

I bleed
From one strong womb
I wish
With one red heart
That you could see me now.

You read it over, then refold the stack of papers and tuck them safely away before you slip outside. The night is clear, and your eyes go straight to the bright full moon. You wander in the trees, waiting, even *hoping*, but there is nothing that needs you here, not tonight. All is well in the woods.

Then, you head to Maggie's house, wanting to see it safe and quiet and shuttered. And that is how you find it, each window dark, a sense of sleep scrimmed across it. She is safe, she is abed.

You could go home. You should, most likely. But you do not. Instead, you picture Graham and the things he has done, and you wonder—though not a wolf, how far off is he from one? Left alone, might he change with the next moon? Or the moon after that? Or five years down the road, when he has, perhaps, moved across the country, or across the world?

What turns someone from man to wolf? And might it be better, even, than slaying a wolf, to catch the boy before he changes? To catch him, perhaps, in the throat? With a claw?

These are dangerous thoughts. And yet, you think them.

You have picked up a slow jog, and then a lope, and then a flat-out run, hands cutting the air like knives, to Graham's house. You've made it your business to know where it is. Why do you run? Why do you run, when Keisha is safe in her bed, when the forest is still, when there is no need for running?

You run because you *want* it—the fight. The kill. The blood.

You stop. Breathe hard.

You are around the corner from Graham's house. The street is bathed in light from the streetlamps and light from the moon, the whole quiet scene glowing and beautiful. Your breath clouds out in puffs.

You *want* it. Whether Graham is a wolf, whether or not he will become one, you want his blood. That is something to consider.

Slowly, now, you walk in the direction of his house. You force your hands into pockets. You stand on the sidewalk, across the street. Though it's late, the windows are bright. There is movement in a front window—the kitchen.

You stand, and you watch the shadow figure in the window as it moves about the room. Fixing a snack, perhaps?

Your nails bite crescents into your palms.

The light goes out. The house is dark. And still, you stand, and you wait, and you watch, and you hope, until the sun begins to rise.

✦ ✦ ✦

Graham is at school the next day. Infuriatingly, there he is, as if he hasn't done *anything*. But he has, even if the police won't press charges, and you feel trapped and powerless and a hot ball of rage fills your throat as you watch him maneuver through the hallway toward his locker.

James is beside you, his hand on your shoulder, and he squeezes, and you know that he is angry, too, restraining himself only because Maggie has asked him to.

Graham is opening his locker, right there in the place you came across Maggie and Tucker, that long-ago day. You remember his hand up her skirt. You remember the look on her face. Shock? Shame? Fear?

And you remember what you did. You turned away.

A sickness spreads through you and you shiver with revulsion. You turned away.

Complicit. That is the word. You raise your hand to James's, resting on your shoulder. You squeeze it. And then you say, "I have to go find Keisha."

She is in the journalism room, sitting at a computer station. Today she is wearing her white frames, and behind them, her eyes stare, unblinking, at the screen. Her fingers hover above the keys as she reads something, then she types, hard and fast.

"Keisha." You weave through the computer stations and

hover over her. "The cops told Maggie there's nothing they can do."

"I know," Keisha says. She doesn't look up from her work.

"They told her to get a *dog*," you say.

"I know, Bisou," Keisha says.

You sit in the chair next to Keisha and lean in. "I went to his house last night," you whisper.

"Full moon," Keisha says, eyes still on her work.

You nod.

"They're not all wolves, you know," Keisha says.

"They all *could* be."

Finally, Keisha turns to you. "Is that really what you think?"

You picture James. His eyes. His hands. The way he looks at you. "No."

Keisha turns back to her work. "Not everything is up to you, Bisou. You're not alone. Maggie's not alone. Remember?"

She looks up, and the lenses of her glasses catch the light, and for a second, they flash, bright as the sun, bright as the moon.

And when the final class of the day is over, and you go out into the hallway, it is to find that Keisha is right.

There is one taped to every locker. SPECIAL EDITION, the front page reads, in extra-large print.

You peel a copy from the bank of lockers.

Incel-ence: An Unacceptable Idea That Deserves to Die
By Keisha Montgomery

If you're an observant reader of this paper—and I know you are—then you have no doubt noted letters we've published from a self-proclaimed incel, a boy who considers himself to be deprived of the sex he believes he is entitled to, and the response I wrote to one of those letters.

This idea is a dangerous virus. No one is entitled to anyone else's body. And I call this a virus because that's what it is: it is a sickness, and when a virus gets into a body, the body is endangered. The body can die.

And not only do we have an incel in our student body, we have among us girls who have been harmed by incel poison. I know one of them personally. She has been threatened and harassed by text and deed; I have seen evidence of this myself. I wouldn't share her name unless she gave her consent, which she has. She wants a voice in these halls, even though she no longer wants to be present here. Her name is Maggie Williams.

Several months ago, Maggie chose to take a break from our school, in part because she didn't feel safe here anymore. That is one effect of the virus.

And in her own words, this is what Maggie has to say:

"Graham Keller has been harassing me since September. He has sent me dozens of texts, even though I told him to stop. After someone put a used condom in my backpack and a picture of a penis and a knife in my locker, I decided I'd had enough and left school. Some of you probably think I'm weak for dropping out, but taking care of myself is the strongest thing I've ever done. I don't know for sure who left me those 'presents,' but I do know that Graham harassed me with unwanted pushy texts and inappropriate behavior, and I'll bet I'm not the only one. The cops say they can't help me, but we can help each other.

"When I was growing up, people taught me all the things I should do to avoid being harmed by men: No short shorts. No belly shirts. Stay with a group. Don't go out alone. Don't say anything if a guy catcalls on the street. Don't be too quiet. Don't be too loud.

"But are people telling guys how to not harm girls? It's one thing to tell a girl how not to get raped or harassed—is anyone telling the guys not to rape us or harass us?

"I'm tired of being quiet. I'm tired of keeping secrets. I'm tired of feeling ashamed for choices that other people make about me and for me. And I'm tired of being tired."

I, for one, am proud of Maggie for speaking up. And we don't have to stand by and watch this virus harm our student body. We don't. There are ways we can fight it, just as the scientific community has discovered ways to combat viruses that threaten human bodies.

Understanding is part of it. We need to understand what motivates and drives toxic masculinity.

We must be willing to look for it and call it out whenever it appears, whether it's presented as jokes or as something else.

And we must act. When we see it, we must protect those who are its victims. We must tell the boys who hold these ideas—the carriers of this virus—to stop. To go elsewhere. To work on healing and educating themselves.

This is how communities stay whole and safe. We all need each other. To see, to believe, to hold wrongdoers accountable. Women and girls are every bit as important and valuable as boys and men.

If you stand with Maggie, if you stand with girls and women, then let's stand up together. Incel thinking is a virus, but we don't have to let it spread.

Tomorrow, let's show the toxic minority how many of us stand against them. If you stand with Maggie, paint your nails BLACK. Let's show them our claws. And from this moment on—today, tomorrow, forever—let's be loud. Together.

You look up from the paper. All around, people are reading—students, teachers. Principal Evans comes out of the administration office, a copy in his hand. He looks around, as if searching for someone—Keisha, most likely—and then heads off at a fast walk in the direction of the journalism room.

You pull your phone from the back pocket of your jeans and send her a text. **Evans is looking for you. Are you going to get in trouble?**

She texts back. **I'm waiting for him in the journalism room. We shall see.**

Next, you text Maggie. Just three words. **I love you.**

A moment later, she texts back. **I love you too.**

That evening, after supper, Maggie and Keisha come over. Together with Mémé, you sit at the kitchen table. You soak your hands in warm soapy water. You push back cuticles. You file and buff. And you take turns painting one another's nails with polish from the same pot. Black.

"So, what happened with the principal?" you ask Keisha, who has clipped her nails short and square. She's stopped biting them, you notice suddenly.

"Principal Evans asked us to go to his office—Ms. Kang went with me—and he didn't sound *angry*, exactly, just worried. He said Graham Keller could have a defamation case, if he or his parents want to get litigious. Ms. Kang pointed out how I had receipts for everything we'd printed. Graham did send those texts, after all, and neither Maggie nor I said he was the one who did those other things, the things we can't prove, but Principal Evans said that we *implied* it, even if we didn't say it outright. And he's not wrong. But I stand by everything I wrote, and Ms. Kang said she'd stand with me. Changes don't get made without people taking risks." She sets down the nail polish. "In the middle of it, Graham's dad showed up all loud and aggressive, and even though Principal Evans's assistant told him the principal was busy, he just burst in like a closed door didn't mean a thing to him."

"What did he say?" Maggie asks. She is holding Mémé's hand and painting her nails, long even strokes of black.

"He saw me sitting there and he asked if I was the trouble-maker who was spreading lies about his son. 'They aren't lies,' I told him, and he said that the police had been satisfied that there was no case, so I was slandering his son. I tried to explain that slander is spoken, that when it's put in print it's called libel, and that it has to be false in order to be considered either one, and anyway it would be up to *them* to prove that what I'd written wasn't true, but he cut me off and said to Principal Evans, 'Even if he *did* pull a couple of silly pranks—and I'm not saying he did, but just for the sake of argument—even if he did, what's the real harm?'"

Mémé's jaw clenches, but her fingers, in Maggie's hand, stay soft.

"Then he said—sorry, Maggie—he said, like, 'It's not like the girl was some prize scholar to begin with, there's no rea-son my boy, who has a solid future, should have his whole life thrown off track just because he has a sense of humor, not that he did those things anyway.'"

"Wow. Sounds like we know where Graham gets it, huh?" says Maggie. Her tone is light, but her expression is strained—brows knit, as if to hold in tears.

"Anyway," Keisha continues, "Principal Evans kind of puffed up after that. He said that you had the right to a safe learning environment, and that the school should have done a better job of protecting you. And that even though they hadn't been paying enough attention *before*, they were now. And that I was totally within my legal rights with my editorial, even if my approach could have been 'less confrontational.'" Here, Keisha rolls her eyes. "Whatever," she says.

Maggie has finished Mémé's last nail, and Mémé holds her hand out to admire them. "Look how pretty," she murmurs. She blows on her nails. When they are dry, she taps them on the table—one two three four, one two three four.

"When I was a girl," Mémé says, "we didn't have the language your generation has. In many ways, the world was a different place. In some ways, it's the same as it's always been. But you girls, you are changing it."

Maggie, Keisha, Mémé. You love them so much that you feel you might break. What a risk it is, loving.

I will do anything, you vow, *anything to keep them safe.*

The next day at school, fingers everywhere are tipped with black. Girls on the bus. Girls in the hallway.

"Bisou," James calls, when he sees you near the doorway to first period. He's standing with Caleb, Landon, and Big Mac. And though they've done a terrible job of it, each of them has black-painted nails.

James grins, that tender sweet smile you love.

It's not enough, all these black nails. The polish will chip, the moment will fade. But it's something, and there can be more somethings, a sea of somethings. For now, for this moment, you go to James, you tilt back your head, and you kiss.

You are right that the nail polish chips. But you are wrong about the moment fading. If anything, over the next few weeks, it grows, it spreads, it waxes like the moon, shining light into dark corners.

In whispered circles, in shared glances, and on the wall in the bathroom, in black ink, girls begin to share.

Graham texted me for six months last year and only stopped when my brother threatened to beat him up.

I never told but Tucker cornered me at a party once and showed me his dick.

When I was a kid, my gymnastics coach kept touching my chest. I finally quit the team.

When I was little, you write, *my father murdered my mother.*

Then you say it out loud, to James. He sits with you in the front seat of his car. He holds your hands, and listens.

"I don't know why I never told you," you say. "It felt like a secret I was supposed to keep."

James pulls you close. The soft flannel of his shirt brushes your cheek. "It's okay," he says into your hair, and his intentions are good, his intentions are so very good. But it's not okay, it's never going to be okay. Some things can't be fixed. Some wounds won't heal. That is the truth.

But *this* is okay, sitting here with James, together. You can't share everything with him—not now, maybe not ever, not because you can't trust him but because you want to keep him safe.

Then, you tell him about all the things the girls are writing in the bathroom in black ink. And James says that guys are talking, too. Or they're starting to. "One of the seniors was talking in the locker room, and he kinda broke down, told us about this time he had sex with a girl at a party, a girl who was really drunk. Too drunk, probably."

A whole world exists in those three words—*too drunk, probably.*

Incels. Gymnastic coaches grabbing little girls. Wolves in the woods. "What is wrong with people?" you say.

"Something," James says. "I don't know. Something."

N'OUBLIE PAS

Just for an hour, you tell yourself as you gently close your front door and jog into the misty velvet darkness. It's a Saturday morning, after midnight, and sleep has evaded you. Mémé won't even notice you've been gone, you promise yourself as you jog out of your neighborhood and toward James's. And, you remind yourself, you left a note on your pillow, just in case she pokes her head into your room. You slip around the side of his house and maneuver between the thorny bushes beneath his window to tap against the glass. She won't even worry.

And then he pushes aside the curtain, and he sees you there, and he grins and lifts the sash, and he leans out the window and helps you climb through, into his room. He's dressed in loose pajama bottoms, and his chest is warm when he pulls you against it, and quietly, quietly, almost silently, the two of you strip naked and slip together into his narrow single bed, him behind you, his arm beneath your head. You feel him shift to open his bedside table and you hear him rustle around, find a condom and tear it open, and his hand slips between you to unroll it before the two of you fit together, his breath in your hair, his blankets up to your chins, and you move together, together, together, until you shiver with pleasure and his breath catches, his hips tighten, and he moans into your hair.

"Shh," you whisper. "Shh."

He moves to take off the condom, and then you lie there together in his bed. Your eyes close. His body fits against the back of yours, chest on your back, hips pressed against your butt, legs bent to nestle just exactly against yours. Your feet are on his feet. His arms wrap around you and his breath slows, deepens, and you lie there, just like that, perfectly held and perfectly safe, and you listen to the rain starting to fall,

He falls asleep. You are tired now, too, and you feel sleep pulling at you like an undertow, but you do not want to be asleep. You want to be awake, surrounded by James's arms, tucked into his bed. You want to feel everything.

And you do. You stay right there and feel everything—James's body, his soft sheets, the press of the blankets. You feel his heart, beating against your back. You feel each of his fingers, woven through yours. You feel him loving you, even in sleep.

Did Mémé feel this way in Garland's arms? You hope so. You hope she felt this way—this exact way. You hope she will again.

And your mother. Did she ever experience this? Did she ever feel safe, and secure, and loved? Nothing in the scraps she's left for you, nothing in her poems, or in your memories, would indicate that she did. Imagine that. A whole life lived, too short, and without this.

You hope you are wrong. You hope your mother did not die without this. You hope she had other parts to her life than the moments you remember.

You breathe in deeply, until your chest is full, and you hold that breath as tight and as long as you can. At last, you let it go.

James breathes heavy into the hair at the nape of your neck. His arms tighten, as if he is holding you in his dream. You wish you could meet him there, in a dream, you wish you could tell him the whole truth of you in the liminal dream-space of sleep. And, perhaps, in real life, too.

Will you one day? You wonder.

And then you must fall asleep, because you wake with a jolt to the loud voices of James's sisters in the hallway outside his bedroom door, arguing about who gets to use the bathroom first, and for how long.

Your eyes open. It's just past seven, his clock reads. You kiss James's hands, crossed around your body, and you climb from that warm perfect nest. You pull on clothes, you tighten boots, you zip your red sweatshirt and turn up its hood against the rain.

"Were you going to leave without saying goodbye?" James's voice is sleepy, and when you turn to him, you see that he's rolled over and he's watching you, his head propped up on his arm.

You go to him in his bed. You kneel beside it and you kiss him, slowly, on his warm full lips.

Then you stand and go to the window. You push it open; a cold wet wind blows inside.

And you say, "Goodbye."

Before you step through the door, you know that something is different. The house lacks something—the particular energy of Mémé's presence. You sit on the mud bench to unlace your boots, then go to the kitchen. There, you find a single sheet of Mémé's stationery, gilded with an *S* at the top, on the table. She has weighted it with the saltshaker.

Bisou, dear one,

Something has come up. It is nothing to concern you. Simply a problem to which I must attend. I will be gone for a few days, no more than a week. Please, my darling, stay put. Invite your friends to keep you company, maybe see about rearranging the pantry while I'm away. It's been years since it had a good scrubbing!

There is money for groceries in the tin by the sink; be a good girl and finish the bread, won't you? The leaven is in the bowl and should be ready for flour and water by the time you are home.

N'oublie pas, dear one. Maggie loves fresh bread and will be so disappointed if you don't finish what I've started.

With love,

M

You read the note slowly. *Don't forget*, she says. The opposite of what your mother wanted from you, all those years ago: n'oublie pas d'oublier.

In all the years you have lived with Mémé, she has never left you. Never. What could have happened to call her away now?

Nothing good.

You imagine her peeking into your room, looking for you.

And finding your empty bed. Your stomach turns as you pull your phone from your pocket. There is no answer—it doesn't even ring before Mémé's voice speaks to you—"I am unable to take your call. Please leave a message." There is the tone, and then blankness, nothingness. It takes you a moment to find your voice.

"Mémé?" You feel your throat tighten, you feel the sting of tears. "Where are you? Where did you go?"

There is no answer, of course, but still, you hesitate to disconnect. This tenuous connection is all you have right now. At last, though, you press End.

You open the garage door. Her car is gone.

Then you send a text to Keisha—**Call me. I need you.**

She doesn't respond; she must still be asleep. It's Saturday morning, after all.

You wander through the empty house in stockinged feet. You run your hand along the mantel, you flick on the table lamp near the couch, then flick it off again. You sit on the couch, and then lie down, and cover your eyes with your arm.

You listen to the ticking of the clock. Minutes later—hours later—you wake with a gasp, your heart clenching and pounding. The quality of light has shifted; it's midmorning now, and you are still alone. You check your phone, but Keisha still hasn't texted back. You feel heavy and awkward from the strange, broken sleep and the strangeness of Mémé's absence, and you make your way to the kitchen for a cup of tea. There, on the table, is the blue ceramic bowl Mémé uses to rise bread, draped in the blue checked cloth. You stare at it stupidly.

N'oublie pas, dear one, her note had read. *Maggie loves fresh bread and will be so disappointed if you don't finish what I've started.*

You pull away the cloth and look at the shiny damp mixture.

Thunder rolls, and the kitchen darkens with gathering clouds.

You lower yourself into a chair and stare at the leaven. The storm gathers outside, and inside, within the walls of your own body, something is gathering, as well. Pinpricks of fear; a constellation of awareness; an answer to a question unasked, just out of your reach. You sit very still, waiting for the answer to come.

But a knock at the kitchen door scatters the constellation, the cursory knock of someone who knows she's welcome any-time, and then the handle turns, and the door pushes open.

It's Maggie, holding a basket, her cheeks red from the cold, and shaking raindrops from her hair.

"Wow, it's getting wild out there!" She's smiling until she sees you sitting at the table, until she sees your face, and then her expression shifts, too, her smile dropping away. "Bisou, are you okay?"

"I don't know," you say, more to yourself than Maggie. "Mémé is gone."

"Gone? What do you mean?" She sets her basket on the table. "Where did she go?"

You open your mouth, but nothing comes out. What can you tell Maggie, without telling her everything?

She asks, "Does this have something to do with your mom?"

"My mother?"

She nods. "It's just—well, I wasn't sure if I should say anything, and maybe you weren't even aware, but this week, this full moon that's coming is going to be an eclipse—a blood moon. And I remembered how you told me about when your mom died, how it happened during a blood moon . . . so I did a chart, see?"

Out of the basket comes a square folded piece of paper, which Maggie spreads flat. It's a circle, rimmed with symbols and crossed over with lines in a rainbow of colors, all of it annotated in Maggie's neat script.

She continues, "So it turns out that this coming moon is the first blood moon in Virgo since the year your mother died. And I thought, I don't know, I thought maybe the energy with that might be kind of hard on you, you know? So here, look . . . ," and Maggie pulls more things from her basket. "I brought you this crystal for clarity, and here, I brought this stone for stillness, and this sage, for clearing. I thought maybe we could get together, the four of us, and we could do a ceremony, you know, to honor your mom? And to ward off anything dark that might come with the Virgo blood moon. Since, you know,

Virgo is a truth teller, and this blood moon that's coming, people say it's a time that will force us to do our shadow work, you know, and deal with truths, even the uncomfortable ones. And, Bisou, I know you don't really believe in astrology like I do, but I figured, it can't hurt, right?"

"A blood moon." Your voice sounds like you are speaking from very far away, from through a tunnel, and you remember your mother sitting by the window, stroking the bump on the bridge of her nose and saying, "Look, Bisou, it's the blood moon."

You remember your mother, minutes later, when twin full moons—headlights—filled the front room. The way she looked at you with unveiled fear. The way she said, "Hide."

"But now," Maggie says, "Sybil isn't here? Where did she go, Bisou?"

You sit very still at the table, eyes closed, feeling as if a memory is just out of your reach, as if life depends on your grasping it.

But it doesn't come; the taste of it fades from the back of your tongue.

You open your eyes. Maggie's hair sparkles with raindrops, her beautiful face slightly quizzical, like she's working out a problem. There on the table is the chart, and the stone, and the crystal, and the sage, all gifts for you, from your wonderful friend.

"Maggie," you say, just that word, just her name.

Secrets, secrets, everyone has secrets. Mémé kept her full-moon life a secret from you for a dozen years. Tucker hid his sexual past from Maggie; Phillip never told the truth about what happened with Cara Lee, or the girl at Berkeley. James is keeping your secret about what happened in the back of his car, and how you ran away from him, through the woods. You're not telling him what happened after you left.

Your mother didn't tell anyone what your father did to her; she ran and hid, with just four-year-old you and no one else. And now your grandmother has let a secret carry her away. A dangerous secret, you are sure of it, and one she shouldn't keep from you.

Maggie once said, *I'm getting pretty tired of keeping secrets.* And she was brave, braver than you, brave enough to say her secrets out loud.

Maggie is your friend, and you want no secrets between you. You are full to the brim with secrets, and now they spill. "Maggie," you begin, "there's something I need to tell you."

She lowers herself into her seat at the table, and her face is open, and she listens.

You hold nothing back—you start at the beginning, with homecoming night, with the way it felt when James put his mouth on you, how good it felt, and Maggie nods like she knows.

You tell her about the full moon and how James looked up from between your legs. When you tell her about the blood on his chin—*your* blood—Maggie gasps a little and brings her hand up to her mouth, and then she pulls you into a hug and squeezes you, rocks you side to side.

You tell her about running away from James. You tell her about the wolf. And then you tell her who the wolf was—that the wolf was Tucker, and Tucker was the wolf.

Her eyes grow as wide and round as moons.

"Oh," she says.

You tell her about Phillip, and Keisha. You tell her how Mémé cleaned the car and burned your clothes. You tell her Mémé's story, too, almost all of it, all the way from the beginning, up to when she came to you that morning to find you in your mother's bloody bed. The broken window.

"A wolf killed your mom," Maggie says, her voice breathy. "Bisou, was your *father* a wolf?"

You nod. "Mémé wanted to kill him. She fought with him, she cut his face, but he ran, and he got away. Then she brought me here, and she's taken care of me all this time. She's kept our woods safe." You feel better telling Maggie all of this, opening up to her. "I'm so glad you know now, Maggie," you say. "I'm so glad you're here, and that we're friends, and that we have each other."

You pick up the stone that Maggie has brought, and as you rub your thumb across it, you think of stones, skipping stones, you think of you and your mother standing by the edge of the pond as she showed you how to curl one finger over the top of the stone, how to bring back your arm, how to flick your wrist, and how to let go. "More stones when the ice thaws," she had promised, but for your mother the ice never thawed.

Your phone vibrates. It's a text from Keisha, at last—**I'm on my way**—and you and Maggie sit together, the stone between you, and you wait.

When Keisha arrives, backpack slung across her shoulder, she finds you and Maggie still sitting at the kitchen table. Her expression is wary. "Hey, Maggie," she says. "I didn't know you would be here."

"No more secrets," you say. "Not between us."

There is a pause before Keisha nods, but she does nod.

"I think I have a problem," you tell her. "I think Mémé needs my help."

"If *you* have a problem," says Keisha, sliding into her seat at the table, "then *we* have a problem."

"And if Sybil needs *your* help," says Maggie, "she needs *our* help."

You take a deep breath. "Okay," you say, and your voice is stronger now. "Listen."

And you tell them how you came home this morning to find Mémé disappeared, which she has never done, leaving you like that. You show them the note that she left behind.

Even before you've finished, Keisha is on her feet, pulling open drawers, looking for something. Anything that could tell her something about where Mémé could have gone.

"Have you looked in her room? Have you checked her computer?"

"No," you say. It hasn't occurred to you to do this.

Keisha must read your distaste in your expression; "There's no time to worry about that," she says. "Maggie, you go through the kitchen. I'll do her office. Bisou, you look through her bedroom. Okay?"

Mémé's room feels as though she has just stepped out for a moment. You stand outside its door, hand on the doorframe. Her bed is neatly made. The drawers to her highboy and bedside table are pushed all the way in. There is no disorder, no suggestion that she might have left in a hurry. You cross the threshold.

The first place you search is in the table next to the bed. Nothing looks amiss—but then you realize that the envelope of cash is gone. Maybe she's put that money in the tin for your groceries, but you'll bet she didn't leave it all. If she doesn't want a record of where she was going, Mémé wouldn't want to use her credit card.

You take apart each drawer, you search through the closet, you put your hand in every pocket.

Nothing.

In Mémé's office, Keisha is going through the filing cabinet, setting aside each folder as she finishes it. "Your grandmother is an incredibly organized woman." Her voice is both grim and full of admiration. "Not much of a paper trail here."

Maggie crashes into the room. "I found her phone," she says, triumphant. "It was in this old breadmaking machine, tucked way in the back of a cabinet."

You'd given Mémé the machine a few years ago for Christmas, thinking it would make her baking easier, but she'd never used it. You'd assumed she'd returned it.

Maggie hands you the phone. You power it on. It asks for a pass code.

"Any ideas?" Keisha asks.

You shake your head. But then you type 020181.

The phone opens.

"My mother's birthday," you say.

Keisha takes the phone, clicks on every icon—messages, mail, notes. Nothing unusual. The most recent texts are all from Maggie. "Sometimes I send her funny videos," Maggie says.

It's a dead end.

"That's it, then." Your knees feel like rubber, and you slide down to the floor.

"I have one more idea," Keisha says, "but we'll have to wipe her phone and restore it. Bisou, does your grandmother back up her phone?"

"She doesn't know how to do anything with that thing," you

say. "But if they helped her set up a backup when she bought it, there's no way she would have switched the settings."

"Okay," says Keisha, thumbing through Mémé's settings and tapping on *Erase All Content and Settings*. "Fingers crossed."

The screen goes blank. She powers the phone back on and begins the setup process. She lets out a held breath when she sees the *Restore from Backup* option. "It was last backed up this morning." She looks up, smiles. "Maybe we'll find something."

You wait together as the phone restores. When it's finished, Keisha clicks on the message icon; this time, there's a conversation above the one from Maggie, from a number you don't recognize. The bottom message, in a blue text bubble, was sent by Mémé at 5:02 a.m.—**By the light of the moon**, it reads.

"Let's start at the beginning," Keisha says, and you are so grateful for her steady voice, her organized way of thinking. You're grateful, too, for Maggie's arm, which she has wrapped around your waist, the way she's pulled you close.

Keisha scrolls to the beginning of the conversation.

It's an old photo. It is you, a small child clutching a blanket; you are on the lap of a young woman whose nose has not yet been broken. Only one person could have sent this picture.

Your father.

"Mama," you say, a word you haven't uttered in many years.

The next message is a response from Mémé: **Who is this?**

The answer: **You know who I am.**

All of these messages have been sent between the hours of three and five a.m. this morning.

"How could he have gotten her number?" you wonder.

"If someone has money, nothing is private anymore," Keisha says. She scrolls to the next message.

What do you want? Mémé has replied.

You.

"It's not your fault, Bisou." Keisha looks up at you, and her expression—is it pity? "You didn't know."

"*What's* not my fault? I didn't *do* anything!" But then you realize that yes, you did. You left two naked, dead boys in the woods. Two wolves. "No," you whisper, but the word is useless against the truth.

Your father, the one wolf that Mémé has fought but hasn't killed, has seen the reports of the bodies. He has put it together, that those naked corpses mean a hunter is nearby. And now he's found her.

"He thinks Mémé is still the hunter."

Keisha nods. "She fought him all those years ago. She scarred his face. And he's angry."

Mémé's next message reads, **Where last we met, I will find you again.**

Then the final message, read this morning at 5:02 a.m. You were asleep in James's arms.

By the light of the moon.

The moon will be full on Monday night. You have sixty hours.

A wave of calm washes over you. It's clear, suddenly, what you need to do. This is better, knowing. And acting on that knowledge. "Keisha," you say, "I need to borrow your car."

She's reading through the messages again. Without looking away from the phone, she says, "You can't do it alone. I'll go with you."

"I'm coming, too," says Maggie.

Part of you wants to refuse them, but Keisha is right; it's too far for one person to drive alone, without taking breaks for sleep, and only two nights separate you from the next full moon. You need them.

Keisha says, "Together, we're better than apart. Sybil said so, remember? We need to go together." She powers down the phone.

"She said it," you say. "But she didn't mean it. Not for herself, anyway."

"She meant it," Maggie says. "Just, not more than she means to protect you, no matter what." Then she turns to Keisha and says, "Keisha, will your car even make it that far? I mean, it's kind of a piece of shit."

In the kitchen, the leaven rests quietly. You carry it to the trash, where you turn the bowl upside down, shake it firmly, and watch as the leaven, which will never become bread, slips from the bowl and lands with a *plop* in the bin.

Maggie has no money, but in addition to the crystal and the stone, she's brought snacks—pistachios and almonds, some cookies, apples and grapes. To her basket, she adds bottles of water and more fruit from the fridge, then drapes the basket with Mémé's blue checked cloth. You take the grocery money from the tin where Mémé has left it, and you put it and all your saved cash into your wallet. You'll follow Mémé's lead and not use your debit card on the road. Keisha has sixty bucks, not a lot, but together, you have enough to pay for gas.

Keisha goes outside to check her car's fluids, adding half a pint of oil from the garage, and takes a quick trip for gas and also to fill the air in her spare tire.

You are itchy and nervous to get going. Every minute that passes closes the distance between Mémé and the full moon. While Maggie packs the basket and Keisha preps the car, you go to your room to gather your warmest layers, for you and for your friends. As you head back out, you see the stack of your mother's poems where you've left them on your nightstand. There's only one left unanswered, the shortest, the final poem. You read it:

V

who's afraid of the big bad wolf

i am afraid

of everything

Pressing your pen into the paper so firmly that it nearly tears, you answer, speaking the words as you scrawl.

Y

Who's afraid of the big bad wolf?

Not me.

Fuck the wolf.

By the time the car is loaded and ready, Maggie folding into the back seat with the basket of snacks, the clouds have thickened to obscure the sun and the growl of the thunder seems a threatening omen.

It is dark, the sky, dark enough even at midday that Keisha pulls on the headlights. They are waiting for you in the car,

Maggie and Keisha, and you take out your keys to lock the front door, standing for a moment on the porch of the home that has sheltered you for the past dozen years, the home and hearth where you have lived with your grandmother, warm and dry and safe from wolves and from memory.

As you stand on the porch, the clouds can hold the rain no longer and it pours down, and you remember, suddenly, the first time you stood in this spot. You were small. Were you frozen? You felt frozen. You could not feel your face, or your hands, or your feet. But that was all right, that was better, because you also could not feel your fear anymore.

It was raining that day—heavy, loud sheets of rain, and Mémé had bundled you in her arms as she ran with you from the taxi to the porch. Then she had set you down as she found her keys, and you watched her pull them from her bag and fit one into the door.

She pushed open the door and turned to you. "It's all right," she had said. "We're home. You are safe here, and you will always be safe. Come inside."

You remember looking through the pushed-open door into the front hallway—the bench with shoes tucked beneath; the long floral rug, extended like a tongue down the shining wood floor; the light up above. Everything clean, everything neat.

You had turned to look back at the street, sleek with rain. The taxi had gone away, and the road was empty. You squinted your eyes and scanned the rain, looking for your mother, who you knew was not there. You tried to remember her face, but you remembered instead her shadowed silhouette as she watched out the window, the way her finger traced a line down the bridge of her nose. You blinked and remembered blood. You blinked again, and you remembered your mother's warm hand upon your own, down by the pond before it froze.

Then you had turned back to the doorway, where Mémé stood waiting for you. And you had gone inside.

So many things are the same, between that day and this. The same porch. The same rain. On the other side of the door, the same bench, and the same rug.

But on this side of the door, things are not the same as they once were.

You are not numb. You feel your hands, fingertips cold. You feel your face. You feel your fear for Mémé—pulsing like a heartbeat, strong and steady.

You are no longer a powerless child.

And you are not alone.

Keisha honks her horn, two short, quick blasts, and you turn the key in the lock.

You tuck your sickle moon into your shirt, you turn up your hood, and you sprint from the porch, away from the house, and through the rain.

OVER THE RIVER AND THROUGH
THE WOODS

"Shit."

You've almost made it to the freeway when Keisha looks into the rearview mirror at the red flashing lights behind her.

She uses her blinker and pulls the Bug to the side of the road. You glance into the back seat, at Maggie, whose eyes are wide and round. Then you look behind her, through the small rear window, at the police cruiser. You watch as the driver's side door pushes open, as a large man ducks out of the car, as he stands.

It's Alan Scott.

Keisha cranks down her window, and frigid wind blows in.

He crouches, hands on his knees, to peer into the car. "Bisou," he says. "We seem to keep running into each other."

"Is something wrong, officer?" Keisha's "adult" game is on point. She has both hands on the wheel, and her voice is low and even.

"Just a taillight." His eyes flick to the back seat. "Hi there, Maggie," he says. "I'm real sorry we weren't able to do anything about that boy. But I want you to know we'll be keeping an eye on him, okay?"

Maggie nods, silent. He does *seem* sorry—sincerely.

Officer Scott's eyes flick around the interior of Keisha's car. "As long as I've got you here," he says, "I wonder if you might be able to clear something up for me. A car like this one was seen on Halloween night, not far from where the Tang boy was found dead. You didn't happen to be parked at the arboretum, did you?"

Maybe he doesn't notice how Keisha's hands tighten on the steering wheel, how there's a pause just a second too long before she says, "Yes, actually, my car had a flat. I pulled over, and then a friend followed me the rest of the way into town, just to make sure I could make it."

"Mm-hmm," the cop answers. "Bisou, I don't suppose *you* were the helpful motorist, by any chance?"

"Yes." Your tongue feels thick in your mouth. "I was."

His face looks troubled, like he's wrestling with something. Rain pours down from the bill of his plastic-covered police hat. He looks carefully at each of you in turn—Keisha, then Maggie, and then you. Finally, he says, "Where are you girls headed?"

You don't have to tell him. You don't owe him anything. But you remember the way he looked at Mémé, and you think of how sorry he looked just now, about the situation with Graham, and you say, "We're going to help my grandmother with something."

"Is that right?"

Behind you, in the back seat, Maggie shifts uncomfortably. In the driver's seat, hands still on the wheel, Keisha waits, too.

"You know," Officer Scott says, "I've lived nearly all my life in this region. My parents moved our family—me and my older sister, Laura—out this way from Alabama when I was a little kid. She was the first person in our family to go to college. And just a few months later, she was murdered." His eyes cloud with memory. "Killed in the woods not far from her dorm room," he says, his voice soft now, and all three of you are leaning toward the window to hear his words. "They brought me and my folks into the station the night she was killed. There was a girl there, a young woman, covered in blood. Laura's blood, it turns out." He shakes his head, clears his throat. "Has your grandmother ever told you about Laura?"

You sit still for a long moment, and then you nod.

As if encouraged by your gesture, he continues. "Your grandmother told the officers that a wolf had killed my sister."

He pauses here, as if he's waiting for you to say something. You don't answer, but you hold his gaze, and it seems that each of you understands the other.

"Later, a man died in those same woods. I remember reading about it in the paper. His name was Dennis Cartwright. His killer was never found. I knew Dennis. Laura dated him on and off through high school. Can't say I was sorry to see him go." A muscle twitches in Officer Scott's face. "Not a good guy." Another moment passes, and he is looking right into your eyes.

He straightens. "Get that taillight fixed," he says, and he taps the top of the car once, twice, and then he walks away.

Keisha waits until his squad car has disappeared before she turns to you. Her voice trembles as she speaks. "That was . . . intense."

"Do you think he knows about Sybil?" Maggie says. "I think he does."

You remember the way he looked at you that day in the trees. Had he been assessing you? Is that why he came to your house that day? Has he known all this time about Mémé? Has he been quietly ignoring her wolf hunting—maybe even helping to cover it up?

"Let's go," you say.

Keisha restarts the engine, looks over her shoulder for traffic, and drives.

It is in Minnesota that the rain turns to sleet. It is wet and sticks to the wipers, a slushy thick mess. You have driven across four states; you have refilled the tank many times. You have wondered a thousand times how Mémé could do this—how she could leave you, after all her talk of togetherness, all her talk of being glad that you have friends, that you aren't alone.

There are no answers—just questions. How could she decide to do this on her own, when she's no longer the hunter? What makes her think she *can* do it, and how could she expect you to go on, if she fails?

You have eaten all the food in Keisha's basket, refilled it, and worked your way through most of it again. You have driven for more than twenty-four hours due east without stopping except to pee, gas up, and buy supplies. At the last stop, near the North Dakota/Minnesota border, you buy tampons along with candy bars and a bag of pistachios.

After you make your purchases and use the bathroom, the three of you stand close together beneath the overhang of the convenience store attached to the gas station, stretching. It is desperately cold, but it feels good to breathe fresh air and to be outside after all the hours cramped in Keisha's tight Bug.

Maggie folds herself in half, bouncing a little as she flattens her hands on the damp concrete. You hear her phone ping from inside her pocket, but she ignores it. Her parents have texted her twice since yesterday afternoon; Maggie and Keisha both told their parents they were staying at your house for a few days while your grandmother left town to see a sick relative, and as long as they have been answering texts, so far no one has seemed too concerned.

"I'll text her when we're back on the road," Maggie says.

Keisha folds her left arm across her chest, and then her right.

"What's the matter?" you ask.

Keisha shakes her head. "I can't believe I didn't think of it before."

"What? You didn't think of what?"

She doesn't answer, just breaks into a run and heads through the sleet to her car, slipping a little but catching herself before she falls. The tank is full, and she puts away the nozzle, twists shut the gas tank, and pulls her car around to the overhang where you and Maggie wait for her.

"We'd better go sit down and talk," she says.

And then you know what she can't believe she didn't think

of before. It didn't occur to you, either. You have been so focused on getting to the farmhouse, on getting to Mémé, on *her* limitations, that you didn't think about your own.

The border crossing.

"We are all minors," you say.

"Yep," Keisha answers.

"Shit," Maggie says.

You drive a short distance to a coffee shop. You and Maggie order three cups of coffee and you sweeten them with cream and sugar while Keisha brings up a map on her phone, tracing her finger along the US/Canadian border.

You hand her a cup of coffee and the three of you sit around a table. You and Maggie wait for Keisha to finish studying the map. She sips her coffee, sighs, and looks up at last.

"Bisou, where exactly is your family's farm?"

You scoot around so that you're looking at the map from the same perspective as Keisha. "It's north of Champlain, New York, just across the border. Here." You point to a spot on the map, just west of Vermont.

"Okay," Keisha says. "This is what we have to do."

The new route will take an just an hour longer in the car. You'll skirt underneath the Great Lakes, staying in the States, then head northeast up the shore of Lake Erie. You'll traverse upstate New York. You'll find a place, as close to the border as possible, to ditch the car. You'll cross, staying in trees as much as you can, hoping no one sees you and calls the police on the US side or the Mounties on Canada's side of the invisible line that divides the trees into separate countries. You'll hope your cell phones still have reception and you'll use GPS to navigate by foot to the old blue farmhouse, the place with the room of ghosts, the place you last saw your mother, in a bed of blood. You'll be racing the moon's rise. Once on foot, you'll have to be fast. And you'll have to be lucky.

Keisha takes a screenshot of the map, her face unreadable.

"You guys don't have to cross with me," you say, though you don't want to go alone. "You can just take me to the border and wait for me there."

Keisha shakes her head.

"Over the river and through the woods . . . ," says Maggie, and she reaches over to take your hand, squeezes it.

The sun is already setting when, on Monday, Keisha navigates her Bug to the dead end of Glass Road. Your cycle has begun, and when you climb out of the car, you are not stiff or sore though you have been sitting for hours, your eyes are not tired though you have not slept.

You feel a buzz of pent-up energy, a calibration of your body to its environment. You smell the air, turn up your face to the sky.

It's maybe thirty-three degrees. Snow and slush crunch

beneath your feet. Night is coming; though the sky is awash in orange and purple and pink, in less than an hour the only light will be from a full moon.

Keisha locks the car; Maggie bends to retie her laces. You scan the tree line to the north. Over there, in those trees and beyond, is Canada, and your grandmother, and the wolf.

"Are you guys ready?"

"Yep," says Keisha.

"Let's go," says Maggie.

There's a big white house near the end of Glass Road, and maybe this will be the only piece of luck you get, but it's a good piece—no one seems to be home. The windows are dark, and only the blackened eyes of the house witness the three of you duck between the horizontal slats of the fence and cut across the grassy field.

With each step you take toward the Canadian border, the sky grows darker. There's a rustling in the grass that makes Maggie suck in her breath and jump closer to you, but you don't flinch.

"It's just a groundhog," you tell her, and then you spy it. "There."

Maggie's gaze follows your hand, and she sees the animal half a second before it disappears into a hole. "How did you know what it was?"

It's the sort of question you have stopped asking yourself.

You don't know how you know, only that you *do* know.

A wind blows from the north. You stop, you breathe it in. Rusted metal. Singed hair.

"We have to hurry," you say, and you begin to run.

WOLF, WHISTLE

The thing is, everything cycles. Your body cycles each month, your uterine wall thickening, then sloughing off. The moon waxes to full, it wanes to new, it waxes once again. You are a hunter; your mother was not; before her, Mémé was. That is a cycle, too, and who knows how many generations back it reaches, the every-otherness of it, the cycle of hunter/not-hunter/hunter. The seasons cycle from cold to warm to cold; the trees cycle from waxy foliage to bare branches and back again.

And you have left the farmhouse, but here you are returning

340

to it, though by a different path—not down the road to its front door as you came with your mother, but from behind, emerging from trees and cutting across a field, dipping between barbed wire fencing and then through another field, feeling your way to the place your personal history of blood began.

The farmhouse is worn and brittle in the moonlight. It is a miracle that you find it, or if not a miracle, then further proof of who you are when you bleed.

Keisha and Maggie do not question your lead; they fall into lockstep behind you, and when you look back once, you see they are holding hands. When at last you see the farmhouse, the moon is nearly risen. The air feels frozen. The moment feels frozen.

You approach the house, coming up from behind and emerging onto the driveway, fifty yards away from the door. There is a car—dirty from the long drive. The sight of it here makes your eyes sting with tears, but you blink them back, you stand still and listen, wait, smell, and feel the air with every inch of your body.

Then comes the roar, a sound that raises up the hair on the back of your neck and fills you deep with dread, but also with something else: fury.

The distance between you and the others doubles, then triples, as you sprint. They're running, too, but they can't possibly keep up, and your head is full of pounding blood and memories.

There are the shuttered windows. There are the sagging stairs. There is a light, glowing, from inside the front room. You take the steps by twos, you meet the half-open door with your shoulder, and you explode into the room.

There—there, thank God, there—is Mémé. She stands with her feet spread, a woodcutting ax hefted over her right shoulder. Your eyes follow the line of her sight; there, at the other end of the room, arms loose at his sides, is a man. Your father.

It is not true that you look only like your mother and your grandmother; you see yourself in this man's scarred face—his nose, and the way his cheekbones jut, and the high arch of his forehead.

You hear, from inside your head, called up from memory, a long, high whistle . . . a warning.

Three things happen then:

First, Keisha and Maggie crash through the doorway behind you, slamming into your back.

Then, the man's eyes begin to shiver, and his arms begin to shake, and his lips pull back from his teeth—no, his fangs—they sharpen and lengthen even as you watch, and his gray-streaked brown hair lengthens and spreads in a crest down his neck, and he hunches and his fingers splay into claws, and he shakes his head and his ears and muzzle lengthen, and in the last moment when there is still something human about him, before his clothes fall shredded to the floor, before his gray-streaked tail wags behind him, the wolf man turns to you, and grins.

The third thing that happens is that Mémé, who has not flinched as the man transformed to beast, hefts back the ax and throws.

Behind you, Maggie screams. The ax strikes the wolf's shoulder; he's thrown back against the piano, which makes a sick tinkle of not-music. But though he's hit, he's not done, not nearly, and as soon as he's thrown back, he's forward again, shaking away the ax with a spray of dark red blood, snarling and angry, and now Mémé's hands are empty, and he's leaping forward, his aim true, he's in the air flying toward Mémé, and you will not lose another person in this house.

You scream as you attack, no time for weapons, no time for fear, no time for thoughts, and as the wolf lands on Mémé, as you hear the sick crunch of his teeth on bone, you are upon him, your own fingers hooked into rigid claws.

You'd like to make him suffer. You'd like to make him pay, as Mémé would have liked to, for what he did to your mother—both that night, while you hid in the ghost room, a terrified little girl, and what he did before that, when he was a wolf but still in sheep's clothing.

And you remember. You remember when the three of you were in the little house, before the memory you thought was your first, that night that your mother snuck you away. In this memory, you were so young. You had a blankie that you've forgotten about entirely, but now you remember—it was red satin, trimmed in blue. You took it with you everywhere, and you would scream and scream if it was missing, until your mother found it.

That night you'd been crying. Blankie was missing. It was *missing*, and you needed it to sleep. And your mother said *shhh* and she looked everywhere—under the couch, in the bathroom, between your little bed and the wall—everywhere she could think to look, but still, no Blankie. And then Mama grew frantic, too, and she begged you to be quiet, please, be quiet, Bisou, we'll find Blankie in the morning, we will, we will, I promise, and you said, no, not tomorrow. Tonight, *now*.

You yelled that word—*now*—and you balled your fist and you stamped your foot. And you watched as Mama's face lost its color, as her eyes grew white-rimmed and round.

You heard a whistle behind you, long and high, and you turned to see Papa, so tall you had to bend back your neck to see his face. And in his hand was Blankie—it must have been in his bed, in Mama's bed, the one place she wouldn't let you look, because Papa was sleeping and mustn't be disturbed.

But he was awake now, and he smiled a sharp smile and held Blankie out to you, and you took it and wrapped it around your shoulders like a cape. And then he turned to Mama and his smile went away.

You went to your room. You sat on your bed. You pulled Blankie up over your head like a hood, and you screwed tight your eyes, and you pretended the sounds you heard were the sounds of the television, and not the muffled cries of your mother.

When Papa had fallen back to sleep, and Mama scooped you from your bed in the deepest velvet of night and cocooned you, wrapped in Blankie, in the back seat of the car, when she rolled the car down the street almost to the corner without turning the key, then made it growl to life, when she turned to look at you in the red glow of a traffic signal just before the freeway on-ramp, and she was somehow both mother and not-mother, the side of her face distorted by blood and the swelling of her jaw, you pulled the blanket up over your head once again and squeezed tight your eyes, and then the car began to move again, speeding onto the freeway and away, away, and that was when you began to forget.

You would like to make him suffer, for that night and all the nights that came before, for the raised bump in Mama's pretty nose, for the way she stroked it as she watched out the front window, waiting for the moment she knew would come, and you would like to make him pay for the moment that *did* come. For the poems she wrote, and all the poems she would never write. But Mémé is beneath his beastly weight, and you are on his back, and his muzzle is in your hands. It is not mercy for the wolf but love for your grandmother that guides you to dig your fingers into the beast's face. You feel the hot wetness of his nose or his mouth or his eye, and you are both wild with bloodlust and driven with precision as you gouge him, as you yank his head, hard and fast and certain, until the wolf is dead.

You scissor the wolf with your legs and you roll him off your grandmother, who is lying beneath him, too still, too quiet.

He is heavy, and for a moment you are trapped on your back beneath the bulk of him on the wood-planked floor of the old blue farmhouse. Maggie and Keisha run up, drop to their knees at Mémé's side.

"Is she dead?" Maggie wails.

For a moment you are paralyzed beneath the weight of all that fur and muscle, and also by your own fear. Better not to know. Better not to see. Better buried here by the weight of so many things than seeing Mémé's slack face, her blood-let body.

The animal above you shivers and transforms, and now you are beneath the naked, broken-necked body of your father, his legs and arms splayed across you, his head lolled back in the crook of your neck, and this you cannot bear, and you thrust him from you, twisting and pushing to emerge from the weight of him, the press of him, and his body slides away, becoming, on the floor, just the corpse of a man, a terrible man.

Maggie is petting the hair back away from Mémé's face, and Keisha is kneeling at her side, looking for the source of all the blood. She moves Mémé's right arm, the one that held the ax, which lies, now, sticky with spilled blood, halfway beneath the tall chair by the window where Mama used to sit and keep watch.

Mémé groans and moves, shaking her head and twitching her arm.

"Oh, Sybil!" Maggie cries, her relief at this proof of life redoubling her tears.

"It's her arm," Keisha says. She rips open Mémé's sleeve from wrist to elbow, and you see a constellation of puncture wounds where the wolf's fangs sank in, an odd looseness of a broken bone.

"We need to get her to a hospital," Maggie says.

"No." It's Mémé, eyes still closed, bringing up her left hand to the back of her head, which must have hit the floor hard when she fell. "Not until after we take care of the body."

Keisha and Maggie help Mémé sit up, propping her against the back of the couch.

There is a moment when you want to scream at Mémé— *How could you leave me? How could you go?*—but you force

347

your pulse to slow, you force your throat to relax, you force your gaze to soften.

"Mémé," you say in a whisper.

"Darling girl," she replies, and her voice is tremulous. "I wanted to spare you this. I truly did. No one should have to kill her father, darling. I am so sorry."

You shake your head, and your tears make the whole room sparkle as if there is magic here, as if this place, this terrible place, is full of wonder, too.

"You didn't have to do this alone," you say. "You aren't alone."

"I tried," Mémé says. "but I couldn't."

You lean forward. You press your lips to her forehead. You close your eyes and breathe.

"You aren't alone," you whisper. "*We* aren't alone."

"Okay," she says. "Okay."

You settle back on your heels. Keisha is there, waiting, and she's holding a dish towel and a dusty bottle of vodka that she must have found in the kitchen.

"Sorry, Sybil," she says, handing you the bottle. "This is probably going to hurt." She ties the dish towel above Mémé's elbow to slow the flow of blood. You twist off the bottle's cap and pour the vodka over Mémé's wounds. She hisses but doesn't cry out. Her left hand, which Maggie is holding, grips tight.

"None of the wounds look that deep, but we've got to splint

it," Keisha says. "Find something to use."

You scan the room, looking for something to use as a splint. There is a small stack of books, the top one a hardcover. Adrienne Rich, the spine reads. *Diving into the Wreck*. Atop the stack is a small pyramid of stones—smooth, oblong, perfect for skipping.

You placed those stones on this stack of books. You remember.

"It's too cold to go to the pond today," Mama had said. "The lake is icy. We'll have to wait for spring to skip stones again."

You had been collecting stones before the last snow came, thick and heavy, a snow that would not melt, not for weeks. And so you'd taken the stones and built this pyramid—carefully, slowly, and full of pride when it did not topple.

It has waited here, all these years, this stack, these stones.

You disturb it now, scooping up the stones and setting them aside, and then you lift the book from the stack.

It's poetry, of course. You flip it open and your eyes land on the end of a poem, these words:

We are, I am, you are
by cowardice or courage
the one who find our way
back to this scene

You turn to the front of the book. There, in your grand-mother's script, is her own name, Sybil Martel.

This was the book your mother read, sitting next to the window, waiting for her death. Your grandmother's book. How did your mother come to have it? Garland, the grand-father you never met, must have given it to her, he must have taken it when he left. Or perhaps it was happenstance that it was among the things in his car when he drove away. And now she is dead, and he is dead, and this story will die with them, you suppose, how this book came to be at the blue farmhouse, what your mother thought of the poems inside, how they may have moved or formed her, how they might have given her the courage, at last, to leave your father and spirit you away. All of that, you will have to accept that it is among the stories you will never know the truth of.

Maybe this is why people make up fables and myths and fairy tales: to fill in gaps. To answer unanswerable questions. To shelter their fears, and their hopes as well. And to con-nect with one another in the only way there is, in sharing their story.

The book will make a fine splint.

Maggie has found a sheet upstairs—from the room of ghosts? You do not ask—and she is tearing it into strips. You take the book to Mémé and kneel beside her. She recognizes it, you can tell, and she smiles to see it, but she doesn't ask questions. She accepts that the book is here, for whatever reason, in whatever way.

You fold it open at its center, and Keisha places Mémé's broken arm on its pages, doing her best to be gentle. Mémé breathes deeply, in and out, and closes her eyes. Maggie brings over the long strips of fabric, and together the three of you tend to Mémé, wrapping each strip carefully but firmly around the book and her arm.

At last, you are done. Mémé opens her eyes. "Thank you," she says. "Now. The body."

WE ARE

We are, I am, you are, by cowardice or courage, the ones who found our way back to this scene. We are the ones who, under the goddess moon, lift the naked man from the floor and wrap him in a sheet.

We are the ones who carry him, together, sharing the burden of his weight, out of the house for a final time. He will never disturb this place again, and the ghosts wave good riddance as we bear him away.

We are the ones who take him to the pond.

We are the ones who fold back the sheet to expose his belly

to the moon, and we are one the ones who use the sickle to slice him open.

We are the ones who fill his belly full of stones, each of us choosing and placing one, the heaviest we can fit, all of us working to wrap the sheet tight when we are done, tying it fast to secure the stones in place.

We are the ones who swing the ax, stained with wolf blood, to break the pond's thin ice. We are the ones who wait and watch and listen as the ice groans, as the crack spreads and fragments and reaches out like fingers, like memories, like hope. We are the ones who strip bare, who tread into frigid water, who swim our shared burden out as far as we can bear, our bodies shivering so violently that our teeth slam together, we are the ones who almost seize with cold.

We are the ones who release him, who paddle in place as the water reaches up and claims him, who watch as he sinks to the murky depths that will keep him.

We are the ones who swim to shore, who stumble from the water, who shiver on the bank, who rub each other dry. We are the ones who go, arms wrapped around one another, away from the water, away from what is beneath it, and we are the ones who don't look back.

We are the ones.

We are one.

ACKNOWLEDGMENTS

"The witch who works with the hands only is a
 laborer;
the witch who works with the hands and the head is a
 crafts witch;
the witch who works with the hands, head, and heart
 is an artist."

In their original form, these words were written by trial lawyer
and author Louis Nizer in his book *Between You and Me*:

"A man who works with his hands is a laborer;
a man who works with his hands and his brain is a
 craftsman;

but a man who works with his hands and his brain
and his heart is an artist."

But we can only wonder where Mr. Nizer may have found the spark of inspiration for *his* words, the sources he borrowed and built on.

All of writing—all of *living*—is an act of creative comingling. My stories come from the novels, poetry, and art I've absorbed, as well as the people I've interacted with throughout my life.

If I work alone, I labor alone; if I acknowledge that my work is not singular, but woven together with the work of others, then, perhaps, I (we) can create art.

Red Hood was not a singular creation. Most notably, I am indebted to my friend Martha Brockenbrough, my sister Mischa Kuczynski, and my editor, Jordan Brown, all of whom read dozens of drafts and offered suggestions, criticisms, queries, and even some killer lines. Thank you.

I'm glad for the friendship of Amber Keyser, who offered keen insight on an early draft, and Brandy Colbert, the first "fresh" reader of this book in its final form. And Ronda Rabe, thank you for suggesting the title.

I'm indebted to the team at Balzer + Bray, who helped turn my story into a book: Tiara Kittrell, whose notes on an early draft were invaluable; Alessandra Balzer and Donna Bray, who have given this book such a wonderful home; Megan Gendell and Renée Cafiero and their eagle eyes; designer Chris Kwon and art director Alison Donalty; and, again, my editor, Jordan Brown, as he deserves double thanks for this one.

I'm grateful, always, to Rubin Pfeffer, my agent and my friend.

And, as always, I need to thank my beautiful little family—Keith, Max, and Davis. Our family, made together, is my favorite creation.

A DARK, TWISTED, UNFORGETTABLE FAIRY TALE.

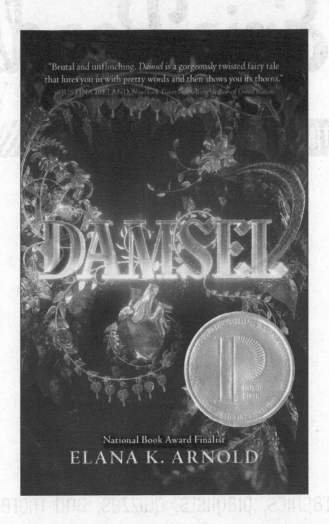

"Brutal and unflinching, *Damsel* is a gorgeously twisted fairy tale that lures you in with pretty words and then shows you its thorns."
—JUSTINA IRELAND, *New York Times* bestselling author of *Dread Nation*

DAMSEL

National Book Award Finalist
ELANA K. ARNOLD